Pleasure

to

Purpose

Based on the True Story of Sex Worker
Scarlett Pereira

By **Elizabeth B. Splaine**

Van Velzer Press
Americana with a Twist

Other books by Elizabeth B. Splaine

<u>Novels:</u>

Blind Order
Blind Knowledge
Devil's Grace
Swan Song
Steel Butterflies

<u>Children's:</u>

Tyrone the Tenor Mouse

Dedication from Scarlett

**To my heart horse, Franco,
the best horse that ever lived,
and to my dad.**

This Story is based on real situations:
Most of the stories in this book are true, though all names have been
altered except mine and Franco.

Before you read on, I want you to understand that I am not a victim. My
profession is by choice and I'm a proud, compassionate BBW (Big
Beautiful Woman) who makes her own decisions and keeps her own
schedule.

Significance of the Red Umbrella

In 2001 during the 49th Venice Biennale of Art in Venice, Italy, sex workers demonstrated against inhumane work conditions and human rights violations by holding up red umbrellas, making this a symbol of resistance to discrimination.

Chapter 1

I find it ironic that some whores don't enjoy sex.

Although Steph's been a sex worker for over ten years, she's mechanical. She goes through the motions without offering what we in the business call the girlfriend experience (GFE). I'm not the only one who finds her work impersonal, there have been complaints online about her enthusiasm deficiency, for lack of a better term.

I watch Steph kiss Jared—no tongue, only closed mouth—then examine the open floor plan of the downtown Boston studio apartment. Mauve walls in need of another coat of paint. A blue, cracked leather couch. A pile of dirty dishes in the sink. Outdated paintings hanging crookedly on the walls scream to be straightened, but I resist the urge as Jared's moan draws me back.

His Viagra-induced hard-on is on full display as he stops suddenly, realizing he's paid for a threesome and isn't getting his money's worth. He motions me over and I oblige, locking eyes and offering a slow smile. A strap of the sheer teddy slips from my shoulder, so I shrug to help it along. In my peripheral vision I see Steph slouch. Jared is choosing me, the new girl, over the sixty-two-year-old pro. She feels slighted, I can tell.

I met Steph online when cyber jerks were advising her to retire. I feel sorry for her, not because society worships youth while efficiently tucking the elderly away, but because she doesn't understand that clients know when you're not into it. Although I'm eighteen years younger, age has nothing to do with the fact that Jared prefers me. He wants me because I provide the GFE: pretending we've arrived home after a few drinks at a bar, we kiss at the door. I place his hands on my breasts, and we undress slowly, that kind of thing. Steph's the opposite. When a client arrives, she tells him to undress and wait on the bed. It's all so generic with her. If I were paying $300 an hour, I'd want more.

Jared moans as his tongue explores my mouth. He's a fifty-something carpenter, lean with average muscle tone and nimble hands that hungrily explore my body. I ease out of the teddy while running my nails through his thin gray hair. I've had sex with better, and I've certainly had worse. Although I enjoy having sex with women, Jared doesn't get off on seeing Steph and I play with each other. He just likes to have us at the same time. He's always been kind, respectful and has never cheated us.

Steph's high-pitched voice cuts through our connection. "Fuck me first," she whines.

I'd almost forgotten she's here. My sole focus is on pleasing Jared, who ignores her while pushing me down. He straddles me while I quickly unwrap a condom and roll it down. My hips rise to meet his as he enters, and everything else falls away.

Suddenly Steph's face is next to mine, staring upward toward Jared. "Me!" she demands. "Do me first!"

Jared holds up a hand, silently telling her to back off. Inside, I feel him wither and my face flushes with anger. I understand Steph's jealousy but she's ruining his experience. Although we've already collected the money, I won't feel right about keeping it if he decides to leave.

An hour would be completely wasted.

A rent payment denied.

I swallow my frustration, remembering that Steph has taught me a lot, including how to count money without the client noticing and how to give a bareback blowjob. "The G spot for men is usually right underneath the head," she had explained patiently. "Massage that spot with your tongue to get 'em going."

Pleasure to Purpose

I reach down to massage Jared's cock, willing myself to focus on reigniting his passion as Steph stands abruptly, clearly put out.

"I gotta pee."

And chill out, I think while cupping Jared's face in my hands and kissing him deeply. He takes a nipple in his mouth, and my back arches as he comes alive again. He gazes at me with earnest gray eyes. I notice sweat beads gathering on his forehead.

"You okay, Jared?"

"Sure. Yeah."

I ask him if he took a little blue pill, and he nods. When he leans back, I prop up on my elbows, noting his pasty skin and staggered breathing. My skin prickles as I ask the next question because I already know the answer.

"Don't you have a bad heart?"

"I just need some water."

He stands, takes three steps, and collapses in front of the full-length mirror. My brain screams at me to move but I can't. Finally, I rise from the bed slowly and watch in disbelief as he starts to convulse. Before I can force sound from my constricted throat, he's in full grand mal seizure. The scene suddenly switches from slow motion to regular time. I scream Steph's name while throwing myself toward Jared. His eyes have rolled back. The tendons in his hands tighten, then contract into claws. His veins stand at full attention as if searching to escape the confines of skin. His neck contorts while his head twists at seemingly impossible angles. Like something out of a horror movie, his involuntary movements force him closer to the heavy floor mirror. Terrified it will shatter, I jump over him and place myself between him and the mirror. As he inches ever closer, I frantically scan the room for my phone.

Steph is just coming out of the bathroom and stops abruptly. "What the hell's wrong with him?"

My words tumble out. "I think it's his heart. We need to call 911. I don't know your address. Where's my phone? I don't know where I put it."

Placing a hand on my chest, I feel my heart slamming against my ribs. I've been in life and death situations before, but never with a client. I force a deep breath, knowing that panic impairs logical thought.

Steph waves a hand. "It's just a seizure. He'll be okay."

Is she serious? I jab a finger toward Jared. "If we don't call and he dies, it'll be manslaughter!"

She turns on me, wide eyes boring into mine. Her pupils are dilated. I wonder exactly what she was doing in the bathroom. "If we call, then the cops might arrest us! No fuckin' way!"

Her tone is harsh, but behind the severity is every sex worker's number one, deep-seated fear. Current law states that someone can be arrested while reporting a crime if they admit to prostitution or are caught in the act. So what's the motivation to report a crime when the outcome might be your own ass sitting in a jail cell?

I glance at Jared, then at my watch. It's been two minutes since the seizure began. If we make the call, my greatest fear of being arrested could materialize. If we don't, Jared could die. I chew my lower lip while staring at the poor man on the floor, his life literally in our hands. After an eternity, my brain catches up with my conscience.

"Steph, we *have* to call! The longer he's not treated the worse off he'll be! Make sure you use your personal phone."

She curses but grabs the phone. "*I* taught *you* that, remember?"

Early on Steph taught me to carry two phones, a "hoe" phone and a personal one. She explained not mixing business with pleasure was the safer move.

Jared's body stills as he drifts into unconsciousness. I check his pulse and am relieved to feel a faint but steady beat, then wrap my hand around his to remind him he's not alone.

"Help is coming, Jared. You're gonna be okay," I whisper, desperately hoping I'm right.

Steph disconnects and glares at Jared like this is his fault. "We gotta get our story straight."

I nod quickly, pushing emotion aside and deferring to her prostitutional wisdom.

She dresses quickly, talking the entire time. "He's a handyman, here to hang some drapes. My regular handyman wasn't available 'til tonight so I hired Jared. I know him through a friend. He was hanging the drapes when he collapsed. We gotta get his clothes on."

After dressing myself, I grab Jared's underwear and manage to slide them up his legs, narrating my actions so he knows what's happening.

Pleasure to Purpose

"He can't hear you," Steph mutters while frantically pacing the floor and chewing a thumbnail.

"You don't know that," I snap. I pull his khakis on, then button his shirt and slide sandals on his feet. He doesn't look much like a handyman, and there are no drapes that he supposedly was hanging, but I keep those thoughts to myself. Steph is waving her hands in the air, quietly freaking out. If I push her, she might walk out, leaving me to fend for myself.

"I hear people coming! Quick, put him by the window," Steph orders.

I hesitate, afraid moving him might do more damage.

"Do it!" Steph hisses.

I don't think it matters where he is when they arrive but I'm in no position to argue, so I drag his limp body and slump it against the wall under the window.

Steph meets the firefighters at the door and tells them the story. If they have doubts, they don't show it. While they give Jared oxygen, paramedics arrive and do an EKG, confirming a heart attack.

"What's his name?" they ask.

"Jared," I answer.

The guy raises an eyebrow, waiting for a last name. I glance at Steph, who's staring at the ground. I shrug, indicating I don't know. The paramedic glances from Steph to me to Jared and back again, clearly evaluating the situation. I've seen the look before and go into defensive mode, holding his gaze and daring him to comment. He averts his eyes and clears his throat, then says that Jared is being taken to Beth Israel Deaconess Medical Center if we want to alert his family.

"His license is probably in his wallet, which is in his back pocket," I say. The paramedic offers a tight smile.

I thank them as Jared is wheeled out on a stretcher, then close the door and exhale the breath I didn't realize I was holding.

"We did the right thing, but that was close," I say.

"What was close?" Steph asks as she reapplies eyeliner.

I stare, lost for words. Finally, I shake my head. "A man almost died, Steph."

She applies lipstick, then smacks her lips together. "But he didn't." She faces me. "*And* we didn't get arrested."

I sit for a moment while adrenaline drains, leaving exhaustion in its wake. I recognize the feeling and let it wash over me so I can be done with it. Closing my eyes, I'm fourteen again with my brother Tyler's hands circling my throat, squeezing. My vision turns blurry, then black around the edges… I force myself back to the present, inhaling slow, deliberate breaths. I'm proud of myself for remaining so calm during the crisis and disgusted with Steph that she considered letting Jared die. Questioning whether I should continue seeing clients with her, I remember that making three thousand a week allows me a masseur, a car and a cleaning service.

You can't place money above humanity, my conscience whispers.

"At least for today I can," I mumble while glancing at my watch. We have four more scheduled clients, and I plan to make the most of it.

Then I'll go solo.

It's time for this bird to fly.

Chapter 2

The next morning I awake thinking about Jared, hoping he's okay. Although I have his cell number, I have a strict policy about not contacting clients in case they're in a relationship. The poor man had a heart attack; the last thing he needs is to be outed for seeing sex workers. So I close my eyes, send him some love and light, then shift my focus to the fun horse day ahead of me.

I dress quickly in black sweatpants and a green hoodie that matches my eyes, then pull on thick rubber boots, knowing I'm in for a day of hay, poop and mud. I smile, a deep understanding in my soul that the rescue is my happy place where I feel most at home.

After brushing my teeth and gathering my hair in a tight ponytail, I catch a glimpse of a book I was given by a child psychologist when I was six.

In the story a young girl relies on magical horses to whisk her nightmares away. In turn, she defends the horses when the nightmares come after them. It's a symbiotic, supportive relationship of mutual protection. I now understand the therapist hoped the book would prompt me to share my feelings about my brother Tyler's sudden disappearance. I don't remember the book being read to me, and my recollection of the therapist is a forty-something, frail woman who seemed nice and spoke in quiet, soothing tones. Although there were several counselors after her, none had such a positive impact, small though it was.

I blink hard to drive away the flashback, but it persists: sitting stiffly on a huge couch, swinging my legs as they hang over the edge. I asked once why my brother was sent away, and no one cared to answer. My six-year-old self concluded Tyler must have been very bad to have been exiled, and I would be good as gold to avoid being kicked out of the family.

The unwanted memories bring a rush of sadness that I shove away, determined to have a good day.

I drive to the barn in an old, rusty Toyota I named after Betty Page, a 1950's pin-up who flirted with photographic and televised soft porn. She was a trailblazer in the industry, setting beauty standards that are still followed today. Unfortunately, like many sex symbols of her generation, her life ended sad and alone. My Betty's been sputtering recently, as if she, too, is thinking about giving up the fight. I ordered her to keep going because I can't blow my savings on a new car right now.

So far, she's obliged.

Exiting Betty, a shrill whistle sounds. I turn to see Patricia Wickford strolling toward me with open arms, her wide hips swinging quickly as she closes the distance in five grand strides. A former large-animal vet specializing in racehorses, Pat founded Sophie's Choice Rescue in response to the mistreatment she observed in the racing world. She contracted with this local farm for space, and after several years of my volunteering, she offered the Rescue Manager position to me. Although I'd like to run a rescue someday, the pragmatist in me knows I don't have enough experience right now. So Pat still comes every day, waiting until I'm ready to take the management reins from her. Like me, she'd rather be here than anywhere else.

As she approaches, Pat's freckles remind me of a connect-the-dots on her sun-kissed face. Seventy-five going on fifty, the best thing about Pat is her hugs. All-encompassing, a reminder that there are people in the world who give so much without wanting anything in return.

"Let me look at 'cha, girl!" She holds me at a distance as if we haven't seen each other in an age. "You look beautiful. Just beautiful!" she gushes.

I crinkle my nose. "I saw you last week, Pat."

Pleasure to Purpose

She lifts a lip and widens her eyes. "Can't a girl compliment another girl when she means it?"

Pat knows my secret. At least I think she does. She's never referenced it, but my hoe senses are pretty accurate and I think she knows. In fact, I think she likes me better because of it.

I shake my head, barely suppressing a grin. "Thanks. You look good too."

Pat's waves a hand. *"Pfft!* You smell that?" She raises her nose and sniffs. "Bullshit." She winks, then grins, and her sparkly blue eyes disappear into a fan of wrinkles under a straight set of pure white bangs.

I raise a hand to shield my eyes as I scan the paddock. "Is Franco here yet?"

"Just got here." Pat points to a dark bay gelding. Shipped from New Zealand to the US when he was young, Franco was retired after a successful harness-racing career and adopted by a woman who boarded him at a small farm somewhat near this rescue facility.

"Apparently, in the ten years Franco boarded, his owner visited only eight times, *and* he never saw a vet or farrier. Not to mention the owner was four months behind in rent," Pat said. "He's supposed to be a wonderful horse. Poor baby."

"Has Xena met him yet?"

Xena, who'd been found tied to a woodland tree with her foal wandering nearby, had been at the rescue for about a year when her stall mate died. When she started exhibiting depression and anxiety, Pat suggested we see if Xena and Franco get along.

"Not yet. I wanted you to meet him first."

We cross to the paddock where Franco stands quietly in the center, his right front leg slightly bent in relaxation. I'm surprised he's not stressed in this new place with strange people. He seems completely at ease as he gazes evenly at me, before shifting his head to follow another horse.

I'm unable to look away as the sun glances off Franco's almost-black body, making him seem even more imposing than his large stature and haughty head toss imply. An uneven white star graces his wide forehead. His brown muzzle has turned gray where he's worn a halter. He's bigger than I'd been led to believe at fifteen hands, three inches, and still carries

Pleasure to Purpose

the dignity of a champion despite the neglect he's suffered. He is, in a word, stunning.

Pat askes, "Well, what d'ya think?"

"He's gorgeous." I literally can't take my eyes from such an exquisite creature.

Pat nods. "Yup."

My hoe phone rings, startling both of us. Pat glances at it. "Take the call. I'll be over here when you're done."

I smile to show my appreciation. When she's out of earshot, I answer. "Hello," I purr.

Heavy breathing comes across the line. Some asshole's version of sexy. I roll my eyes and try again.

"How can I help you, handsome?"

The caller grunts, making me wonder if he's jerking off. It's a fairly common occurrence. A guy wants to hire me but doesn't have the cojones to say it out loud. Or it's a teenager completing a dare. Or just some horny guy who can't afford me but wants to get off.

Suddenly the guy screams something unintelligible into the phone, surprising me with his intensity. Before I can respond, he disconnects. The interaction was odd enough that I click on recent calls to memorize the number in case he tries again.

"You okay?" Pat asks, her eyebrows raised. "I could hear the caller yell from over there."

I pause, wondering why I feel uneasy about the call. I've gotten hundreds of prank calls and have never felt unsettled afterwards. But something feels… off.

I briefly consider confiding in Pat, then decide I'm being dramatic.

"All good."

"You sure?" Pat's eyes drill into my soul, and I know she knows. I place my hand on her arm.

"I appreciate your concern, but I'm really okay."

She narrows her baby blues. "Okay, but if you ever need anything, I'm here. Got it?"

I want to burst into tears. The kind of fat, blubbery tears you reserve for the times you've held it together for so long that at the first touch of kindness, you fall apart. Instead, I nod. "Got it."

Pleasure to Purpose

"Good. Now, let's meet your new horse."

That sobers me. "My new what?"

Pat rolls her eyes. "Just follow me, sweetheart."

I follow Pat toward the paddock while reaching into my bag for a large slice of apple. Holding it in my outstretched hand, I'm in awe as I approach. "Good to meet you, Franco."

He shifts his head dismissively, then detects the apple and grabs it with his lips, chewing heartily. His soft nose returns to my hand, seeking another treat. Finding none, he turns away. I step forward and run my hand along his neck. He flinches and pulls away. I try again, softer this time. He swings his head around and, for a moment, I think he might sink his teeth into my arm. But I stand my ground, continuing long, slow strokes down his side. He watches me warily as his entire body shivers, not in exhilaration or joy, but because he's not used to being touched. I tamp down anger at the prospect of such an amazing creature being neglected. After several tense moments, he turns his gaze straight ahead and the shaking ceases, indicating silent acceptance. Horses are surprisingly humanlike, absorbing our emotions as we interact with them. They then mirror those emotions back to us through their behavior, often without our understanding what's happened. In this case, I hope he's intuited my love and respect for him. Either way, I'm humbled by his trust as his massive shoulder muscles relax under my touch.

"He's perfect, Pat."

She squeezes my shoulder. "They all are. God's creatures. It's us who fuck 'em up."

Franco's teeth are filthy, his matted mane and tail need a good brushing, but his eyes are clear and bright. Despite the stressful situation, I can already see why Pat thought Franco's calm, confident nature would make him a good companion for Xena. I take his lead rope from the barn hand and guide him to a section of the paddock, then close the gate.

"Where's Xena?" I ask.

On cue Xena appears through a separate entrance, allowing them to meet each other across a fence in case they don't get along.

I bite my lip as I watch them notice one another. Neither rushes to the fence that separates them. Instead, they graze, lifting their heads every now and then to glance at each other. Xena's anxiety is exhibited through

Pleasure to Purpose

jerky movements and eye contact avoidance. After fifteen minutes, Franco walks slowly to the barrier. He dips his head repeatedly to get Xena's attention. She responds by sauntering over in a serpentine pattern to elongate the inevitable. They stand face to face, neither looking the other in the eye, until Franco closes the remaining distance. He touches her nose with his and she accepts his overture by returning the nuzzle. An unspoken agreement has been brokered. My shoulders drop in relief. Xena has found a friend.

Pat and I share a moment of triumph before I remove the temporary fence, allowing the two horses to spend the next hour grazing quietly, occasionally touching one another. At one point Xena runs away and Franco follows, creating an impromptu game of tag. I lean on the perimeter fence, marveling at their ability to find such happiness in the moment. Their contentment brings me joy, a reminder that a good friend, food and shelter should be all we need. They play for another hour while I prepare Franco's stall, then return to the barn, where they spend the rest of the day alternating between staring at each other and eating—the way a horse's life should be. I watch them for a bit, then muck other stalls and haul fresh hay bales from the storage area. The work feels solid and real, grounding me and reminding me what's important.

I approach Xena and stroke her nose. "See, girl? Things can work out. Franco's a keeper." I glance at Franco, who whinnies boldly. "He's already claimed you, Xena. Friends for life."

My memory returns to the book on the shelf as I realize that Franco looks exactly like the horse on the cover. Rich, chocolate brown with an uneven star on his forehead and white socks above all four hooves. I shiver in the morning heat, determined to put those memories in a mental box. Before I can, another memory surfaces unbidden.

My mother's blue dress drapes over the edge of the bus seat as I sit quietly beside her, matching her demeanor and tone. We ride the bus for what seems like hours without speaking, Mom staring blankly ahead and me looking out the window, excited to be going on a trip to visit Tyler. Mom hasn't told me exactly where we're going, so when we arrive at a mental hospital that smells funny and has dirty, black and white tiles on the floor, I feel cheated. Of course, I didn't know it was a mental hospital at the time. All I knew was sometimes we'd arrive to find that my ten-year-old brother had lost visitation privileges because of bad behavior. My mother would accept the news without comment, swallowing the anger and frustration she must have felt, and we'd return home without seeing him. Although I remember feeling disappointed, I didn't complain or cry; that might land me in the smelly, dirty place with Tyler.

Pat sidles up next to me and bumps my hip with hers. "So?" she asks.

I look at her sideways. "So… what?"

She pulls away and crosses her arms, head tilted to one side. "If you want Franco, he's yours. God knows the current owner won't be upset."

Although I've volunteered for some time, I've never been financially liable for a horse. I've always been able to come and go as I please, making choices specifically so I'd be responsible only for myself. The weight of potential horse ownership settles between my shoulder blades. Owning a horse is a major commitment and I'd have to commute to the barn every day. *How will I balance clients and Franco?*

I glance at the magnificent animal who's staring directly at me, daring me to reject him. Love floods me the way I imagine a mother regards her newborn. *How could I have lived without you for so long?* There's an undeniable connection, and whether I'm ready or not, Franco is my heart horse.

I look at Pat, waiting patiently, and the words come out before I process them. "I want him, but only on a foster basis. In case things go wonky, I want to be able to give him back. Deal?"

Pat smirks knowingly. "Yeah, deal."

I feel strangely euphoric as I cross to Franco's stall. He stares at me gravely, as if he knows his fate has been handed to a horse-loving, wannabe rescue owner who has big dreams but little experience and even less money. Tension creeps into my lower back, a sure sign that I've acted rashly. As if reading my mind, he leans forward and places his chin in my hand.

I'm struck at his vulnerability and openness; we've just met yet he trusts me blindly. I run my thumb across his lips, and they quiver. I examine his beautiful face, noting the years of neglect and the toll they've taken. Closing my eyes, a vision appears: a man in a yellow baseball cap holding a riding crop, slashing at Franco while he's secured in a stall. I don't know where the vision came from, but I can hear the crack of the crop finding flesh and smell the overripe stench of the paddock. I *feel* Franco's terror as he tries to escape the torment.

I'm trembling when my eyes fly open, startled by images so real I wonder if Franco just revealed his past. The former champion gazes at me evenly with honest, soulful eyes. Anger at his mistreatment quickly hardens into resolve.

"No matter what, I'm going to take care of you. Got it? It's you and me against the world. You have my word."

Pleasure to Purpose

Chapter 3

After a glorious afternoon tending to the horses, I say goodbye to Franco and return to Betty. On the way, the farm manager appears, a fist planted on her bony hip that's jutted precariously to one side. Serenity's raven hair is plaited into a braid that hangs across her left shoulder. Fake lashes resemble black caterpillars devouring her eyes. Though her name implies stillness and a grounded sense of self, the only child of the farm owner is a thirty-something college dropout with a large ego and not much to back it up. Managing the farm where Sophie's Choice Rescue rents space is a means to an end for her, a mostly cash business that feeds her clothes habit. Several months ago, Pat discovered Serenity was stealing cash from the rescue. She asked if I would keep an eye on the books. Serenity found out and has held it against me ever since.

Serenity gives me the up/down, the same look I get from women whose husbands' eyes wander my way.

"Pat told me you're adopting Franco."

I nod.

"Well, he can board rent-free if you cover his other expenses."

I pause, momentarily surprised by this generosity. Then I realize Serenity does nothing out of kindness. She'll expect something in return.

Cross that bridge when you get there, I advise myself. *Franco has a home.* I paste on a smile. "That's really nice."

Serenity flounces away, her perfect braid bouncing with her gait.

I plop into Betty and sigh heavily, hoping she'll start. I smell like horse and am exhausted from a hard day's work. Despite my fatigue, I'm elated Xena accepted Franco, who settled into his new home like he's been here forever.

Without paying board, expenses will still be very tight. But I'm determined to swing it. I learned the importance of tucking money away after rescuing a bunny whose vet bill totaled over five thousand dollars. Jessica Rabbit ended up dying but left me the gift of preparedness. Now I keep an *Oh, Shit!* fund that currently has several thousand dollars in it.

While driving home, I do some math. A horse Franco's size consumes a half bale of hay per day, and one bale costs five dollars straight from the field. If a barn has to store it, it costs $6.50 a bale. I add in his dietary supplements, and I'm already in the hundreds of dollars per month. Vet bills can range dramatically, especially considering Franco's received no care for ten years, and a farrier for his hooves every other month will cost about sixty per visit. The bottom line is that between Franco's vet, farrier, food, supplements and bedding, my fund will dwindle quickly.

I grip the steering wheel while considering luxuries that'll have to go: massage, cleaning service.

"It was nice while it lasted," I mumble while pulling up in front of my apartment, careful not to ding an old Mercedes as I slip in behind it. The car's occupant stares at me in the rearview as a text appears on my hoe phone.

I want to fuck with you.

I glance at the number. It's the heavy breather from earlier. I read the sentence aloud. "I want to fuck with you." *Odd wording. Does he want to fuck me or fuck with my head?*

My horse-related euphoria fizzles while deciding how to handle this. I could ignore him, but then Franco's expenses flash in my mind. Although my hoe senses scream to steer clear, I text back asking him where and when, then watch three gray dots sprinkle across the screen as he composes a response. After several seconds, the dots evaporate. A frisson of relief shakes my body, surprising me with its intensity. *Do not engage with him,*

Pleasure to Purpose

pops into my head, then vanishes as the Mercedes driver waves to get my attention.

"Shit," I say aloud while waving back. I lost track of time at the rescue and need to shower. My personal phone rings. I hold up a finger, asking the client to wait. He gives a thumbs up.

"Hi, Princess. It's your dad."

"I know, Dad. Your name pops up on my phone. Hey, can I call you back? I'm kind of busy." I glance at the longtime client who waits patiently, unlike the younger ones who can't wait to pounce.

"Sure."

"Just give me an hour."

"An hour, huh?"

Is that sarcasm? When my father asks what kind of work I do, I tell him I hold several minimum wage jobs. The frequency of the same line of questioning makes me sure he doesn't believe me.

"Yes. I'll call you in an hour."

I disconnect while shaking off the nagging feeling about Dad, then approach the Mercedes, acutely aware of how horsey I smell. It's been about three months since I've seen Mike, a beanpole-thin, married seventy-seven-year-old who loves to be spanked. I'm not talking a couple of light taps on the behind. I mean, full out, arm-drawn-back slaps with an open palm or riding crop. He once told me that as a child he purposefully got in trouble so he could enjoy the punishment.

"Hey stranger. It's been a while. How's Lizzie?"

Normally I don't invoke a wife's name during a session, but Mike's situation is unique. His wife was his personal dominatrix before she had a stroke, and although I've never met her, she must be some sort of fabulous. When she became too weak to administer to Mike's needs, she gave him permission to see me, as long as she didn't know when he visited, and the session left no visible marks. I can count on one hand the number of wives that would extend such grace to their husbands.

His rheumy, sky-blue eyes hold a mischievous sparkle. "She's good. Asked me to give you this." He holds out a white box tied with a red ribbon. A pink envelope with beautiful cursive lettering is tucked into the ribbon.

I accept the gift, then tell him to give me time to shower. He makes a show of sniffing, crinkling his bulbous nose.

23

"You smell like…"

"Horse," I finish. "Twelve minutes."

Over the years I've morphed getting ready from an artform focused on creating allure to a science based on fuckability. I used to take an hour to create the illusion of Scarlett Pereira. But I quickly realized it's less about what I'm wearing and more about how I treat the clients. Now I have it down to twelve minutes. If surveyed, I'm sure clients would prefer I spend time *with* them instead of preparing *for* them.

I climb the stairs of our three-family house, the television glowing through my mother's first-floor window. Passing the door to my uncle's second-floor apartment, the day with Pat and Franco is still fresh in my mind, filling me with a happiness that spills over. I'm also thrilled to be earning money tonight. So, I shower quickly, brush my teeth and apply eye liner before slipping into a black lace bra and leather pants. Not the pants with a slit so I can be taken from behind. That's not Mike's thing. In fact, he can't really get it up anymore. He's here for the arousal and potential blow job.

At twelve minutes on the dot, Mike is at the door waiting respectfully to be let in. His thin lips are parted in anticipation, revealing uneven, yellowing teeth. He smiles and raises his eyebrows, as if asking permission. Skipping the small talk and very much in character, I guide him to the sex room and push him onto the bed.

"Strip," I command. Although I speak quietly, the tone is firm and unyielding, leaving no room for negotiation or discussion. The threat of punishment for noncompliance heightens Mike's arousal as he eagerly removes his pants. While maintaining eye contact, I grab a riding crop from the assortment hanging on the wall. It's a fiberglass cane sheathed in brown leather, thick at the top and narrow at the bottom, and ending in a leather tassel called a keeper.

"You've been a bad, bad boy, Michael," I whisper sternly while slapping the crop against my open palm. The sting on my hand reminds me how painful whipping is, but I push the thought aside while rounding the bed to focus on Mike, whose pupils dilate as his breath comes in staccato bursts.

"Assume the position for punishment, Michael."

Pleasure to Purpose

Breathless, he rolls over to expose his butt then I mount him from behind, grinding against him. While he moans, gripping the sheet and twisting it, I remove two protective pads from under the pillows and lay one on his lower back and the other across his upper thighs.

"Are you ready, you *bad* boy?"

"Yes."

His voice is raw with desperation. I know from experience that his eyes are screwed shut as he anticipates the intersection of pleasure meeting pain. Permission granted, I breathe deeply to steel myself against the pain I'm about to cause, then draw my arm back and release a major blow. He gasps as the crack of the crop reverberates through the small, dark room. I pause to verify he wants to continue, and two seconds later he whispers through gritted teeth, "Again."

I repeat the process many more times, alternating between my hand, the crop and a paddle board with small round holes to maximize pain. After ten minutes I draw his attention to a welt beginning to form. However, like an autoerotic asphyxiate who accidentally kills himself, Mike's too far gone to care. Against my better judgement, I agree to keep going. But after another smack, the welt weeps a clear fluid—a precursor to blood—and I lean back on my heels, panting from exertion.

"Again!" he orders in a tone reminiscent of the high school principal he once was.

I don't want to disappoint him, but Lizzie and I have an unspoken contract. I remind him of her rules and his head drops. He's frustrated, but not half as sad as he'll be if we ignore his wife's explicit instructions. Not only is it the right thing to do, but he won't be able to come back if he breaks the rules.

I examine his pale, lean body and sticklike arms gripping the black, iron spindles of the headboard. His back is broad. Thin skin succumbs to gravity, sliding down his sides and between his thick rib bones. He's older than my father but possesses the stamina of a bull.

"Sorry," he says, regaining his breath and composure.

I remove the pads and toss them to the floor. "No need for sorry," I say, gently turning him over for a hand job. As I work, I consider how kind Mike is, how different he is from other clients I no longer see.

Pleasure to Purpose

BDSM stands for bondage and discipline, dominance and submission, and sadism and masochism. It's been around for millennia and enables taking control through roleplay, freeing wild fantasies in a safe space without judgment. It's about trust, acceptance and release. Although I'm naturally the submissive as a paid participant, I don't particularly enjoy playing that role. Luckily for me, most men want to be dominated.

Early in my career I agreed to play a submissive with a client named John. Although we agreed on the rules, he quickly went from light hand slaps to hard whipping with a riding crop. The lashes stung like hell, but when I turned around to confront him, his massive erection made it apparent he was enjoying my pain. I allowed it to continue but felt physically and emotionally terrible afterwards, even though he apologized for getting carried away. Later I learned that some clients mask their penchant for abuse behind domination games. John continued to contact me until I blocked him, and I vowed not to be that vulnerable again.

Mike moans. I know from past sessions that he's had enough. I lean back into the pillows while he waggles his eyebrows, his lips curling into an impish smile.

"You gonna open the gift?"

I'd forgotten about the box. I retrieve it and open the card.

Dear Scarlett,

Thank you for taking care of Mike and for honoring my wishes. I know the flowers happened because of you so I wanted to give you something in return. This has been in our family since shortly after we were married.

Sincerely, Lizzie

I nod, remembering Mike's last visit when I ordered him to buy a huge bouquet of Lizzie's favorite flowers, along with a card saying how grateful he is to have such an empathetic wife. Seems he'd completed the assigned task. You can always tell the character of a person by how they treat their significant other; Mike didn't disappoint. I glance at him as he lies sprawled on the bed, grinning like a proud child.

"What are you so happy about?" I ask, although I'm secretly pleased he followed my advice. He shrugs, then wags his hand impatiently at the box. I remove the thick red ribbon, then pull off the top. Inside, laying against white sateen, is a brown leather riding crop, frayed on the edges from years of use. My jaw drops as I look to Mike for verification. He nods.

"This was Lizzie's and my first riding crop. We kept it for sentimental reasons, obviously."

Mike and Lizzie have been together almost fifty years. I'm incredibly touched that she trusts and respects me enough to share such an important memento of their most intimate moments. I do calculations in my head, wondering if I'll still be whoring when I'm Lizzie's age. Although it sounds improbable, there are many GILFs (Grandmothers I'd Like to Fuck) making a strong living. I know a *very* popular woman called Toothless Mary who removes her dentures to perform oral sex. The reality is that demand for our services will never dry up, even if it wanes in winter when testosterone is lower and at the end of each month when most paychecks have been spent.

I smile at Mike and tilt my head. "What a thoughtful gift. Please tell her I'm grateful."

Mike asks if I want to take the old, new crop for a spin. I cut my eyes and shake my head playfully, amused at his boyish enthusiasm and *joie de vivre,* then remind him of the welts I know he'll feel when the adrenaline settles. He pulls a face in disappointment but agrees, making me promise we'll use it next time. I make a show of hanging it prominently among my other toys and tell him I'll use it only on him. Satisfied, he rolls onto his stomach and asks for some water.

I return with a bottle of water to find him snoring lightly. Glancing at my phone, I note he still has fifteen minutes remaining in the hour, so I cover him gently with a blanket and tiptoe out of the room, pulling the door closed behind me. Normally I'd wake a client and ask him to leave, but Mike is special and has been with me for several years. Besides, the man's seventy-seven-year-old heart has withstood some serious strain for the last forty-five minutes.

Thinking about Mike's age has reminded me to call Dad, so I step outside. As I take a seat on the wooden stairs, I notice an older, green Nissan driving very slowly down the street. Rust outlines the wheel wells and the

27

underside of the doors. The driver's dark, wavy hair curls around the edges of a bright red baseball cap.

As his gaze meets mine, I'm drawn to his intense brown eyes like being pulled toward the edge of a sheer cliff.

A promise of danger leaves me shuddering in the warm evening air. But before I can coordinate these jumbled thoughts, he flashes a beautiful grin, tips his cap, and speeds around the corner.

Chapter 4

Shaking off the weird vibe Nissan guy gave me, I unlock my phone to call Dad.

My parents married under the delusion that life follows a predictable path—one grows up, marries, has kids, and lives happily ever after. My parents never should've married in the first place. After my father burned down their convenience store for the insurance money, he was caught and claimed mental incompetence. While he was in a psych ward, Mom filed bankruptcy and divorce papers in the same week. I was two and have no memory of ever living with my father. After Dad left us, he hopped from job to job, state to state, occasionally popping into our lives, but leaving my mother with three challenging kids, including a daughter she never really wanted.

Dad picks up on the third ring. "Hiya, Princess."

"Hey, Dad."

"How ya doin'?" His tone is flatter than usual.

"I'm good. You okay?"

Ignoring the question, he says, "Penny says hi."

No, she doesn't. Penny is Dad's third try at blissful matrimony. Although she's infinitely more tolerable than the second wife, she's always seen me as competition for Dad's heart, which has contributed to our lukewarm relationship. Penny is a caricature come to life. She has a nasal, high-pitched voice, dyed blond hair piled high, lots of rouge on a wide face and an overbite in a mouth with too many teeth. Her clothes border on tight because she gained weight and refuses to acknowledge it. Her laugh is more like a guffaw. She has no filter between her brain and mouth. In short, she always feels like… too much. I never understood what my father sees in her, but he genuinely loves her, so I try to be good.

"Tell her I say hi too," I say while watching the neighbor's obese cat sink into a crouched position to stalk a bird. My cat, Don Rickles, would never consider chasing a bird because it would require far too much effort. A stray who decided I was his person, Don appeared in my life by literally walking through my door last summer and laying on the wood floor, sprawled out in a warm sunbeam that shone through the window. Later that night, after sharing my dinner, he curled around my head like a halo and purred his way into my heart.

"So, what're you doing for work these days?"

Wow, he went right to it. "Oh, you know, walking dogs and temping. Stuff like that."

Although lying about my work has become second nature, I feel guilt pluck at my conscience every time. Not with everyone, just with my dad.

"But you're okay for money?"

"Yeah, I'm good."

When I was a senior in high school Dad and Penny moved to Delaware. I don't know why. Dad was a trucker and worked construction, so he could do that anywhere. But since the move, I speak with him even less than when he lived locally. Although I appreciate the phone calls, we don't really know each other, so we've mastered the art of avoidance. We discuss money, the weather, my brothers, anything but the glaringly obvious emotional gap in our relationship. Well, that and my real job.

"You seem to make a pretty good living walking dogs."

There it is again. The implication. In general, my dad is relatively openminded, certainly more than my mother. If I shared the truth with Mom, she might kick me out of the apartment I rent from her, then I'd be homeless again. Dad obviously suspects I'm lying and is pushing our boundaries. He seems to intuitively know I have another income source, so

Pleasure to Purpose

continuing the ruse seems somehow immoral. Plus, he's recently made a real effort at building a relationship based on trust and honesty. *Shouldn't I do the same?* I bite the inside of my cheek, wondering why I'm nervous. After all, he did the bare minimum in terms of parenting. Yet for some reason, I still crave his approval. Or, at least his acceptance. I take a massive breath, then exhale slowly to calm my galloping heart.

"Here's the thing, Dad. I'm a… an escort."

Dad inhales a slow, wheezing breath. After several tortuous seconds, I release my balled-up fists. I've done my part. Now it's his turn to accept me or not. When he speaks, his voice sounds small.

"An escort… like…"

"Yes. Like that."

"So… you sleep with men for money?"

And women, I think, though I omit that tidbit. No need to rock a flooding boat.

"Yes."

The giddy release of a long-held emotional burden lifts me like a helium balloon. I watch the neighbor's cat shift its stance, edging ever closer to the oblivious pigeon who pecks manically at some crumbs left in a Dunkin bag. I'm not sure if I'm rooting for the bird or the cat.

"But you're safe, right?"

My heart skips a beat. I stare at the phone like I'm gazing into my father's haggard, round face. Despite our fractured relationship, he's concerned for my safety.

"Yes. We meet in my apartment or at nice hotels. I'm safe."

He grunts as I imagine him rubbing his gray, stubbly chin while processing that his only daughter has sex with strangers.

"You could be arrested or go to jail."

In revealing the secret, my unease has been magically transferred to him. Now he must decide what to do with it. Perhaps he's worried my arrest might reflect badly on him, highlighting his subpar parenting.

"I'm aware, Dad. But I've been doing this for a while now. I'm good."

He asks if Mom knows. When I answer no, he instructs me not to tell her because she'd judge me. No surprise there. I've been disappointing my mother since I was conceived.

31

After a failed attempt at modeling, Mom decided to become a nurse but discovered she hated the sight of blood. She settled on working as a full-time medical secretary while managing her unpredictable husband and two sons. When an unplanned pregnancy entered the picture, she decided to abort. Although my father convinced her to carry to term, her emotional connection to me has always been tenuous at best.

I snap back to the present to see the cat lunge for the pigeon, missing by a substantial margin. Although he never really had a chance, I admire his spunk.

Dad asks why I do this type of work, and I tell him I don't want to be homeless again.

"What do you mean, again? Your mother wouldn't kick you out."

When I was eighteen, I was accepted into eight of nine colleges. With dreams of becoming a veterinarian, I attended a school in Western Massachusetts, a lush, green paradise compared to the cramped three-family house where we were intermittently on welfare. I ended up dropping out but didn't want to return home, so for the next year I worked five jobs and lived with friends. When their hospitality dried up, I lived in my car.

"You're wrong, Dad. Mom would absolutely throw me out. In fact, she did."

After totaling my car, I was truly homeless. I stayed with a gay couple I befriended until I saved enough to buy another car. I returned home to find the extra apartment was now occupied by my grandmother, who kindly let me stay with her until I saved enough to afford a place of my own.

Dad grunts again, then draws a ragged breath. Stumped for words or maybe wondering why I didn't reach out to him when I was homeless. Either way, it's time to change the subject.

"You sound tired, Dad. What's going on?"

He doesn't answer; my skin prickles.

"Are you not sleeping well?"

"I sleep about eighteen hours a day, Princess."

Even though he has heart stents and leads a sedentary lifestyle, Dad's only sixty-nine. He should have more energy. "That's not normal. You should see a doctor."

He says his brother, Jay, told him the same thing. My father is a smart man, but I come by my stubbornness honestly.

Pleasure to Purpose

"So go!" I order.

"Okay, okay," he mumbles.

"I gotta go, Dad. I'll call you soon. Love you."

I disconnect, then realize I forgot to tell him about Franco and Xena. Although he doesn't understand my love of horses, he would enjoy the story.

Mike wanders out, yawning and smiling.

"I can't believe I fell asleep."

"You needed it," I say, reaching out to pat his leg. "Remember to thank Lizzie for me."

"Will do," he answers, already heading down the stairs.

I turn to go inside and spy the neighbor's cat cleaning himself. Leaning back provocatively, his large belly exposed, he licks his outstretched back leg. He stops and throws me a dismissive glare only cats can muster. I smile, loving his kick-ass cattitude, then go inside and sit down at the computer.

Before I register what my fingers are typing, I've entered the phrase "heart, fatigue and the elderly." A deluge of information appears, from heart disease to diabetes to Chronic Fatigue Syndrome. After several, stress-inducing minutes I realize I won't find an answer to Dad's fatigue without understanding his other symptoms. So, I resolve to follow up with him and switch to a chat room in which sex workers discuss clients. While reading about a young man who's robbed two prostitutes, a banner scrolls across the top of the screen:

Sex Worker Support Group meetings.
Click here for more information.

My curiosity piqued, I click.

Pleasure to Purpose

Chapter 5

After stumbling on the open invitation, I learn the group meets to discuss challenges, share advice and offer support to people in the sex trades. I am, by nature, a soloist, choosing to tackle problems myself. I cringe at the idea of sitting in a circle, sharing my feelings and experiences for others to judge. But recent events—Jared's heart attack, Pat's kindness with Franco, Dad's fatigue—remind me that I can choose to give and accept help. It's scary, but I don't have to go it alone.

I Google the group and learn that it's run by an escort named Anne who works out of her apartment. In addition to sex work, she volunteers with a non-profit called COYOTE (Call Off Your Old Tired Ethics), an organization founded in 1973 to support and promote sex workers' rights. According to multiple sources on the internet, Anne is a force of nature, an intelligent entrepreneur with an analytical mind who enjoys bringing people together to affect change. From all accounts, I pity the client who messes with her.

The next day, as I climb the stairs of a converted Victorian home that serves as the local women's center, my feet slow as excitement turns to apprehension. Sex workers can be competitive, so I wonder what it'll be like to sit in a room full of them. Will each of us tell stories, trying to outdo one another? Or is it a group whose true intent is help and support? One thing is for sure, my trust must be earned. So I plan on being careful with what I say and to whom I say it.

I enter the brick-floored foyer and cross into a large living room. Small, lead glass windows line the walls, allowing muddy sunshine to poke through. Couches and chairs in various colors and styles, some from days long past, are arranged in a circle around a worn Chippendale coffee table. A small kitchenette floored in mustard yellow linoleum lies to the left. As I pass, the aroma of freshly brewed coffee borders on smelling burnt and a plate of doughnuts arranged in a pyramid sits on a Formica counter. The artwork on the cream walls is shabby chic, most likely collected over decades. Women of different ethnicities, ages and sizes mill around, most choosing to remain apart except for a set of twins who warily watch the group, whispering to one another. They're young, maybe early twenties, but could pass as teenagers with too much make-up and little life experience. I wonder if that's how they market themselves, if they work together, and how much they charge.

A woman claps her hands and introduces herself as Anne. Lithe and light of build, she appears younger than her sixty years. A dyed ginger pixie cut frames her oval face. Large green eyes with no make-up but long, lush lashes add to her youthful appearance. Only the fine lines and settling midsection betray her maturity. Once breathtaking, she seems to have settled into an aging beauty who is comfortable exactly where she is.

As she invites us to sit, the group moves slowly, negotiating seating like a game of musical chairs. Once settled, we eye each other before Anne draws our collective attention by saying she knows each of us has a story to tell. She keeps introductory remarks short, her warm openness already putting people at ease.

"Let's begin by saying your name, your preferred pronoun, what type of work you do and how long you've been doing that work. Okay?" She points to a twenty-something trans woman with close-cropped hair, a huge chest that must draw clients, and the kind of deep brown eyes that keep them coming back. "Why don't you start?"

The woman seems caught off-guard, pointing to herself with manicured, raised eyebrows. Anne nods encouragingly.

Pleasure to Purpose

"Hi, um, my name is Camille and I'm new to this. I prefer they/them and let's see… it's been about four weeks I'm doing this. I offer all services and… um… I had a problem recently where…" She trails off as her gaze drops to the floor and my heart goes out to her. She deals with a whole other group of haters. Never mind the people who see our work as dirty or beneath them. This poor woman contends with being called names I'll never encounter.

"This is a safe space, Camille," Anne offers.

Camille nods, then raises her chin.

Good for you. Be the queen that you are.

A tear escapes but Camille quickly swipes it away. "This guy, a client, cheated me. After we were done, he gave me wadded up money and beat it out of there. Turns out he was sixty bucks short. I usually don't feel cheap, not even when they call me a name when they're done, but… I got mad, ya know? Really angry. I mean, this is work, right? This ain't some charity."

I look around the group. Everyone nods because we've all been there. After being cheated by one of my early clients, I learned how to differentiate between the weight of three hundred and four hundred dollars, whether it's in tens, twenties or fifties. I discovered how to count money without the client noticing, because he can never think it's about the money. I memorized the feel of the metallic stripe on a hundred-dollar bill. If it feels wrong, the bill is counterfeit. It's amazing how one cheating jerk changes you, and how quickly you learn so it won't happen again.

"What did you do?" I ask.

She looks at me with wide eyes and says she ran after him, demanding the money. He pushed her and told her to call the cops, then laughed and drove away.

"I felt so…"

"Invisible?" I offer.

Anne intervenes, reminding us to allow others space to think and work through mental minefields. She asks us not to interject, even if we're trying to help. I grit my teeth in frustration. Being a fixer, it's a challenge to stay quiet when I see an obvious solution.

Perhaps sensing my impatience, Camille takes my hand. I smile and squeeze, implying she's not alone, then violate Anne's request by offering my thoughts on how to count money without the client noticing. Afterward

I glance at Anne to ensure I haven't overstepped. She's nodding along with many others, silently reinforcing the advice.

"Thank you for sharing, Camille. Do you want to add anything else?" Anne asks.

Camille shakes her head, looking a little more confident.

"Who else?" Anne asks.

A scrawny white woman with shoulder-length, dyed platinum hair raises her hand. Her hazel eyes are rimmed in red, her teeth stained and uneven. Her sallow complexion reminds me of a heroin addict I did a threesome with who ended up screaming at our non-English-speaking client. Upon closer inspection, however, I realize this woman's eyes are bloodshot from crying. I chastise myself for such quick judgment. Although her emaciated frame might be a result of drug usage, her muscular calves and expensive sneakers suggest she's a serious runner. I settle in with an open mind as she presents a situation I've never considered.

She's in a long-term, same-sex relationship but sleeps with men for money. She differentiates her two lives by rationalizing that as long as she sleeps only with men, she's not cheating. She tells us she's here because she can't discuss her work at home.

"In other jobs if you've had a bad day, you can vent to your partner. But my wife doesn't want to hear the details of a guy whose dick was so big it hurt. I understand her point, but it's hard not having someone to talk to, you know?" Her anguish is apparent and completely relatable. *Maybe that's why I'm here. To have someone to talk to.*

"Anyway, I don't have anything in particular to talk about, just that it's hard to do this work and be in a committed relationship."

Anne asks, "How many people here are in a relationship right now?"

I'm astonished when half the women raise their hands. Although I would've liked a relationship and children, that boat sailed when my fiancé left and I got into sex work. Several clients have proposed, but never someone I felt was worthy of giving up my career. In fact, there's been only one client I'd ever seriously consider dating.

Thomas reached out to me several months after his wife passed. A stocky, bald man, he was shy and nervous when we first met, an endearing quality as compared to more aggressive clients. His nervousness dissipated as we kissed. He ended up being incredibly thoughtful and sweet in bed,

Pleasure to Purpose

making sure I came before he did. Over the ensuing months he treated our transactions as so much more than that, and I found myself looking forward to seeing him. But when he suggested taking our "relationship" to the next level, I shut him down. He stopped seeing me then, perhaps embarrassed or unable to continue because of his strong feelings. If I'm honest, I miss seeing him and still think about him every so often.

As for me, I just don't believe I could be in a committed relationship and be a sex worker. Although I'm pretty good at compartmentalizing, that would be a whole other level. And honestly, could a man really accept that his partner is fucking other people? Once the mystique of dating a sex worker wore off, he'd be left with a girlfriend who cheats on a regular basis. It's a thin wall we construct in this business to keep our true selves tucked away from the client. But it's a wall, nonetheless. Sure, there are times I lower my guard a little when I chat with a regular client about my day or an issue I'm trying to resolve. It's rare though, because when I become Scarlett, I'm a listener, a caretaker and a pleaser. I'm whatever the client needs me to be at that moment.

A woman who looks no more than twenty raises her hand. Her hair is streaked with blonde highlights and is cut bluntly, requiring lots of maintenance. Her make-up is subtle but perfect and her silk blouse hugs factory boobs. Long, lean fingers with manicured nails grip a Gucci bag close to her flat stomach, perhaps afraid one of us might steal it. In short, she's the kind of girl who can charge a hell of a lot of money. She introduces herself as Lauren and says she's been with a guy for over a year who pays her expenses and visits twice a week.

"When I made this deal, I was a kid, ya know?

She still looks like a kid, but I keep my mouth shut. Her voice is high-pitched and breathy. I wonder if it's real or if she's perfected it to appear young and naïve.

"But now I think I'm worth more than I'm earning."

Lauren is a sugar baby, her comfortable lifestyle funded by a man who keeps her on call for whenever he gets the urge. She's playing the long game, betting her future on one man.

Not me. Unless there's a serious commitment from a guy... not necessarily a ring, but a defined, monogamous relationship, I prefer the short game, seeing clients who are in-and-out, pun intended. No muss, no fuss, and no entanglements. I stare at her while wondering if she signed some sort of contract. If she did and breaks it, I don't know how the guy could bring her to court without getting arrested himself. But who knows? Maybe he's a lawyer and knows how to beat the system.

"I mean, I went on Tryst and saw another girl kinda like me who's earning twice what I am. That's just not right."

Tryst is a website where clients can find willing participants of every age, race, sex and specialty or fetish. If you can imagine it, you can find it on Tryst.

"But I don't know how to raise the issue without seeming greedy or pissing him off," Lauren finishes and slumps in the chair, her perfectly glossed lips forming a well-practiced pout.

There's the problem with having a sugar daddy. She's afraid to anger him because she could lose everything. With no backup plan or money stashed away, she's vulnerable.

"Thoughts? Suggestions?" Anne asks.

I raise my hand and suggest she broach the subject when he's in a relaxed state, like during sex.

"You could whisper in his ear, 'You know what's sexy? Being able to pay my phone bill.'" Light chuckles from the group, along with serious head nods. "He might laugh but he'd get the point, and you've made the request in a nonconfrontational way." I shrug while watching Lauren process the idea.

Anne asks if anyone else would like to speak. When no one responds, she announces a ten-minute break and tells us to mingle. People are slow to rise. Speaking in a group is one thing, but sharing intimate stories one-on-one seems somehow more daunting.

I examine the interesting, intelligent group of women as they start to chat and move toward the teetering pile of doughnuts. I was anxious about coming here, worried what it would be like to be surrounded by people like me. But these women aren't like me, and I'm not like them.

Offering advice to those less experienced reminds me how far I've come in my professional development. Although we perform similar work, each has a unique story through which we gain perspective when shared.

I hold my head a little higher, proud to be a part of something bigger than myself.

People have it wrong when they refer to us as sluts.

Sluts are people who sleep around and don't get paid. If you're going to have a lot of sex, you may as well leave the slut life behind to become a sex worker.

That's the smart thing to do.

Chapter 6

I spend the next week seeing clients and creating a financial plan to support Franco's needs. In five days, I earn over three thousand dollars which sits tucked away in a closet. Some of the cash comes from a client who gets off on crossdressing while being guided publicly on a leash, a dog collar cinched tightly around his neck. He says he feels safe, protected and loved when he's wearing a collar. But I think it's the humiliation and attention that excite him. After the perp walk, he's always rock hard. So we return to my apartment, where he asks, "Am I a pretty girl?" I shower him with praise to reinforce his femininity, then we have sex.

He once told me that as a business executive, he comes to me because he's tired of being in control. He wants someone else to make decisions and he's so desperate to be free that he's willing to be recognized in public. The money he pays me for this form of liberty is then used to pay for the care of another creature who also wants to be free. The difference is that my client made a devil's bargain when he entered the business world—money, control and power in exchange for his autonomy. Franco didn't make a choice. He was born free but dominated from an early age. His wild spirit was broken early, forced into a harness and trained to run around a track to please someone's ego and wallet.

It occurs to me that all of us are like lumps of clay. We're born without limitations but slowly molded by expectations until we either fit in, opt out or crack under the pressure. My client fits in during the day but opts out at night by coming to see me. I tried to fit in by going to college and working regular jobs.

It didn't work out, and I've never been happier. Franco was forced to fit in for a while, but I imagine he's more content now that he's opted out through retirement. The more I consider it, the more I realize that Franco and I are kindred souls whose spirits remain vibrant despite best efforts to the contrary. How can I not love him unconditionally?

I'm jittery with anticipation as I drive toward the rescue. Although I've already spent time with him, today's the first day I meet Franco as his new mom. When I offered to make daily runs to the farm, Pat told me that she'd tend to him while I got my "financial horse in order," a terrible joke that consistently makes her laugh until she snorts. I spoke with her every day and was thrilled with the final report on Franco and Xena.

"I've never seen two horses bond so quickly or so completely. It's like they were looking for each other their whole lives."

I'm beaming with pride and happiness as I make the turn down the long driveway leading to the barn. Passing the paddock where Xena and Franco graze peacefully side-by-side, I wave to Pat, then join her at the chipped, wooden fence, watching the horses and enjoying the sunshine warming my back.

"You look… rested," she says.

I don't feel rested. In fact, I'm really tired. But I nod while closing my eyes and breathing deeply, inhaling the scent of manure and hay. Completely at peace, I listen as Franco stomps the hard earth, then open my eyes to find him nuzzling Xena. A soft blanket of contentment drapes over my shoulders, instilling confidence in the choice to adopt this glorious, gentle giant.

As if reading my mind, Pat leans into me. "You made the right decision, ya know."

I face her. "Thanks to you."

A loud "Hey!" breaks the spell. I turn to see Serenity approaching in new designer boots. I stifle a smirk, wondering aloud how much they'll depreciate the first time she steps in horseshit. Pat spits a laugh, then walks away before getting in trouble.

"Hello," Serenity says, throwing a raised eyebrow Pat's way.

"Serenity."

She joins me at the fence where the horses glance at us sideways, choosing to remain aloof while enjoying each other's company. "Seems like Franco's settling in pretty well," she says.

She's extending a verbal olive branch. "Yeah. Thanks for taking him in."

"Sure, sure. Hey, listen, I know Franco is staying here free of charge, so I'm gonna need you here every day to feed and water him. Plus, if you could help out with some other stuff every once in a while, that'd be great."

I consider her request and agree that it's fair. I planned on daily visits anyway, so doing some additional work isn't a big deal.

"Great! You can start by unloading hay from that truck and piling it in the barn."

I follow her pointing finger to see a pick-up truck piled high with hay that will take more than an hour to unload and stack.

I stare hard at her, realizing she set me up, then check the time. I'll need to reschedule a client, so I send him a quick text promising to make it up to him. Serenity walks away, her mission complete.

I return my attention to Franco, who has walked away from Xena and is struggling to urinate. The dark orange liquid comes out in spurts, reminding me he hasn't received healthcare in years. I remove my phone and call Dr. Styles, a local vet who tends to other horses at the rescue.

She agrees to see him the following week.

Franco finishes peeing and breaks into a beautiful trot around the paddock, his elegance resembling a dressage champion. He rounds the bend and stops, sniffing cautiously before recognizing me, then dips his huge brown head so I can stroke his velvet nose. Over the next several minutes he falls asleep, the long, slow strokes lulling him into a comfortable trance. I marvel at his ability to trust so quickly in spite of the abuse and neglect he suffered. I hope he feels how much I care for him. Horses are known to read humans' emotional intent and character, so I'm humbled. I only hope I can live up to the faith he's unknowingly placed in me.

Pleasure to Purpose

He pulls away and looks me squarely in the eye. "Hey, handsome." I laugh, realizing that's how I greet most of my clients. He nuzzles my shirt, searching for a treat. *Smart guy, remembering from the last visit.* I remove half an apple from my bag and feed it to him, reveling in the sound of a crunching, happy horse. **My** horse. Xena wanders over, no doubt drawn by the apple, so I feed her the other half. Franco steps forward again, leaning over the fence.

"I don't have anything else to give you, buddy."

He bobs his head as if to ask, *Are you sure?* then presses his head against my cheek. A rush of emotion tackles me as I wrap my arms around his neck. I dreamed of this as a little girl, a moment of unconditional love where everything makes sense. In the horse book the therapist gave me, the girl's nightmares are carried away by horses. They protect her as she protects them. I wasn't always protected as a child, but I could always rely on my horse dreams to whisk me away to a safe place.

The moment fades as Franco slowly backs away and resumes his slow trot along the fence, Xena by his side. He hugged me, no doubt about it, and I swipe tears away while walking toward the pick-up. Reality steps in as I realize there are at least fifty bales of hay to be dragged down and then stacked, each weighing about fifty pounds.

I slide on some leather work gloves and lug a bale from the truck, then pick it up by the twine that binds it. I'm immediately struck by a tobacco smell, a unique scent that's associated with mold. Although the hay looks dry on the outside, it might have become wet and didn't dry out thoroughly. Horses can develop respiratory and liver issues from being fed moldy hay, so I break open the bale to investigate. Inside I find telltale signs of mold: gray fibers that resemble a spider web.

I glance at Franco, who's slowed to a walk as Xena leans into him, as if relying on his strength. Franco is a born leader, a champion in harness racing and in life. If he were human, he'd be the quarterback who volunteers for Meals on Wheels while maintaining a 4.0 GPA. He certainly didn't survive ten years on the harness racing circuit to live the rest of his life eating moldy hay.

Not on my watch.

I pull out my phone and text a guy in Maine who produces pristine hay. He promises to deliver some bales specifically for Franco by the end of the week. I then text Serenity who asks me to check each bale thoroughly and stack the moldy hay outside the barn.

I swear under my breath. Her request will add at least an hour to this chore. But she knows my conscience won't allow the horses to eat compromised hay, so I drag another bale off the truck and break it open. No mold. I repeat the process many more times. Luckily most of the bales are free of mold, so I stack the moldy bales outside the barn to be dealt with later and return to stacking the healthy bales inside the barn.

While I work, I estimate how much money I'll be spending on the vet and Franco's hay.

"Well, I guess it's hoeing-for-horses time. There ain't no horse without no hoeing," I mutter, determined to make the finances work. A bale rolls from the pile because I've over-stacked. I sigh heavily, frustrated I've made more work for myself. Franco whinnies loudly, drawing my attention. I smile broadly as I feel his joy and freedom.

"It's worth it," I call to him. "You're worth it, buddy!"

Pleasure to Purpose

Chapter 7

After stacking the hay, I muck out Franco's stall, fill it with a double-thick pile of fresh wood shavings, then refill the water and food buckets and hayrack. I brush him thoroughly, bribing him with treats as I remove underlayers of fine fur and work through knots in his mane and tail. He tolerates the attention for a while before pulling away, a sign that he's done for the day. After giving Pat a big hug goodbye, I kiss Franco's nose, whisper how much I love him, then begin the drive home feeling happier than I can ever remember.

Caring for Franco and being responsible for something other than myself has injected me with an energy I didn't know was missing. I've had other animals. Franco is special, very majestic; we relate on a spiritual level. I arrive home that evening smelling like I had a roll in the hay, a bad pun I never tire of considering.

As I exit Betty, my back prickles.

I turn quickly to scan the surroundings but see nothing out of the ordinary. In fact, the street is empty except for a guy with his back to me wearing low rider jeans and an army green hoodie. Although he's arguing with someone on the phone and not paying any attention to me, I eye him a moment to determine if I've seen him before. *Is that the Nissan guy?* I wonder as my hoe phone rings. His dark hair is wavy, yet considerably shorter than the man in the car.

I continue to watch him as I answer. "This is Scarlett. What's your pleasure?"

Heavy breathing comes across the line. I pull the phone away and check the number. *Same guy.* I've dealt with men who won't take no for an answer, cowards masquerading as tough guys. When they're called out on their bullshit, they slink away. This guy is different in that he's not bothered by my anger. He seems stoked by it.

That behavior is troubling and potentially dangerous. I don't want to admit it, but the calls are getting under my relatively thick hoe skin.

"Listen, asshole, either man up and say something or stop fucking calling me!"

He grunts, then disconnects. I chastise myself for letting my guard down and not checking the number before answering. Safety has to be a sex worker's first priority, and I've become complacent. Swinging back around, I'm relieved to find hoodie guy has disappeared. My radar tells me that something about him isn't right, so I file him away in my memory.

Climbing the steps to the third floor, my momentum slows as I notice the apartment door is slightly ajar. It occurs to me that hoodie guy might've broken in and was hanging around to see how I'd react.

I scan the street again.

Completely empty.

I've felt unsafe with a client only once before, when his drug dealing thug friends showed up at my apartment. Although I politely asked them to leave, and they did, I threatened to report the client to the police if he contacted me again. He obliged but I'll never forget the look he gave me. Hurt and anger roiling like an enraged pimp on crack. Too much money and power concentrated in one egocentric ass.

That incident replays in the reptilian part of my brain as I remove a can of pepper spray from my bag. I quietly tiptoe to the door and listen to objects being moved. Heavy footfalls suggest the intruder is unafraid of being heard. I momentarily consider calling the police but quickly dismiss the ridiculous idea, having learned not to trust the police when I was a teenager.

Pleasure to Purpose

I take a deep breath and hold the pepper spray at arm's length, then push the door open quickly. It slams against the wall, drawing the stumbling intruder from the sex room.

Anger quickly replaces fear.

"What the hell are *you* doing here?"

Steve is my mother's brother. A single, ridiculously tall, bald man whose clothes are chronically too large for his emaciated frame. Although he holds a good job, he somehow manages to come across as destitute and needy. After selling his house outright, he came crying to my mother that he was homeless, asking if he could rent the second floor of the three-family building until he found another place. That was six years ago. I've tried engaging with him many times, but we have absolutely nothing in common. So we exchange neighborly chitchat but maintain distinct bubbles that rarely intersect. Until this moment I would've said he's an okay guy.

Using only a pointer finger and thumb, he holds a dildo aloft. Pristine in his cleanliness, I'm shocked he's touching such an object considering where it's been. I watch in grim satisfaction as I see the thought enter his mind. I hold the upper hand, though, because only I know how thoroughly I disinfect my toys.

His thick black eyebrows are drawn so far up they look like wayward woolly bears negotiating the desert of his bald head. "What's this?" he asks, trying to reclaim the moral high ground.

His smugness is repulsive. I consider using the pepper spray after all. "Do you really need me to explain it to you? It's a—"

"I know what it is."

Then why did you ask?

"Why do you have it? And what the hell are you doing with *this*?" He holds up the riding crop Lizzie gifted me. "It certainly looks… well-used."

For a moment I'm six years old, being chastised for asking about Tyler's sudden disappearance. That curiosity landed me in a psychiatrist's office. But I'm not six anymore. I pay rent, and this jerk is manhandling a special token entrusted to me. I snatch the crop and tuck it under my arm.

"None of your business. How'd you get in here?"

He reaches into a pocket and pulls out a string dangling a single key. Only two people have a key to the apartment: me and my landlord, who

Pleasure to Purpose

happens to be my mother. Mom and I have our differences, but why would she violate my privacy by giving Uncle Steve my key?

"I always wondered why men are coming and going at all hours. You're not actually a—"

"Get out!" I order, holding the pepper spray toward him.

He throws up his hands to shield his face, slamming the dildo into his forehead. "Jesus! Relax! I'm leaving."

He throws the dildo on the bed, then maintains eye contact while walking past me. I recognize false moral superiority in his gleeful gaze, otherwise known as the *I got you* look. He thinks he has something on me now, knowledge he'll keep hidden until it suits him to drag it out.

I know this game. Although I don't like to play it, I'm quite adept.

Looking at him intently, I deliver an ultimatum in a calm, clear voice. "If you ever come into my home again, I'll call the cops."

His eyes grow dark, surprising me with their intensity. "You sure about that?"

I deal with a fair amount of arrogance in my clients, but I refuse to tolerate it when I'm not being reimbursed for my time. I lean forward, my face an inch from his. "*Dead* sure. Try me."

He holds my glare, then starts to walk out, the key swinging from his left hand. I snatch it before he reaches the door. He pauses to say something, then thinks better of it and descends the stairs while whistling casually. I wait until I hear his apartment door close before I take the steps two at a time to ground level. After knocking twice, I enter to find my mother watching Wheel of Fortune in the family room. She's dressed in jeans and a white button down, her shoulder-length blonde hair gathered in a low ponytail. Her large green eyes, once vibrant, now seem dull above dark circles that belie life's disappointments. She has a stunning smile, though I can't remember the last time I really saw it.

"Did you give Uncle Steve the key to my apartment?"

She shrugs a narrow shoulder without looking at me. "What's the big deal?"

"Mom, I pay rent. I'm a tenant with rights, and one of them is that people can't enter my apartment without my permission."

The scariest facet of my mother's personality is that she can go from zero to sixty in a millisecond. There's no giveaway, no tell to prepare you

Pleasure to Purpose

for the crazy about to explode. But I'm furious, so I'm willing to take her on.

"I'm speaking to you!" I bark.

I brace for the worst. Instead of flipping out, she lifts the remote and yells at the television, calling the contestant an idiot. I'm not sure which makes me angrier, being yelled at or being ignored. I walk forward, blocking her view.

"Move!" she orders. My mother is a conundrum. She apologizes all the time for absolutely no reason.

Except with me.

With me she can be aggressive and offensive. If she treated everyone in a similar manner, I couldn't find fault. I've been living with this emotional albatross for as long as I can remember.

"Look at me!" I demand.

She narrows her eyes while folding skinny arms across her ample chest. Mom used to be overweight, now she's lean. She also used to be a redhead.

"Don't ever give my key to anyone again. Please. Got it?"

She lifts a drawn eyebrow and leans back into the couch. "It's my house."

The reality is Mom could demand much higher rent for the apartment I occupy, so I check my temper. That still doesn't give her the right to hand out my key to every Tom, Dick or Steve. I bite my lip, considering a different tack. "Why did you give him the key?"

She shrugs again. "He wanted to see how your place compares to his."

Bullshit. Steve saw my apartment when my ex-fiancé and I invited him to dinner after he'd just moved in. Today's visit was simply a fishing expedition for proof that I'm a sex worker. Mom looks at me and I suddenly wonder if she's the person seeking the truth. Maybe she's behind the surprise visit. I consider telling her to unburden myself. But the moment vanishes when she breaks eye contact and I realize how foolish I'm being. This secret is best kept quiet.

My brother William walks in, his thinning, light brown hair standing at odd angles. Wearing what I've come to call the uniform—khakis with a blue, short sleeve, button down—his gray eyes look tired as he runs a hand over his face. The family affectionately refers to William as a neatnik; his closet is organized with several of the same shirts lined up neatly next to perfectly folded khakis on a shelf. His pants hang low on his frame, making me wonder if he's recently lost weight or perhaps forgot a belt. Although he holds a prestigious IT position at a local university, like most of the men in my family he can't seem to find a way to stand on his own two feet and lives with my mother rent-free.

"What's going on?" he asks through a yawn.

"Your sister's throwing a tantrum," Mom says, waving the remote in my general direction.

I throw up my hands, feeling like the only family member who accepts responsibility for choices.

It occurs to me that maybe I should change my attitude. Maybe being responsible and independent is the wrong answer. When you swim upstream for so long, you can't help but question if it might be easier to allow the current to carry you for a while.

My brother ignores both of us and returns to the cocoon of his room. I turn my gaze to Mom who's lost in the game show, she's already forgotten about me.

A sense of weightlessness and emptiness carries me out of the apartment and slowly up the stairs. I'm physically tired from a hard day at the barn and emotionally drained from dealing with my family. My thoughts wander to my dad. I'm thrilled to be rebuilding a relationship with him. I hope someday Mom and I can find common ground.

My mom's mother was not an easy person to like; her sharp tongue and quick slap could draw breath from your lungs. But when she was diagnosed with Alzheimer's, Mom and I worked side-by-side to care for her. Ironically, she became kinder as the neurological disease ravaged her. My concerns that she abused Mom as a girl (concerns Mom never addressed) faded to the background. Mom and I took turns caring for her, reporting to the other before signing off for the shift. We were a solid, capable team, and I felt valued and important. But with the passing of my grandmother, so died Mom's kindness and openness toward me. It was as if her passing signified the death of the new relationship we'd forged.

Pleasure to Purpose

I pass Uncle Steve's apartment, where he's sitting in a recliner by a window. I don't recall the chair being there before and wonder if he's angled it to get a better view of my visitors.

Sighing heavily, I cross him off my mental list as my personal phone dings with a text.

Call me I have news

Chapter 8

I enter the apartment and heat some frozen penne with red sauce. While the microwave works its magic, I call my dad's cell, praying Penny doesn't answer.

"Hiya, hon." My head drops.

"Is Dad there?"

Penny clicks her tongue. "He's sleeping."

My stomach shifts. *He just texted me and now he's asleep?*

"Have him call me when—"

"The text was from me. He saw the doctor."

I brace for bad news as my overactive imagination shifts into high gear. I don't want to have this conversation with anyone, but especially not Penny.

"He's anemic. That's why he's been so tired."

I press the phone to my ear, thinking I've misheard. "That's it? Anemic?"

"Yeah."

I close my eyes in relief.

The microwave beeps. I remove the pasta, stir it, then put it back in and set the timer for thirty seconds while she tells me he was prescribed iron supplements.

"What about his heart? Did they check that?"

Several years ago my dad had a heart attack. I only found out after it happened in a Facetime call that ended with Dad defending his unhealthy lifestyle choices even as he lay in a hospital bed hooked up to six machines.

"I'm sure his heart's fine."

That's code for: Dad didn't want to go through the testing and Penny went along with it. Although he's never going to win a father-of-the-year award, he's all I've got. I'll kick his butt if it ensures his health.

I hear my father in the background, asking for the phone as the microwave beeps again.

"Hi, Princess." He breathes in short bursts and sounds exhausted.

"I hear you're anemic."

"Mmm." He's annoyed Penny gave an update without his consent.

"Did they test your heart?"

In my forty-four years I've seen two friends die long, slow deaths. The first was my best friend diagnosed with cancer in her twenties. She was given several weeks to live but made it eleven years before her body gave in. She was a strong, courageous woman who sold weed to pay her outrageous medical bills when she could no longer work a regular job. The second person was another tough woman who ran the horse rescue before Pat. When she got sick, she asked me to step in and help oversee things. Though I was making great money, I cut back on my clients and never regretted a single moment I spent helping her or the horses.

"You worry too much."

"You didn't answer the question. Did they test your heart?"

"My heart's fine."

I grit my teeth as anger swells. Jared's heart attack looms in my mind as I marvel at Dad's ability to ignore the obvious. Plus, knowledge I gained working in a nursing home tells me that with Dad's medical history and current symptoms, he should have a full work up.

"You can't know that, Dad. You need to go back and ask for more tests."

54

He grunts, effectively ending the conversation. I briefly consider going to Delaware and forcing the issue, but I have Franco to consider now. It's one thing to ask William to watch Don Rickles for a couple of days. But my horse?

In the background I hear Penny say he's missing their favorite show. That's Penny for you. We're discussing my father's failing health, but she pretends everything is normal. I flash to my mother two floors down, hunched in a recliner, staring intently at a screen. *Is this my future? Comatose in front of the boob tube?*

"Just promise me you'll see the doctor if your symptoms get worse, okay? And take the iron pills, Dad."

"I will."

"I'll call you next week."

He clicks off without responding. I stare at the phone screen with my gut in a knot. I text William to update him on Dad, hoping he'll call so I can share the burden. He responds with a thumbs-up emoji. I stare at it for several seconds, wondering what the hell it means, then retrieve the overcooked pasta.

I wonder how long Dad was feeling tired before seeing the doctor. I know some people avoid going because they're scared of hearing bad news. But when it comes to serious concerns, isn't it better to understand what's happening so you can educate yourself and form a plan? That's why I get tested for STDs every month at a local hospital. Sandy never judges as she takes blood and urine. She always asks if I'm safe and happy, reminding me she's only a phone call away if I need her.

Don Rickles winds around my legs, reminding me it's time for dinner. I lean down to pet him, calmed by his gentle purr, then fill a bowl with wet food and place it on the floor while considering my role in our fucked-up family.

By the time I was eight I'd accepted the role of protector. I was hypervigilant regarding Tyler, having developed a sixth sense for predicting with startling accuracy when a rage was coming. It would often start with him breaking something. I'd scoop up the cat while urging William to join me in a bedroom, then lock the door behind us as Tyler stomped up the stairs, searching for a target. We'd listen to my mother trying to reason with him as he punched holes in walls and threw things. As we sat huddled

Pleasure to Purpose

together in the closet, Tyler's manic rage eventually abated like a waning tide returning to the sea. Although the episodes were terrifying, I managed to funnel my fear into action. Mom didn't seem able to take care of us, and Dad simply wasn't there.

I suppose I appointed myself caretaker out of necessity. That's how I became a doer.

Stirring the pasta, I realize I've completely lost my appetite. I turn to throw it away and see the dildo and riding crop on the bed. I hang the crop on a hook and replace the dildo on the shelf, smiling as I recall Uncle Steve's face. Maybe I'm relieved he knows. Maybe I'm not. One thing's for sure, though. Between taking care of Franco and Dad's health, I need to earn more money. The upcoming vet and farrier bills will be expensive and although I don't know my dad's financial circumstances, he might ask for help at some point.

I cross to the closet to remove a box from the top shelf. Inside is approximately five thousand dollars, a large sum that will disappear quickly given current circumstances.

I've learned to live by three critical rules that keep me safe and solvent:

> Never be desperate.
> Never be complacent.
> Don't ever count the money before it's in your hand. It'll disappoint you every time.

Although I'm not desperate, I definitely feel pressure to earn money. Maybe that's why I forget the rules when I receive a call later that night.

Chapter 9

If you make a decision out of desperation, you're putting yourself on defense from the start; you must act in order to survive. If you become complacent, you might place yourself in danger. Finally, if you rely on income you haven't earned yet, you're setting yourself up for disappointment and potential debt. Some sex workers don't have the luxury of applying the rules. A street walker who works so she can eat, for example. But, if possible, the rules help keep us safe, secure and solvent.

These hard-earned words of wisdom are forgotten when my hoe phone wakes me from a deep sleep at 2:17am. Sometimes calls at this hour are a gag. A horny teenage boy completing a dare from another equally as horny friend. Other times they're legit, so after ensuring it's not the heavy breather's number, I answer.

When I don't hear giggling or someone in the background egging the caller on, I assume the call is real. The guy says he saw one of my ads and "needs to see me" at his place.

His voice is deep and raspy, making me wonder if he's been drinking. If he has, he might be asleep by the time I arrive. Or worse, he might forget he called me, leaving me tired, angry and money-hungry.

"It's so late," I grumble as a recent sweet dream tugs at my eyelids.

"C'mon," he urges. "You're so hot."

I open my mouth to decline, then remember I make $350 an hour for an outcall. I adjust my attitude and turn on the charm. "You got it, handsome. Just text a picture of some mail and I'll be right over."

I request a piece of mail with the client's name on it to verify his identity and address. Although it doesn't assure my safety, at least I know the location is legitimate and the client is willing to share his name. That is, unless he's in someone else's house or using someone else's name, which has happened. If a client is in a hotel, I call the front desk and request the particular room to verify there's someone actually there.

"I'm in a short-term rental. No mail to send you."

I waver. It's 2:20 and I can't validate anything about him. Being awakened from deep REM has my brain foggy. But then Franco's beautiful face pops in my head.

"Okay. Text me the address." My phone dings immediately. It's only twenty minutes away by car. Even if it's a scam, I can be home and asleep by 4:20.

I dress in a sheer teddy and throw on an overcoat to ward off the early morning chill. After brushing my teeth, I run a comb through my hair and tiptoe down the stairs, careful not to alert Uncle Steve. The street is barren save a skittish raccoon who scares the hell out of me by toppling a trash can. Betty's engine almost floods before finally turning over, so I add a new car to my growing list of financial concerns while making my way across town. Boston is a beautiful city, especially when it's quiet and dark. The streetlights cast an eerie glow as I travel between their pools of light, making me feel like I'm in a crime novel. **Scarlett Pereira, sex detective.** Kind of a has a ring to it.

I stop in front of a completely dark two-family house. Normally I don't park directly in front of a meeting place because I don't want to draw unwanted attention to the client or myself. But at 3am I take the risk. After examining the windows and seeing no one eagerly awaiting my arrival, I consider leaving. But I've come this far, so I apply lip gloss, wipe mascara from under my eyes and exit the car. The air is chilly, so I pop my coat collar and tighten the belt while climbing the steps of the old brownstone. I ring the bell and wait a full minute before slamming a fist on the door, anger tingling my scalp.

Pleasure to Purpose

Nothing. I remove my phone and text him.

Here. Where r u?

No answer. *What a dick!* I chastise myself for believing him. I turn to leave and my phone rings.

"Boston Police. How can I help you?" the caller says.

I shake my head in confusion. I didn't call the police. They're calling me. Working through the situation logically, my stomach drops when the realization hits home.

I've been set up.

Adrenaline floods my body as fingernails sink into my palms. Sirens sound in the distance, their unmistakable wail crescendoing as I whip my head around to search for the cops who will drag me down the stairs, throw me to the ground and handcuff me. They'll recite Miranda rights as images of my devastated mother cloud my vision.

She'll come to the jail cell where I sit on a bench with other sex workers and shake her head in disappointment. She'll bail me out but remain mute on the way home, her silence a powerful condemnation. Or worse, she won't come at all, leaving me to rot in a dungeon.

As I spin a dramatic tale in my head, the sirens fade away, replaced by the relative quiet of an early Boston morning. Only seconds have passed, but it feels like an hour. As the pulsing in my ears evaporates, I realize something critical: I haven't done anything wrong. I'm simply a woman knocking on a door. I am in a teddy, but still…

"Boston Police. How can I help you?" the cop repeats.

I jump, forgetting I was still on the call. Before I can respond, I hear labored breathing on the line. Tilting my head, I listen while staring at the phone screen. In a heartbeat, adrenaline is replaced by rage. It's the heavy breather. The sicko used a different phone number to contact the police and has conferenced me in. I suddenly remember his text: ***I want to fuck with you.*** At the time I questioned the wording. I now realize he meant exactly what he wrote.

I could just hang up. I could go home and resume a restful night's slumber. But now I'm angry. I've never backed away from a confrontation. I won't start one. But if I'm challenged, I'll see it through. Plus, I want to

59

teach this dick a lesson. He picked the wrong mo fo hoe to fuck with, literally and figuratively.

"Hi," I say to the patient officer. "It looks like my friend is playing a trick on me and put us on a three way call. Sorry to waste your time."

I am sorry. This poor lady is working the night shift, sitting at a phone bank answering crank or legitimately terrible calls. Either way, she has it way worse than me right now.

"You sure you're okay, ma'am?" she asks.

I'm touched. She sounds like she actually cares. Must be a rookie.

I paste a "I'm-pissed-off-and-somebody's-gonna-pay" smile on my face to psych myself up. "I'm good. Have a good night."

I disconnect and am halfway to the car when the heavy breather texts, asking when we can meet. I shake my head, legitimately confounded. I ignore it and try to start Betty while the word "asshole" runs on repeat in my mind.

The engine makes a heaving sound as it attempts to turn over. "C'mon, girl. Now's not the time to poop out on me." I try again, and she sputters and coughs, then dies as my phone dings again.

Seriously When can I see you?

Seriously, you're an asshole! I curse my stupidity. I've broken all of my rules, and I'm paying the price. I should've listened to my gut and not accepted the outcall. But hell is paved with should haves, so I own the mistake and vow to do better.

A stooped man nears my car, slowing as he passes. I freeze, wondering if he's the heavy breather. His long gray hair is unkempt and the blue sweater he's wearing under a worn suit jacket has a large hole. He stares straight ahead, seemingly unaware of my presence. "That's not him," I whisper while surveying the street.

It's empty.

I'm completely on my own if things go any more sideways.

After the man passes the car on the driver's side, I check the mirror and see him stop. He looks up and down the street, then looks straight at Betty. My heart lurches as he turns around and starts back toward me. *He may not be the breather but he's still a threat*, I think as shallow breath leaves me lightheaded. Watching him in the mirror, I try Betty again, only to have her heave and surge without starting.

Pleasure to Purpose

"C'mon, c'mon!" I urge.

The man stops a few feet from the back of Betty. Every muscle in my body tenses as he squints, trying to get a better look. He starts to turn away, then suddenly changes his mind and resumes his approach. His eyes meet mine in the side mirror. My heart hammers as I curse under my breath and reach into my bag to retrieve the pepper spray.

The man peers into the backseat, then places his hands around his eyes to get a better look inside before rattling the door handle. I love Betty, but the only thing protecting me from certain assault is a flimsy, unpredictable lock and a thin pane of glass. For the second time in three minutes, I feel adrenaline flood my body, fueling it for a fight. I slam a fist hard on the window and scream like a maniac, my stress and terror releasing.

The man jumps straight up, then scurries down the street, probably afraid the crazy lady might follow him.

After he turns the corner and I'm confident he won't double back, I beg Betty to start. Holding my breath, I try her once more and laugh out loud when the engine turns over. "Yes! That's my girl!" I say, while patting the dash and pulling away from the curb. I scream when my hoe phone rings, the sound too loud to my hypervigilant ears. Seeing it's the breather again, surprise twists into anger as my trembling hands swipe to answer.

"Fuck off!" I yell.

"Sleep with me."

What started as a money-making opportunity has morphed into the beginning of a B horror movie. It occurs to me that he staged the entire escapade so he could watch me get out of the car, go to the door and receive the police call, all the while getting off on my fear and anger. That just pisses me off more so I choke out a surly laugh.

"You missed your chance, buddy." I disconnect. I feel wired but overtired, like I've drunk too much coffee on too little sleep. Betty's wheels squeal as I take a turn too fast. I force myself to ease back on the accelerator. With any luck, which seems to be in short supply tonight, I'll be asleep in twenty-two minutes.

The phone rings again and I almost run a red light as I beat him to the punch. "Stop calling me, asshole!"

"I have video of you I'll send to the cops."

So, he was watching me. Filming me! Was he in the brownstone after all? Or across the street? Why didn't he just answer the fucking door? Maybe he *was* the guy who tried to get into Betty.

Although fear nips at the heels of my anger, when presented with a choice between the two, I'll choose anger every time.

Fear stifles action.

Anger fuels it.

"Let me get this straight. You have video of me walking up to a door and ringing the bell, then taking a phone call on the street?"

He's silent.

It empowers and calms me. The tide has shifted. I'm now at the rudder of the little boat in which we find ourselves. He probably expected me to panic or perhaps he thought I'm stupid and would sleep with him. To be honest, now that I'm driving and the crisis has passed, I feel remarkably composed. It's the same feeling I had when Tyler would have an episode. I learned how to harness anxiety and use that energy in a proactive way.

I hang up and drive in silence while replaying the evening.

I broke all three of my rules and will never do it again. As I park in front of the apartment, I glance up at the front window and see a light. *Did I leave that on?*

The phone rings again. I click the speaker button but remain silent, my eyes glued to the lighted window. If the asshole is in my apartment, I don't think he could stop himself from standing at the window to check for me. Heavy breath comes across the line. It suddenly occurs to me that maybe I simply left the light on. Or, what if he's smarter than I thought and lured me out so he could follow me home? I whip my head around to examine the surroundings. No one's skulking in the shadows. My gaze returns to the window. Or, I flip-flop, maybe I was right the first time, and he's in the apartment waiting for me. Anger builds as I stare at the window.

*This is **exactly** how he wants me to feel.*

On edge. Indecisive. Second guessing myself so I make a tactical error. I'm genuinely scared, but there's no way he's going to know that.

"Fuck you!" I scream, hoping it sounds more angry than frighted as I disconnect. The curse and accompanying anger bolster my courage as I jump out of the car. Fear takes a back seat to fury as I slam the car door,

Pleasure to Purpose

then stomp up the stairs. I feel reckless and bold. Until now he's been in the driver's seat. For this to end, I have to take control. If he's in the apartment, I want him to hear me coming. Because given my current state of mind, he should be scared. I pause on the top stair and remove my phone. In case he's watching, I pretend to dial 911.

"Yeah, hi. There's an intruder in my apartment. Yeah, I can stay on the line." My voice is raised so he can hear, but level and even as I rattle off the address. "Hey, asshole!" I call toward the door. "The police are on their way!"

I stand back from the door to give him a chance to run.

When nothing happens, I clutch the pepper spray and bounce up and down several times to psych myself up. I run in place to quiet my trembling knees while blowing out several lungfuls of air and envisioning how I'll hit him square in the face with pepper spray. He'll fall to the ground writhing in pain and I'll—"

What? What will I do then?

I can't call the police. Exhaustion overwhelms me as I realize I'm losing momentum. So I take a deep breath, push logic aside and try the handle. Locked. With trembling hands, I retrieve the keys from my bag and gently unlock the door. Then, holding the pepper spray directly in front of me with both hands, I breathe slowly to calm my panicked heart. *It's now or never.* Gritting my teeth, I burst into the apartment, waving the can wildly to cover the entire entryway.

Although the front door was locked, I remain taut and tense while conducting a thorough search. I yank open every cupboard, thrusting the spray forward each time. When I open the hall closet, a broom falls forward, sending me into a tizzy as half of the spray ejects. I snatch the shower curtain aside with such force it rips from the hooks, leaving it hanging sideways. I drop to my knees to search under beds and grab chairs to check top shelves. After exhausting all potential hiding places, I fall into bed, wishing I could've reached out to William or Uncle Steve to escort me upstairs. But I certainly don't want to give Steve fodder for his meddling, and I don't feel comfortable asking William. Besides, how would I explain why I'm out in a teddy at three in the morning?

Pleasure to Purpose

As I begin to drift, my hoe phone rings. Completely spent, I let it go to voicemail. After several minutes, however, unable to let it go until morning, I listen to the short message.

"You *will* sleep with me."

His tone has altered. The timbre is flat, devoid of emotion, which feels somehow more disconcerting than if he were yelling. The sentence is a declaration. It's an inevitability, as if he has nothing to lose.

In my experience, it's the people with nothing to lose who are the most dangerous. The manipulative event he choreographed tonight launched him into a new category. He's no longer just a heavy breathing nuisance. He's a full blown stalker.

I want to scream or throw the phone across the room, but I don't. We all deal with work-related issues we'd like to ignore or leave behind. Mine just happens to be a horny, relentless, crazy stalker.

Physical and emotional fatigue overwhelm me.

For the first time since entering the business, I silence the ringer on my phone. Don Rickles jumps on the bed and curls himself around my head. I fall asleep dreaming of a beautiful farm where Franco, Xena, Don and I live in blissful peace.

Chapter 10

Over the next several days I see as many clients as possible. Not only to increase my *Oh, Shit!* fund, but also to keep someone in the vicinity in case the stalker knows my address. Although I never answer, he calls and texts repeatedly, alternatively threatening, then begging.

In an honest moment I admit I'm over my head. In addition to saving the voicemails and texts in case something happens to me, I consider seeking assistance. But from whom? I can't go to the police because I might be arrested. I can't tell Dad because it would confirm his concerns about my work, and pride prevents me from telling Uncle Steve. I even consider telling Pat until I realize she doesn't deserve to be dragged into this drama. Still, she clearly senses something when I ask her to attend to Franco because I'm sick.

"What kind of sick?" she asks. "Like, sick and tired? Or physically sick?"

Smart cookie. "Can you take care of Franco for me, Pat? Please?"

She pauses a long time before answering. "'Course I will. But promise you'll reach out if you need anything else. *Anything.* Got it?" The way she says *anything* makes me wonder if there's more to Pat than meets the eye. But I decide to tuck that away for another time.

The fact that I can't approach the police is a serious flaw in our legal system. There should be some type of amnesty for sex workers to report a crime, a demilitarized zone where they can report things without fear of retribution. I think about how long Steph and I waited to report Jared's heart attack and the trans worker who got cheated out of hard-earned money. The law enforcement road being closed to me, I even consider contacting one of my clients who told me he'd "take care" of any problem I encountered. Knowing his personality, I'm concerned he'll go too far. Instead, I remain vigilant, checking the street for strange cars, jumping each time a client knocks on the door and generally becoming paranoid as the days pass. My only recourse is hoping he'll eventually tire of the sick game.

A week later I'm stir crazy from being inside so long. When Covid lockdown flashbacks infect my restless sleep, I know it's time to move forward. Besides, I won't allow anyone else to oversee Franco's medical care and his appointments with the farrier and vet are today.

Although I haven't yet met the farrier personally, Scott has a great reputation and I trust him to thoroughly examine Franco's hooves. Yesterday over the phone I explained how long Franco has been without hoof care, and after cursing the previous owner under his breath, Scott agreed to see my boy immediately.

Betty cooperates fully, starting on the first try. I encounter no challenges getting to the farm despite checking the rearview about eighty times. The stalker seems to be taking the morning off, allowing me to focus on my upcoming joy: being outside in the warm sun with the smell of hay, dung and mud surrounding me. When I arrive, Scott is waiting by the paddock where Franco and Xena graze. Franco whinnies loudly when he sees me, as if asking where I've been, then saunters over to accept a treat. Xena remains close to him, nosing my hand for the other half of the apple.

Scott watches the exchange with a huge grin on his tan, weathered face. Thick brown hair styled in a bedhead motif sits above bright, crescent-shaped eyes that sparkle in the sunlight. Rough, calloused hands round out the cowboy appearance. He seems completely at ease on the farm among the horses as he shakes my hand. "Like two peas in a pod, these two, huh?"

I smile proudly while Scott holds his other hand toward Franco's nose to encourage trust.

"Anything I need to know before I go in?" he asks.

I flash back to the vision of Franco being slashed with a crop. It certainly isn't hard evidence, but I don't dismiss it either. "He may have experienced some physical abuse, so just be gentle."

Scott nods, then enters the paddock and traces his hand down Franco's side. Franco watches the newcomer closely. His flank shivers, then stills.

"I think he likes you," I say, feeling my shoulders relax.

Scott runs a hand down one of Franco's legs and gently lifts a hoof. Hooves are made from the same substance as human fingernails. They can grow unevenly, often causing problems if they're not cleaned and trimmed. Much like humans, if horses alter their gait to accommodate hoof pain, over time other ligaments, tendons and muscles can be affected as well.

Franco stands perfectly still, impressing me with his stoicism. The fact he's allowing so much touch given his background reinforces my opinion of his resilience. I hover, waiting to hear Scott's initial opinion. The vet is coming in an hour, but I arranged the farrier visit first because I wanted to start from the bottom up.

"He looks pretty good considering how long it's been," Scott says.

I purse my lips, sensing there's more.

"Xena, though… she doesn't look so good," he adds.

As Franco and Xena walk away, I notice she's favoring her back left leg. I don't recall her limping before and wonder if Serenity is aware. As the rescue manager it's her responsibility to ensure that horses without owners, like Xena, are given basic care.

Scott taps the fence. "I'm not here for her, but I have to check it out. Can't leave the poor thing like that. God knows it might get worse."

I whistle. Franco turns to see me holding a carrot. He tosses his head, then trots over and nibbles the vegetable from my outstretched palm. His whiskers tickle my hand and I laugh.

"You've got some smile," Scott says.

My cheeks get hot and I wonder if he somehow knows what I do for a living. Xena interrupts, reaching her large head over the fence rail. "I have one for you too," I say, offering another carrot.

We each take a horse, guiding them back to the barn. I secure Franco to the crossties in the alleyway while Scott puts on a leather apron that holds his tools. He pats Franco's withers, then runs a hand down the horse's leg, grabs the fetlock, and gently lifts the foot. He removes a pick from the apron and quickly digs dirt from either side of the frog, the center of the hoof that helps to provide traction. A medium-sized stone flies out. I wonder how long Franco's been living with that irritation. When I think about the last time I had a pebble in my shoe and how aggravating it was, anger flares again at how long Franco went without proper care.

Scott replaces the pick and brings out a hard-bristled brush which he wields like he's buffing a shoe. After that, he whisks out a knife and a nipper to shape the hoof before filing it down with a huge rasp. He moves with precision and care, yet makes the work look effortless. Seven minutes later, he lowers the hoof and straightens, then runs a forearm across his forehead to wipe away sweat.

"As you know, wild horses cross uneven terrain, so their hooves usually harden and stay trimmed. But farm horses walk on dirt, grass, straw and wood shavings all day, often stepping in their own feces. If the hoof isn't cared for, it can grow too long or become infected. In this case…" he pats Franco's shoulder, "his frog is a little swollen, but not infected. The sole of the hoof looks surprisingly good."

I nod encouragingly, breathing a little easier.

"No shoes, right?" he asks.

Although some horses wear shoes for therapeutic, protective or performance reasons, I don't like them. If the 2021 Swedish Olympic jumpers didn't wear them, my ex-champion won't either. "He doesn't need them."

Scott nods and moves on to the next hoof. The process repeats until all hooves are cleaned and shaped. As Scott repacks his tools and removes the apron, he comments on Franco's composure. I outline his history, finishing with the newfound friendship with Xena.

"Oh, yeah. I forgot. Let me check her out while I'm here."

We cross to Xena's stall where her head hangs over so she can keep an eye on Franco. She whinnies as we approach. Franco responds, as if to say, *It's okay.* We enter her stall and speak quietly, then gently stroke her neck, flank and withers to warm her up to our presence. When she calms, Scott lifts her back leg as I scratch behind her ear. I'm completely at peace as I place my forehead against her nose, inhaling her scent while surreptitiously examining Scott.

Pleasure to Purpose

Not only is he a cowboy with strong forearms, but his can-do attitude and kind heart make him incredibly attractive. As I watch his jaw muscles tighten and release in concentration, I feel myself soften, then remember I'm committed to being single until I retire. When I settle down, I want to leave the whore life in the rearview mirror. And honestly, I'm not ready to do that yet. So, Scott may be handsome and kind, but he's not an option for me.

"Ah, here it is." He holds up a chestnut that had lodged between her frog and sole. "She should be good to go," he announces.

He stands, brushes off his jeans and leaves the stall.

"How much do I owe you?" I ask.

"That depends. I was thinking maybe we could go for drinks or something."

Dammit! My face must reflect my thoughts because he lifts his eyebrows, looks away and nods, intuiting my negative response.

Embarrassed, he kicks the dirt with his boot. "Okay then. That'll be sixty for today."

I should've accepted the drink. I pay him in cash and thank him as I watch him walk toward his truck.

"See you in a month or so?" I call out. He waves a hand without turning, a sign I've offended his manhood.

I return to Franco, tell him what a good boy he's being and remind him that the worst is yet to come. The vet. Poking, prodding and general unease. But all for his own good.

"Kind of like a pap smear, buddy," I explain.

The vet's pick-up rumbles down the dirt road, a hand poking out to wave to Scott as they pass. Dr. Styles parks, yanks her bag from the back seat and walks toward me, hand extended. She's tiny and lean, with a large, freckled forehead and stringy blonde hair that's drawn into a business ponytail. Her blue eyes crinkle as she smiles.

"Lisa Styles, nice to see you," she says.

We've met before, but never when I was the horse mom paying the bills. I shake her hand. Clean with short nails. Her grip is surprisingly strong for her size, exuding confidence and competence. I've placed my trust in the right hands.

Pleasure to Purpose

A young man no older than twenty appears behind her. He's large and round-shouldered with messy, straw-colored hair and a goofy grin. He towers over Dr. Styles while raising a hand in greeting.

"This is Casey, my tech," the vet explains. "He's here for… well, whatever I need. Right, Case?" She turns to him, he gives a thumbs up.

"Good to meet you," I say.

"Casey's learning quickly. Been with me… what? Eight months now?" Dr. Styles asks.

Clearly shy, Casey nods while blushing.

She turns back to me. "I saw Scott, so I know the hooves are all set. Where's the patient?"

I lead her to Franco who waits quietly in the warm sunshine. I thought he might be nervous at her approach, but perhaps Scott's visit prepared him. Dr. Styles runs her hand along his side, patting him hard. Franco remains calm, sensing her expertise or, perhaps, feeling my trust in her. She evaluates him from every angle before removing a stethoscope from her bag and looping it around her neck. I update her on Franco's background as she listens attentively. When I'm finished, she sighs.

"Unfortunately, I see neglect way too much. But at least he has you now."

I smile proudly, promising to keep up with fur and skin maintenance.

Casey secures Franco while Dr. Styles examines his teeth, eyes, nose, heart, lungs and joints. The tech definitely knows his way around horses. The stern but caring manner in which he handles my champion makes me even more confident that Franco's care is in the right hands. After twenty minutes of being poked, Franco spreads his back legs and drops his penis, urine releasing in spurts. He shifts his weight from side to side, trying to avoid the splatter, but the urine is coming out so unevenly it's impossible. Dr. Styles steps back and watches, a furrow in her broad brow.

"How long's he been peeing like that?"

"Since I got him, but I don't know how long before that."

She crosses her arms and places a hand on her chin. "I'm going to draw some blood today, but we may need a full work-up at my office, including a bladder ultrasound. It could be something as simple as a UTI. Bloodwork will tell us more."

Her words sound hopeful, but her tone implies something more serious. I look into Franco's eyes, remembering my promise to take care of him. He stares back evenly, not a care in the world.

"It would be expensive, but I think you know that," she adds.

I nod, thinking it's just my luck that my first horse is a money pit.

As Casey prepares to draw Franco's blood, an unknown number appears on my hoe phone. I excuse myself to take the call. I'm grateful for the distraction, hoping it's a client requesting a sleepover for a fifteen-hundred-dollar paycheck.

"Hello, this is Scar—"

"Listen, bitch! You're gonna sleep with me or else!"

The world contracts to a pinpoint. My heart races. For a glorious, fleeting morning I'd forgotten the stalker existed. I glance at the screen. He changed his number again, knowing I'd answer.

Then, just as quickly as it appeared, suddenly the fear evaporates, leaving behind a wrath that rumbles like violent thunder during a humid, summer storm.

Something has shifted. I'm done being scared of this guy. I'm not sure what I'm going to do, but it's going to end this ridiculous game. Gritting my teeth, I hiss, "If you don't stop, I'm gonna make you stop!"

"Are you threatening me?" he taunts.

His audacity fuels my rage, and I laugh—a bitter, hard sound that surprises me. "I'm not threatening you, you dumb prick. I'm warning you."

Chapter 11

The next day I'm sitting on the hardwood floor in my living room contemplating how to handle the stalker. When no obvious solution presents itself, I allow my eyes to wander the mostly empty space. My maternal grandfather was a Sicilian master carpenter whose craftsmanship is on display in the extensive, intricate woodwork throughout our three-family house. He was a meticulous, careful man whose eye for detail is undeniable. But he also had schizophrenia and received shock therapy at a local mental hospital. I've often wondered what it was like for my mother growing up. But despite numerous attempts to draw her out, Mom remains secretive, including why she refers to her father only by his first name. Never as Dad, always as Vinnie.

Although I've lived in the apartment for years on my own, I've been slow to decorate. First, I didn't have the money. Then Aaron moved in, and we were going to decorate together. When he absconded with our savings, I was broke again. After that, I started doing sex work, and it just seemed like a waste to spend money on things when I could take care of animals and enjoy massages. But I've reached a point in my life where I want to be comfortable and surrounded by things that bring me joy. So as I stand up and brush off my jeans, I decide it's time to create a warm, inviting space. Plus, a project will distract me from the stalker.

Over the next few days I scrub dirt and dust from the walls and radiators, answering my hoe phone only when I recognize a regular client's number. I paint the living and dining room a light yellow that compliments the sunlight pouring through the oversized windows. I give away my old sectional and hang new white, cotton curtains. Finally, I arrange artwork on the walls, including some of Sonya's drawings from college.

Sonya and I met during preseason soccer. My nervous, quiet nature was drawn like a magnet to her dynamic personality. A brunette force of nature with an Indian father and a Jamaican mother, her hazel, almond-shaped eyes radiated warmth. She was as kind as she was smart, and everyone wanted to be her friend. For reasons I'll never understand, she chose me. Whether it was transforming hidden dorm rooms into party caves or hacking into the grading system to change our test scores, we became inseparable.

Diagnosed with cancer in sophomore year, she faced the news as she did everything else: as a challenge. Her wit was intact to the end. Sonya's assigned nurse was so attached to her, administrators switched the woman to another unit for fear she'd be devastated at Sonya's death. That was the impact Sonya had on people. She was my rock. Her passing affected me like nothing else in my life. I don't remember a lot about the time immediately following her death. I do remember the emptiness, the void that expanded inside me until I thought I'd be hollowed out. Though she died many years ago, I miss her like the sister she was, and tears sprout as I recall the last time we spoke. She said she was fine (she clearly wasn't), told me I shouldn't worry (which made me worry more) and died the next day.

Sighing heavily, I think about my recent conversation with Dad. Like Sonya, he said he's fine. A heaviness invades me that mirrors the feeling I had when Sonya was diagnosed. Shaking my head hard to banish the negative thoughts, I focus on my next big project.

Although I have a bedroom dedicated to seeing clients, I'm considering splurging on a sex couch as another option. The week I stayed home I amassed ten thousand dollars, bringing my savings to fifteen thousand. I figure I can cover Franco's expenses, help Dad out and give

Pleasure to Purpose

myself a little treat as well. *Besides, I can always write the couch off as a business expense,* I joke to myself.

The couch I want is purple, with multiple restraints and several reclining features that encourage creativity. I usually use cash for purchases in order to remain untraceable, but because I'm buying it online I need to use some type of card. I live a debt-free, card-free life, so purchasing online requires a fair amount of coordination. Then there's the additional problem of working with banks, even using cash. I can't go to a bank and repeatedly deposit thousands in cash without raising eyebrows. At some point a nosy teller or supervisor is going to spot a pattern in my deposits and raise a red flag with the IRS. That's how Eliot Spitzer, disgraced ex-governor of New York, started his fall from grace. One would think that the treasury department has better things to do than go after a small-time sex worker, but I'm not taking any chances. Instead of trusting my money to a bank or credit card company, I use PayPal, Visa giftcards or CashApp to stay under the radar.

My hoe phone buzzes. I wince, expecting to see a text from the stalker. The amount of time and energy he's spending makes me think he's legitimately out of his mind. I breathe a sigh of relief when I see it's not from him. It's from Shawn, a fifty-something regular who calls every few months. He's a divorced father of two who's incredibly disorganized but has a generous heart. He's always on time, respectful and clean.

Available today?

I reply with a thumbs-up emoji, appreciating how easy it is to coordinate with clients. In earlier days, I would've received a phone call. Before that, I suppose clients would've just shown up, hoping I was available, and queueing to wait if necessary.

Shawn immediately responds, asking if he can come over now. I agree, then jump in the shower. Like most clients, Shawn prefers me hairless. I made the mistake of waxing once and burned myself in the process. After that painful disaster, I take great care to shave until I'm smooth, then apply lotion.

As I'm applying lip gloss, Shawn knocks twice and enters, a wide grin fixed on his tan face. He's a tall, burly man with large hands and chest hair that sprouts from the collar of a tight, black t-shirt. I try to find something sexy about each of my clients. In Shawn's case, it's not difficult. He's

Pleasure to Purpose

incredibly manly without exuding testosterone until it tips beyond a pheromone into a stink. As I approach, his dark blue eyes devour me, lingering on hard nipples popping out over the rim of a half-cup bra. I lift a leg and swing it wide to reveal crotchless panties.

His breath catches. "Hey, beautiful."

"Hey, handsome. How was your day?"

"Certainly better now."

I kiss him deeply while unbuckling his pants, then reach inside to feel a rock-hard cock.

"Somebody's ready for me," I whisper before leading him to the sex room where a black satin-sheeted canopy bed awaits.

Shawn loves that I have a room dedicated only for sex. He isn't into BDSM or being pegged with a dildo I strap on. He prefers the girlfriend experience.

He hands me three one-hundred-dollar bills. I feel for the silver streak, not because I don't trust him, but out of habit. I place the money on a shelf, then slowly unzip his pants while exploring his mouth with my tongue.

"I'm gonna make you feel so good," I moan in his ear before biting the lobe.

His jeans fall heavily to the floor as I lick my way down his chest, taking my time around his nipples. His breath comes faster as I trace a finger along the elastic of his boxers, tugging gently, teasing. Eventually I kneel, pull down his underwear, and take his generous hard-on in my mouth to warm him up. He grabs the bed's footrail and thrusts forward, but I hold my ground while luring him to the brink several times. He pulls me up while his tongue traces my ear, then travels down my neck, and across the top of my breast as we fall into bed. I straddle him, rolling down a condom with my mouth while fondling his balls, then lower myself onto him and rock slowly until he comes, which happens more quickly than usual. Whether he took a blue pill too early or really needed the release, we're left with another forty minutes to complete the hour. For all I know he may want a repeat performance in twenty minutes or so. But for now, we lay side by side, staring at the ceiling, both breathing a little heavily.

"That was something!" he says.

Pleasure to Purpose

"Sure was," I say in response. He's not wrong. I came when he did. Maybe I needed the release too.

"What's new in your life?" he asks.

Sometimes when we have extra time, a client makes small talk to be polite. But when Shawn asks, he really wants to know.

"Lots actually."

He props up on an elbow, gazing down at me. "Like what?"

I look around, unsure where to begin. "Well, my dad's sick with anemia, or that's what the doctors are saying. But given his heart issues I'm wondering if it's more than that. My horse might be sick because he's peeing funny, and I have a stalker who won't leave me alone."

Shawn stares at me, then blinks. "Sorry about your dad. I didn't know you have a horse… and a stalker?"

I explain how I came to take care of Franco and how expensive it might be, then describe the tenacious ass who wants to sleep with me. Shawn lays back down. "Do you need me to get involved?"

I watch a mosquito float lazily through the air, then shift my gaze to the ceiling, thinking I should put a mirror above the bed. It's a little obvious, but it could be fun.

"Why would I want you to get involved? It's not your problem."

I feel him shrug next to me. "Well, I am a cop."

My entire body tenses while flashes of being arrested fly through my mind. Then I relax, realizing I'm losing my edge. Shawn's been seeing me for years. There's no way he's a cop. I slap his leg. "A cop. Yeah, right. You scared me!"

He turns his head to look at me. "You knew that."

Um… nope, is all I can think as my adrenaline spikes again.

When I first became an escort, I'd scroll through clients' social media accounts to identify red flags. But I quickly learned that people post only what they want you to know, and certainly not the things they wish they hadn't done. When I commented about this to Steph, she told me about a guy named Joey the Player whose online profile painted him as a successful entrepreneur who gave back to the community and was involved in the church. In reality, the native New Yorker traveled through Boston and New Hampshire raping and stealing from high-end escorts.

Pleasure to Purpose

I stopped prescreening after that, instead paying attention to my gut, to any niggling feeling I got that something isn't right. We all have it, but the more you cloak yourself in false safety nets, the less attention you pay to it. If I have concerns about a client, I ask for the number of a former escort under the auspices of learning what he likes. But I've had no concerns about Shawn, so I didn't research him.

I sit up quickly, trying to find a way out. There isn't one. "I didn't know you're a cop."

"You didn't look me up on KYG?"

KnowYourGuy is a site where sex workers chat about and rate their clients, like transportation apps where drivers rate passengers.

I shake my head, shocked that my radar has dimmed so much. But if I'm going down for sex work, I'm glad it's with Shawn. At least he has the decency to pay for my time instead of demanding it in exchange for keeping my secret.

I extend my wrists toward him. "You gonna arrest me?"

His eyebrows come together as he pushes my hands down and pulls me close. "Are you nuts? No way."

He tells me I'm the kind of sex worker he's not worried about. When I press him on it, he ticks off a list.

"You don't do drugs, your services are offered behind closed doors and you don't have a record. You're good. Besides…" he squeezes a nipple, "then I'd miss out."

I consider what he said, realizing that if he'd met me on the street instead of through an app, he might have arrested me when we first met. But he didn't, and maybe I can use the new knowledge to my advantage. Information is control, and control is power. I straddle him, brushing my breasts against his lips.

"Wanna go again?" I whisper.

He's less hungry this round and takes his time, making sure I come before him. Afterwards, as we lay side-by-side, I twirl his chest hair around my fingers.

"How easy would it be to take me off the police's radar?"

He's quiet a moment. "You mean make you a confidential informant so you'd be protected?"

Pleasure to Purpose

I smile and shrug. That's exactly what I was thinking, but now it's his idea.

He looks at me sideways, then glances at his watch. "I gotta go, but I'll see what I can do."

He dresses, goes to the door, then gives me a wink. "See you soon?"

"I hope so." I smile and blow him a kiss.

As he descends the stairs, I'm proud of myself for turning a potentially terrible situation into a unique opportunity. My hoe phone rings, I grab it thinking Shawn's forgotten something. Heavy breathing comes across the line and I remember Shawn's offer of help, lost amidst my fear of being arrested.

"Listen, asshole, I don't have time—" I start.

"Who's the dick just left your house?" His voice sounds primal. Low and deep. Almost a growl. I register how angry he sounds, even as I realize…

My stomach clenches, then expands, leaving behind a wave of nausea. I sprint to the window to see a green, rusty Nissan pull away from the curb across the street. The driver is wearing a bright red baseball cap and an army green hoodie. We make eye contact, he glares, then throws me a stunning grin as the battered car zooms away. I recall the first time I saw the Nissan and realize he's playing the long game—the heavy breathing calls, surveilling my house—first in his car and then in person the night Uncle Steve was in the apartment. Finally, his *coup de grâce,* drawing me out in the dead of night to rattle my nerves and keep me on edge. He's not just smart. He's patient and cunning. Worse yet, his erratic behavior is escalating.

My instinct is to call Shawn and beg him to find the guy, but I know that's panic talking. Plus, I'm already asking a lot of him to make me a CI.

I close my eyes and breathe deeply, willing my befuddled brain to think logically. The gut that failed me with Shawn is on high alert now and I've no doubt the stalking will become even more bold.

What's his end game? To rattle me? To kill me?

Don Rickles meows loudly, drawing my attention. With trembling hands I scoop him up, allowing his warmth and softness to calm my frayed nerves. For several minutes I bury my nose in his long fur, stroking him while I stare at the spot the Nissan occupied. The vision of being locked in Betty, slamming my fist in terror as a man peered through the glass, plays

Pleasure to Purpose

on repeat in my mind. That's exactly how I feel: trapped and helpless. Two things I swore I'd never be, and the exact opposite of how I view myself.

The epiphany wraps a vise around my skull. I swallow my pride and march downstairs to ask Uncle Steve to look out for a rusty green Nissan. His eyes narrow but he agrees.

"What do you want me to do if I see it?" he asks.

I examine his face for smugness but see only curiosity and, unless I'm mistaken, genuine concern.

Thrown by his compassion I say, "Just text me if you see it." Then add, "Thanks," before returning upstairs to secure the door. I take a steak knife from the kitchen and stuff it under my pillow, then grab Don Rickles before locking the bedroom door. I lie on the bed, an arm under the pillow for easy knife access, then get up and complete the dramatic scene by dragging a dresser in front of the bedroom door.

Only then do I settle into a restless sleep.

Chapter 12

The next morning I wake up groggy, having repeatedly dreamed of Franco being stolen. I dress for the barn, then stare obsessively out the window while scarfing a bowl of Captain Crunch with one hand and gripping pepper spray with the other.

I slurp the leftover milk, then place the bowl on the floor for Don to finish. While descending the stairs and thinking about the calming effect Franco has on me, a car backfires and sends my heart soaring. I sprint to Betty and drop the keys trying to unlock the door, then throw myself inside and slam the lock. I sit quietly, my knuckles stark white against the black of the steering wheel. I wonder if I'd feel more secure carrying a gun. I've never considered the idea before and realize how out-of-control I feel. Still, the thought boosts my confidence and gives me something to focus on as I arrive at the barn and take care of my boy.

Later that day, I decide to attend another support group meeting. Although I don't have an agenda in going, once there I realize I'm seeking solace in solidarity. Only another sex worker can truly appreciate my stalker situation. I recount the story, partially to alleviate my stress but also as a learning tool for the younger girls. They listen with wide eyes, probably reassuring themselves that something like this will never happen to them because they're careful or clever or smarter. While that may be true, it escalated because I violated my rules when I agreed to meet him that night. If I hadn't been desperate for money, I would've listened to my gut and turned him down. But I didn't, and now I'm paying the price. Do I deserve what happened? No. Do I take responsibility? You bet I do, and now I choose to pay it forward.

"Remember, never be desperate, never be complacent and don't ever count the money before it's in your hand."

A young, new-to-the-business member scrunches up her face and yawns, clearly bored. It's ironic, because as a newbie she's the most in need of advice.

"What are you gonna do?" a small voice asks.

I turn to face a huge pair of deep blue eyes, opened wide in anxiety and curiosity. Randy sits ramrod straight. A nineteen-year-old, full-lipped, petite, natural blonde whose resemblance to a doll must bring in a lot of business. When we introduced ourselves, she told the group she's been on the streets for over three years. It must have been pretty bad at home to have left so young, but she's obviously a survivor. You wouldn't think so based on her looks, but perhaps that's her superpower. Many of us are tougher than we look. We have to be.

"Obviously I can't go to the police," I answer.

A large woman named Marty blows out air in frustration. *"Psshht! That's just bullshit is what it is! The fact you can get harassed and maybe raped and you can't do nothing about it? Fuckin' ridiculous. These laws have got to change!"*

I consider telling them about Shawn but decide to keep that information to myself. I don't want them to know I'm sleeping with a cop, even though many of them probably do too. Nor do I want them to know I've requested what amounts to amnesty.

"Marty's right," another woman comments. Grumbles of agreement rumble like thunder.

"I've considered getting a gun," I say, testing the idea out loud to gauge the reaction.

"I'd zap that motherfucker," one girl says while removing a taser from her bag. Her eyes are wild as she examines the device, making me wonder when she last used it. If I were a betting woman, I'd say recently.

Pleasure to Purpose

Clearly, she hasn't thought it through though, because to taze him I'd have to be—

"Stupid! That'd mean she'd have to be close to him!" Randy spurts. Like I said, she's a survivor.

Anne interjects, reminding the group to allow people space to finish their thoughts and to speak in an inclusive manner.

"Anyway, I know I'll come up with a plan. It just might take a while to execute," I finish.

"My pimp could execute him." We turn in unison to a monotone, wigged brunette who refused to introduce herself. When no one responds, her eyes dart defensively. "What?"

I almost burst out laughing, but that would be rude. Instead, I lean forward, trying to keep my voice level. "I'm not executing *him*. I'm executing a *plan*. Carrying out a plan."

At first she doesn't understand, then her mouth forms an *oh*. She nods, then retreats into the safety of silence.

Anne clears her throat. "Anyone else?"

A girl named Misty raises her hand. She's big boned and strong with deep lines in her face. Her long nails are yellowed from smoking. I wonder how much experience she carries in the bags under her eyes. She's probably forty-five but looks sixty. "You know the Sex Work Study Commission?"

Although several people nod, most of the group stays mute.

"Can you tell us about it?" Anne asks, reading the room.

Misty sits up straighter, proud to share her knowledge. "There was this group that studied racial equity and health laws that affected people like us. It was a really good idea, but it turns out that the lawmakers didn't really listen to what us sex workers said. So nothin' changed."

When the commission's findings were first released, I read the entire summary and was disgusted that so much time, money and effort resulted in surface resolutions that lacked operational detail.

"Go on," Anne urges.

"Anyway, I heard they're thinking about having another commission. This might be a chance to make our voices heard. We need to write our reps. Tell 'em what we think."

Anne looks around the group, some of whom have leaned forward. Because sex workers are used to operating in the shadows, it's not in our natures to seek the spotlight. As I evaluate my peers, I realize a tipping point has been reached. I consider Misty's idea and a tiny nugget of determination begins to form. At the very least we should be able to report a crime without fear of retribution.

Anne returns to Misty. "What do you think we should say to our representatives?"

Misty recounts a situation in which spa owners waited too long to report the fatal shooting of one of their massage therapists. They didn't know she was offering Happy Endings to her clients and were afraid the business would be shut down if the truth came out. She also recounted a 2021 ruling against a spa in which the owner had to shut down and pay a $650,000 fine after being found to employ three prostitutes, 80% of the fine went to the local police precinct and 20% went to the attorney general, leaving nothing for the legitimate massage therapists who lost their jobs.

"How does that help anybody?" Misty laments. "The sex workers went to jail and the massage therapists got their lives ruined. The only winners were prosecutors and cops."

"And what about the cops?" the wigged brunette mutters. "They can get their rocks off and then arrest us so we get fucked twice? Kinda doesn't seem fair."

Eye rolls and nods all around.

"Not to mention the October round-ups. I mean, what the actual fuck?" another girl offers.

Before the Heaux app was shut down, rumors were posted about upcoming sting operations. A lot of them happened in October, like the cops had a quota to meet before the end of the year. I've heard that precincts receive funding based on how many girls they "save" from prostitution, so maybe that has something to do with it.

The group devolves into a bitch session about cops, making me glad I didn't mention Shawn.

"I'm from Rhode Island. They recently closed a loophole that allowed brothels if they weren't in plain sight, like sex rooms in the back of clubs. They were legal as long as they weren't seen." The girl laughs derisively. "How stupid is that? Just decriminalize it already!"

Anne holds up her hands for silence. "How many people have witnessed a crime but not reported it for fear of being arrested?"

Pleasure to Purpose

Seven of ten people raise their hands. Seven crimes that might've been addressed if we weren't scared of the police.

"Okay. I don't normally do this, but I'm assigning homework. You don't have to do it, but Misty's right. If we want things to change, we can't sit on the sidelines. I want each of you to write a letter to your respective representative outlining what you'd like changed. If you don't know who your rep is I can help you. The letter doesn't need to be long, but I want you to write it. Got it?"

Everyone nods. I'm a little surprised but proud of our group. What started as a gaggle of strangers is quickly becoming a unified force.

"I'll gather the letters at the next meeting and submit them to the COYOTE president to share with the reps. If Misty's right about another commission, our timing might be perfect."

Anne ends the meeting and asks us to take a business card to spread the word about the support group. Most of us run our businesses as solo enterprises, so not surprisingly, only two people take a card, Misty and Randy. I avoid the doughnuts, opting only for a cup of lukewarm coffee. Randy walks over, grabs a doughnut, and stares at me until I face her. She's impossibly tiny, reminding me of a bird. Her large eyes and delicate bone structure make her seem even more fragile up close.

"Can I help you?" I ask.

"You're independent?"

I nod.

"How long?"

"A while."

"You like it?"

"Yeah."

She's probing because she's looking to get out from under a pimp. To go where? Another pimp? Not likely because her current enforcer would hunt her down. To be on her own? Not without some serious protection. She's tough, but in this business brawn often wins.

I regularly receive texts from pimps telling me I should "join the winning team" and "there's no I in team." It's as if they're hiring for a call center position or something. When I engage in text conversation, they usually say I need protection in case someone tries to kill me. When I don't bite, they hurl insults or threaten physical or sexual assault, becoming the

Pleasure to Purpose

very thing they say they want to protect me against. Their egos are astonishing. One time a pimp came to me as a client and left his Rolex behind as payment. Turns out it was fake. Since then, I've steered clear of all of that. Sure, I could work for an escort or dominatrix agency, but they'd take forty percent. I'm happy on my own.

I feel sorry for Randy as she nibbles the doughnut, taking little, mousy bites. Turning slightly, I justify my withdrawal by remembering that life is full of choices, I'm responsible only for mine. Besides, I have enough on my plate without accepting responsibility for a late-teen hooker.

"Maybe you and I could work together," she offers.

"You have a pimp?"

She nods, her sincere gaze holding mine.

I look away. "Maybe." She looks so hopeful. I want to be kind, but there's no way I'm seeing clients with someone who works for a pimp. When pimps ask me to train their girls, the answer is always the same. If I'm training them, why wouldn't I become a madame in my own right? The answer is, I want to be responsible only for myself.

She holds up the business card. "I might tell my cousin about this place. Maybe she'll come to the next meeting."

I nod to be polite, wishing I could find a way to end the conversation.

"You feel safe?" she asks quietly.

"Pretty much." *Until recently.*

She stuffs the business card in her pocket and places the rest of the doughnut on a napkin as my phone rings. I was planning on calling Dad on the way home, but he beat me to it.

"Sorry, Randy. I gotta take this." I turn away, grateful for the interruption. "Hey, Dad."

"It's not your dad. It's Uncle Jay."

"Why are you calling from—"

There are several moments in my life when I can remember my body suddenly turning cold, like the blood has drained quickly, leaving a skin suit behind.

This is one of them.

"What's wrong?" I ask, my blood pressure spiking.

"Don't get upset."

"What's wrong?" I repeat.

"It's your father…"

Uncle Jay has a flair for drama, but his tone is serious right now. My jaw muscles tense. "Well!?"

"He had another heart attack."

Chapter 13

Uncle Jay is the eldest of five siblings on my father's side. A self-described hippie, he's a barrel-chested, pony-tailed yogi who drinks too much and swears like a sailor. He's acerbic and witty and super fun to be around. He's been with Brian, his opposite in every way, for fifty years, way before I understood what being gay means. If I ever settle down, theirs is the relationship I'd look to for guidance. They're the healthiest, most solid couple I know. In short, I love him.

I step away from the group to find some privacy. "Is he—"

"He's in surgery, hon. They found some blocked arteries and they're putting in stints."

"Stents."

"That's what I said."

After completing rehab following his last heart attack, Dad was given a clean bill of health. You'd think the close call might have prompted a healthier diet or increased exercise. It didn't.

"I'll call when I have news. He's gonna pull through, hon."

"Yeah… okay." I hang up and turn to see Randy staring at me. Tears sting but I swipe them away.

I recall the last conversation with Dad when I asked about testing his heart. He dismissed the idea and now he might die. *I should've pushed harder.* I feel detached as my eyes travel the room but land nowhere. I was looking forward to building a stronger relationship with Dad. Fate may steal that opportunity, leaving me alone with a mother who offers my key to a nosy uncle. I feel a sudden urge to drive the ten hours to Delaware, but then remember Franco's follow-up appointment. He needs to see the vet. *Am I placing my horse's health above my dad's?* On the other hand, Dad is safe and being taken care of. My presence isn't going to make any difference between his living and dying.

"Everything okay?" Randy asks, stepping closer.

I don't feel like sharing but appreciate her kindness, so I briefly explain the situation. She shrugs, tells me she never knew her father, then walks away as my phone rings again. Dad's number is on the display.

"You have news already?"

"It's Penny."

I squeeze my eyes shut, unsure I can handle her right now. She starts crying, saying she can't lose my father, and how he's everything to her. She ends with, "So when are you coming to help me?"

Guilt seeps in slowly like a spilled jar of syrup. But there's something else nipping at the edges. Anger. Dad might have avoided this attack if he'd listened to his body. Instead of debating the idea with Penny, who would only make excuses, I explain the Franco situation.

She explodes. "It's just like you to put yourself first!"

I stifle a retort while a childhood vision appears: three kids sitting on hard, wooden stairs with packed bags, waiting to be picked up. Although hours pass, none of us dare leave our posts as we shiver in the early evening chill, afraid we'll miss Dad's big car that matches his big smile. At 7pm Mom receives a call saying Dad isn't coming because Penny decided it's not a good weekend for her.

"I'm hanging up now," I say.

"Don't you dare hang—" I press the red button, silencing her threat, only to hear my stressed heart pulsating in my ears.

My father lost two brothers, one to a massive heart attack at the age of twenty-seven and the other to suicide. Although I was a child at the time,

Pleasure to Purpose

I have distinct memories of my parents' sadness at both deaths. Instead of discussing it, though, a vacuum of silence followed.

My phone rings again and I snap, "What, Penny!"

Deep laughter comes across the line, followed by a gravelly bass voice. "Is that how you're greeting clients these days?" I pull the phone away and glance at the screen. STAN.

There are very few clients who have my personal cell number. Stan earned the privilege when he passed the four-year mark of monthly visits. I haven't seen him in the past few months because his security firm was working a gig abroad.

I smile as an idea begins to form. Stan once told me, "If anyone ever bothers you, a phone number's all I need to take care of it." I remember saying I could take care of myself and wouldn't need his services. But I tucked the offer away, just in case.

"Hey, stranger. What's up?"

"Me, so I want to come over. That okay?"

I ask if he wants to meet in a local park, his favorite place to receive a blowjob or have sex. Not during-the-day public sex where anyone can see. He enjoys the dark, after-hours, thinned-out park crowd. He likes hiding behind bushes so the sounds might draw onlookers. It's the rush of potentially being caught that gets him off.

"I'll head to your place," he says.

Perfect! "See you in thirty minutes."

While I help Anne clean up, she reiterates the importance of writing the representative letter.

"You've helped girls here with your advice, Scarlett. Just think what you could do with a larger platform," she adds.

I feel a rush of pride and appreciation, then wonder if I want a larger platform. The idea makes my heart trip a little. I can't discern if it's excitement or apprehension. Deciding I'm getting ahead of myself, I promise to write the letter.

Betty starts on the third try and clunks all the way home, reminding me to come up with a plan before she kicks the bucket. Although I don't want to spend the money, she's sending me clear messages that it's time to move on.

I focus on sending Dad positive vibes the entire trip home and scan the surroundings before exiting the car, my hand tightly gripping the pepper spray. The street is quiet except for some loud music and two teenagers arguing about Taylor Swift's impact on the world. I decide to stop by Mom's apartment to tell her about Dad. When I relay the news, she waves a hand without taking her eyes from the TV. I wait, hoping to have a real conversation. She may no longer love Dad, but she shares three kids with the man. After several moments of being actively ignored, I shrug.

"Just thought you'd like to know," I say before turning toward William's room and knocking on the closed door. Receiving no answer, I consider calling him, then decide I'll tell him tomorrow. Or, perhaps he already knows and doesn't care.

I run upstairs to brush my teeth and change into a matching red lace bra/panty set I know Stan likes. When a knock sounds, I lift my breasts and push them together to achieve full impact, then open the door to find Stan leaning against the jamb with an arm above his head. His white-blonde, straight hair is longer than I've ever seen it. He sports a broad mustache I find irresistible. His Swedish complexion, naturally ruby red lips and impossibly high cheekbones give him the appearance of an aging model. Although I don't know his exact age, I'd put him at a young fifty-five. He's still strong because he works out, but he's starting to lose the effortless beauty youth affords. His intense brown eyes bore into mine as he walks in and closes the door. While handing me the money, I glance down to see that his jeans are unfastened. When I meet his gaze again, he smiles lasciviously, then whips out his mushroom-shaped cock and starts masturbating. Stan's not a chitchat kind of guy. He's all business until we're done. I lick my lips and watch him play with himself.

"You like watching?" His voice is husky, breathless.

I step forward quickly and grab his hand to still it. "I'd rather be involved," I whisper.

He presses me against the wall, but I slide down and take him in my mouth. He grabs the top of my head and pushes me down while lifting his hips, trying to thrust deeper into my throat. I don't enjoy being face-fucked. In fact, it's one of the limits I set early on with clients, and Stan knows better.

Pleasure to Purpose

Tamping down my annoyance, I remove his hand from my head and stand, commenting on his aggressiveness. He apologizes, takes my face in his hands and kisses me tenderly. I lead him to the sex room where he bends me over the footrail, pulls down my panties, and takes me from behind. I barely have time to register how hard he's thrusting before it's over. When he's done, he steps out of his pants and throws himself on the bed, splayed like a starfish.

I lean against the footrail while thinking how aggressive he was. "Someone's been watching a lot of porn."

He raises a hand. "Guilty as charged."

I examine him before joining for a cuddle. "You okay?"

"Yeah. I'm good. Just a lot going on at work."

"Wanna talk about it?"

He shakes his head.

"I have a lot going on too," I say.

He grins, highlighting the gap in his front teeth. "Wanna talk about it?"

"I do actually. Remember when you told me to ask if I ever need help?"

"Sure."

I relate the entire stalker saga while he listens intently. Before I'm finished, he sits up quickly like a dog excited for a car ride.

"You got his number?"

"Not his license plate but I have his original cell number. He's gone through several since this began."

Stan grins wickedly, making it look more like a sneer. His eyes are wide with enlarged pupils, and I suddenly realize how little I know about him. *Is this a mistake?* I don't want the stalker killed, just scared off. Too late now. The request has been granted. Stan asks me to wait a few days, assuring me he'll "take care of business." I start to ask what he means, then think better of it, finding another way to use my mouth instead.

He prepares to leave a half hour later, much more relaxed than when he arrived.

As he descends the wood stairs, I hear footsteps walking up. I grab a robe and close the door to the sex room, just in time to see William finishing the climb. He jabs a thumb toward the stairs. "Who's that guy?"

Pleasure to Purpose

"Just a friend." He glances at the sex room door, making me wonder if Uncle Steve blabbed. If William knows, then Mom knows too. The idea makes me shiver, but I mask my discomfort by opening the French doors leading to the living room, implying he should follow. He glances at the fresh paint and new curtains.

"Looks nice."

"Thanks." The sex couch hasn't arrived, so the room is devoid of furniture, not allowing him to become comfortable. A part of me wishes we could sit and have a lengthy conversation, but the part of me that operates in the shadows knows that's a bad idea.

"Mom told me about Dad."

"Yeah. It sucks," I say.

"At least Tyler's there."

In a group home where he resides as a ward of the state, I think. Tyler's so medicated he's unable to leave the grounds without being accompanied.

"Remember when he almost killed you?"

The swift topic change catches me off guard. I reluctantly remove the memory from the mental closet where I've so carefully stored it.

It was a hot summer day. We were bored, our tempers on edge. Tyler was picking on William. When my mother came to his defense, Tyler turned his aggression on her. I yelled to distract him and time suspended for a split second as silence replaced chaos. His wild eyes found me, then his six-foot frame descended with the speed of a viper. The pain was unbearable as his thumbs pressed on my larynx. I can still hear the guttural grunts as I desperately struggled for air, more confident with each passing second I was going to die right there in our living room. I tried to pry his hands loose; they were unrelenting. Seconds ticked by. The world contracted. First came pinpoints of light, followed by flashes of color, then black, blissful silence. I remember floating above my body, observing the horror with detached curiosity. His hands on his mouth, William stood mutely in the corner watching as Mom spoke to the Department of Social Services. Suddenly Tyler relented. My body dropped to the floor. Mom was standing over me sobbing and screaming, "You killed her!" I remember wanting so much to remain a floating light above the mayhem, but I felt a pull to re-enter my body. I reluctantly returned and awakened, coughing and gasping for breath.

Pleasure to Purpose

A shaking hand involuntarily finds my throat. "Yeah. I remember."

"That was some crazy shit, huh?"

No crazier than Tyler feeling me up and hounding me to have sex with him when I was fourteen. "It's part of his pathology," is how his terrifying behavior was explained to me by a therapist.

"Crazy is the operative word, William."

"When are you going to Delaware?"

I consider telling William about Franco, but something stops me. William and I were close as kids, bonded by negotiating the emotional minefield that was our brother. When Tyler left for good, we discovered we didn't have a lot in common. I love him, but I wouldn't call us friends.

"I'll try to get down once he's home from the hospital."

William nods and turns to leave. He stops at the door, his hand on the knob.

"I know he's not a great dad, but…"

He leaves the sentence hanging, and although I wonder what he was going to say, I simply nod.

Sometimes words aren't necessary.

Pleasure to Purpose

Chapter 14

I spend the next few hours pacing the apartment, cleaning Don's litter, sweeping the floors and reorganizing closets so my nervous energy doesn't spill over. Between worrying about what Stan has planned and Dad's surgery, my skin feels like it's going to crawl away.

An incoming call startles me, I dive for the phone. Uncle Jay's name is on the screen. *Dad must be out of surgery.* Terrified to hear bad news, I remain rooted to the spot, listening to *Dancing Queen*, Uncle Jay's chosen ring tone. I force myself to swipe right just before it goes to voicemail.

"He's okay," Uncle Jay says. Overwhelmed with relief, I drop my head in my hand, not appreciating until now how worried I was. "They put in another stent so he'll be in the hospital for a bit. But he'll be alright."

"Should I come down?"

Uncle Jay huffs. "Not much to do around here unless you wanna deal with Penny. Uh oh, speak of the—"

A rustling sound as Penny grabs the phone. "Hi honey, your father's gonna be fine, thank God! I honestly don't know how I would've… how I could…" Her voice trails off as she begins to sob. I hear Jay consoling her, saying the worst has passed.

Uncle Jay has a way of making everything feel good, even when it's not. When my grandmother pushed me down the stairs for talking back, Mom didn't take me to a doctor because she was afraid they'd tell the authorities. Instead, Uncle Jay took charge. In my ten-year-old mind, the zoo and accompanying ice cream made everything better, despite an ankle sprain that lasted weeks.

Uncle Jay snags the phone back. "As I was saying…"

"Sounds like you have things under control."

"Yeah, stay in Boston. Call him in the next few days if you like, but he's pretty weak right now. Love ya."

I disconnect, feeling much lighter. I decide I'll celebrate Dad's successful surgery by ordering takeout. As I pull up the menu for my favorite Indian restaurant, Dr. Styles calls to say she's been rethinking Franco's symptoms and wants to do a full work-up. My momentary euphoria dissipates, replaced by a pit in my stomach. I tilt my head back, wondering at the haphazard nature of the universe.

One second I'm surfing the waves.

The next I'm at the bottom of the ocean.

"What do you think?" Dr. Styles asks.

I sigh heavily. "I think I have to know what we're up against, so let's do it."

I call Pat to update her about Franco. She offers me her rig.

"Thanks so much, Pat. I really appreciate it."

"No worries. Don't worry about a trailer either."

The next day I arrive at the barn to find the truck waiting for me, already hitched to the farm's trailer. I smile, picturing Pat negotiating with Serenity to borrow the trailer for the day. I cross to the paddock and spot Franco standing proudly among the other horses. I'm struck with his coloring and stature. Even now, so many years in retirement, he carries himself like a champion. The curve of his neck, the rippling leg muscles, the way he throws his head when he's annoyed. I'm so proud he's mine and so grateful our two wounded souls found each other. I turn my attention to Xena, still limping as they walk side-by-side, nuzzling each other now and then. I was hoping the farrier visit would have resolved her pain. Clearly the root issue remains untreated. If I had the money I might adopt Xena too. But as of now, she's technically property of the farm.

Pleasure to Purpose

Serenity walks up and removes leather gloves. "Happy to lend you the trailer," she says, reminding me of the favor.

"Yeah. Thanks."

I point to Xena. "What's with her limp? It's not going away."

Serenity follows my finger. "She looks okay."

"Serenity." My tone forces her attention. "You need to get her checked by a vet."

She shrugs. "Pat's a vet."

I roll my eyes. "But she's no longer practicing, and Xena isn't her responsibility. She's yours. Scott said Xena's hoof looked okay, so the limp has to be caused by something else."

Serenity picks at a nail. "Fine. I'll call the vet."

"Thank you."

We stand in awkward silence until a voice calls out, "I'll help you load Franco!"

We turn to see Pat approaching, her arm raised in greeting. Serenity looks from Pat to me, begins to say something, then thinks better of it and walks away.

"That girl needs some work," Pat mumbles. "Can't find her way out of a paper bag."

I thank her for lending me the truck, then grab Franco's halter and guide him toward the trailer.

"Are you feeling better?"

"Better?" I ask.

"You were sick, right?"

"Oh… yes. Much better. Thanks. Things are definitely looking up." I flash to Stan, who's God knows where doing God knows what to my stalker.

"Good. You know… you don't have to do everything on your own. I know you're worried about Franco's health. How 'bout I tag along to the vet for moral support?"

I make a clicking sound asking Franco to stop, then walk back to Pat. "Why are you so nice to me, Pat? Don't get me wrong. I really appreciate it. Just, *why?*"

Her eyes crinkle as she grins and shakes her head. "Oh, sugar. Don't you see how special you are?"

My mouth opens and closes in stunned silence. No one has ever said something like that without wanting something in return.

She crosses her arms and tilts her head. "You don't, do ya? You really don't see it."

I shake my head and look away, not trusting my voice.

She sighs heavily. "Not everybody should be a scientist or a teacher or a banker. Some of us offer gifts in other forms. Like empathy, listening or companionship."

My eyes fly back to her, and she lifts her chin. "You offer beautiful gifts that help many people. I'm sure of it. And so is that guy." She points to Franco. "Trust yourself, hon. You've got a good head on your shoulders and a good heart in your chest. Just keep doing you and you'll be just fine."

Suddenly I want to tell her everything—Dad's surgery, the stalker, the letter Anne asked me to write. I open my mouth to speak but nothing comes out. It feels like a plastic ball is lodged in my throat. If the ball were removed, I'm sure a dam of emotion would burst forth.

Seeing my dilemma, she waves toward Franco. "Now go, dammit! You're gonna be late."

I hold her gaze for another moment. "Thanks, Pat."

"Nothing to thank me for, hon. See you soon."

I watch Pat walk to Xena, then take a deep breath to harness my emotions. I grab Franco's halter and guide him to the trailer. As he steps onto the ramp, Xena whinnies.

"It's okay, girl," I hear Pat say. "He'll be back soon."

I feel Xena's worry that I'm taking her best friend and leaving her alone. As a child, I felt the same way when Tyler vanished with no explanation, only to reappear months later. Horses are intuitive and smart like children. Xena is communicating her anxiety at Franco's impending absence.

"He'll be back soon. I promise," I call out.

Pat waves. "Good luck!"

I wave back, grateful for her friendship, then turn my attention to Franco.

As I load him, his large hooves clopping on the steel, Serenity reappears to ask me if I've seen her Facebook post. I shake my head.

"I'm advertising for kids' riding lessons," she says.

I take a moment to process this while closing the back of the trailer and sliding the windows open to provide Franco fresh air.

"Using which horses?"

She points to Franco and Xena and my eyebrows come together.

"Didn't we *just* discuss Xena's limp?"

Serenity whips around. "Yes! And I said I'll call the vet!"

I look away and bite my lip. I know from experience there's no sense escalating the situation. "Well, until you do, she certainly shouldn't have anyone on her back. As for Franco, as a harness racer he never had anyone ride him. We have no idea how he'll react, especially with unpredictable kids."

She stares at me for a long time, then shrugs. "He stays here free."

"It's not free. I do work to cover his board. That's our deal."

"Your chores don't cover the total, so…" She scoffs, then walks away, leaving me speechless and unable to understand how a person who manages a rescue can value money more than the horses' health. She's supposed to save them, not use them. As I drive to the vet's office, I consider asking Pat to speak to Serenity, then decide she's done enough for me. I'll handle the situation on my own.

We arrive fifteen minutes later. Casey leads us to a paddock. Although Franco was fine with the tech at the rescue, in unfamiliar territory it's a different story. Franco's eyes are wide as he pulls and tosses his head. Casey grabs the lead from my hand and walks away, urging Franco to follow. As they walk in tandem, I hear Casey speaking to Franco in a low, even voice, communicating calmness and confidence. When they complete the circle, I smile.

"You're really good."

He shrugs without making eye contact. "Thanks."

A man wearing a yellow baseball cap approaches to ask Casey a question. Franco's demeanor shifts dramatically as he yanks his head back and stomps his hooves.

"Whoa, buddy. You're okay," I say while approaching him.

He continues to huff, so I place my hands on either side of his head and lean my forehead against his, willing him to absorb my calmness. I stroke his cheeks as we share breath and after several moments, he stills. As we stand there, a picture pops into my head: Franco restrained in a stall,

Pleasure to Purpose

being beaten by a man in a bright yellow baseball cap. This time though, the image is startlingly clear, and the colors shockingly vibrant. Sensing my emotional shift, Franco pulls back and starts to rear up.

I turn to the person talking to Casey. His yellow cap doesn't exactly match my vision but it's close enough. "Take off that hat!"

"Why?" the man says.

Casey doesn't hesitate. He grabs the guy's hat and tosses it to the ground. The man looks angrily at both of us before snatching his hat and walking away.

Franco stops pulling and huffs, then nuzzles my cheek. I stare at him in amazement, wondering if I connected with him on some unseen level. It wouldn't be the first time something like this has happened to me, but never with an animal.

When Aaron and I lived together, I visited Salem on Halloween night. The next day Aaron called me at work to say he heard a child's laughter in the apartment. Doors were opening and closing on their own and our dog Roger was barking and running in circles. Strange occurrences continued for several days: cabinets propped opened at exact angles, the dog's leash suddenly swinging like a pendulum. Having never experienced this type of phenomenon, the timing of my Salem visit couldn't be ignored. I spoke to a friend who suggested my presence on Halloween—when the veil between the living and the dead is thinnest—might have opened a spiritual door through which a deceased soul entered. On her advice, I asked the spirit to communicate with me and learned that ten-year-old Josh was born in 1945 and was searching for his mother. My friend advised me to direct him toward the Light, and after several tries, eventually things stopped moving on their own and the apartment felt brighter. The atmosphere felt lighter as well, like gravity took some time off. Both Aaron and I felt it, as did Roger, who slept soundly for the first time in several days.

"Thanks for doing that, Casey." I stroke Franco's nose again, feeling Casey's unspoken question. "He doesn't like yellow hats," I explain, keeping the rest to myself.

Dr. Styles appears, breaking the tension. "How's Franco today?"

99

I consider telling her about the vision but decide against it. One person's psychic experience is another person's schizophrenic episode. "Pretty good."

"Let's get a picture of that bladder." She inserts a long needle into a glass vial, then slowly pulls back on the plunger to fill the barrel. She taps on it to remove any air, then injects the liquid into a neck vein. While we wait for the sedative to take effect, she asks what I do for work.

I pause. "I'm a massage therapist."

"Good to know. What do you specialize in?"

"Pain management." It's technically true.

"Great! Maybe I'll book an hour with you. I've had a strained muscle in my neck for about a week."

After several minutes Franco's shoulders relax. Dr. Styles comments on what a lightweight he is considering his size.

"I thought I'd have to give him more, but it seems like he's all set."

She turns on the ultrasound machine and lubricates the wand before pressing it against Franco's belly, then moves in slow circles until an image fills the screen.

"See this line? That's the edge of the bladder. It goes around like this." She points to the screen while manipulating the wand, pointing out a white blob surrounded by black. After several minutes, she removes the wand and cleans it, then wipes Franco's belly. He doesn't acknowledge her touch, completely at ease.

"No sign of infection and no mass. Looks good." Her words are positive, but the inflection is flat. She sighs heavily, using her wrist to brush wayward hair to the side. "He probably has a UTI. But there might be another issue too."

My mouth becomes suddenly dry. My horse-owning dream is fraying at the edges like a children's book clutched by small, anxious hands for too long.

Dr. Styles tilts her head. "You look so worried! I'm just thinking he might have an obstruction in his urethra that could cause the penis not to drop completely. It would certainly explain urine leakage."

I wince, remembering a kidney stone in college. The nurse told me the pain of passing a stone ranks almost as high as giving birth.

"I'd like to insert a catheter to see if there's an obstruction."

I look at Franco, who seems oblivious to the bad news dropping like rain around him. Drugs can do that. "Let's do it."

She removes a long, narrow tube and gently inserts it into Franco's urethra, careful not to put herself in kicking territory. Franco doesn't move, making me marvel at both the sedative and her dexterity. She steps away, and we watch deep yellow, grainy urine dribble from the catheter, forming a large puddle in the dirt. I cover my nose and mouth against the ammonia stench, but Dr. Styles seems immune.

"It wasn't easy to insert the catheter. I think he might have an obstruction."

She removes the catheter, then squeezes some lube on her hand and massages his penis until it drops a little. The professional side of me admires the technique as I try to commit it to memory. But reality drops a bomb when Franco grunts and a hard misshapen mass falls into the vet's hand. She holds the mass up to the light to examine it. It looks like a warped, dirty golf ball.

"It's called a bean," she explains. "It's made of dirt, urine and smegma. Sometimes when horses don't drop their penises completely to urinate, they can end up peeing inside, which can cause beans like this. If Franco hasn't had vet care for ten years, you're lucky it wasn't worse than this."

The scariest part of owning a horse is that my ignorance could cause him pain, or even his life. I've owned Franco for one week and I've already learned more than I thought I ever would. As my boy throws his head back and whinnies, I feel his relief mingle with my own. Two stressed souls suddenly free of a burden. I was so scared he was really sick. This is a reminder that good things can come from bad.

"I want him on antibiotics for a week, just to make sure we cover any potential infection. Who knows how long that thing was in there?"

She strokes his side, impressing me with her commitment and bedside manner. She's the kind of dedicated vet I like to think I would've been if my life had turned left instead of right.

"So, you think he's gonna be okay?" I ask. The high pitch of my voice betrays my worry.

Dr. Styles nods. "Franco's relatively young and strong. I think he'll be fine."

The situation reminds me of when I asked Mom if our dog Bruno was going to be alright. I was five. He'd been sick for days.

I found the dog the next morning, dead on the kitchen floor.

Chapter 15

After returning Franco to the rescue and ensuring he's settled, I clean some stalls and refill water buckets. The number of times Serenity just happens to "need" something from the barn while I'm working makes it clear she's checking up on me. After the third appearance I ignore her, choosing to enjoy the afternoon taking care of Franco and the other glorious horses.

Physically tired but emotionally energized from a day at the farm, I start the drive home. On the way I receive two texts from the stalker promising to fuck me one way or another if I don't respond. I find grim satisfaction that my lack of engagement is driving him crazy. Trusting that Stan is on the job, for the first time I'm able to push him from my thoughts.

"You're not gonna know what hit you, buddy," I say while arriving home to find a cherry red Tesla Y parked in front of the house. Having never seen the car before, I glance at the driver and curiosity turns to recognition.

The last time I saw Lucas the Dutch prince he'd just lost a lung to cancer. He's been absent for several years, probably lounging at one of his family's numerous European estates. His eyebrows shoot up in greeting as he powers down the tinted window to reveal Caribbean-blue eyes with near-white lashes under a full head of tousled ginger hair. When he grins, his wide face expands like a flesh balloon.

The muck boots and sweatpants I'm wearing don't inspire sexuality, not to mention the strong stench of manure. Still, I lower my chin, shove a hip to the side and smirk mischievously. Sometimes a little attitude can work wonders.

"Good to see you, handsome. Do we have an appointment?" I ask, knowing full well we don't. Lucas is definitely an ask-for-forgiveness-not-permission kind of guy.

He shakes his head with a fixed grin, then holds up an open box. "No, but I brought you a gift."

I glance in the box to see a dark brown dildo, at least a foot long and four inches in girth. I look at his hopeful face, then back at the ridiculously large toy. As my analytical mind starts calculating how something that size can actually... *Just go shower. We'll figure it out.*

"Great!" I manage. "Just give me twelve minutes, okay?"

I've had vibrators, dildos and all manner of body parts stuck up my hoohah, but I've never considered putting anything *that* big inside. Although I'm not opposed to spontaneity and creativity, the idea of inserting that thing is simply asinine. But Lucas has been a good client, I don't want to disappoint him so I put on my big girl panties and take a deep breath as twelve minutes later on the dot, he waltzes through my door with the enormous dildo in hand.

Lucas found me several years ago through an ad I placed on Tryst. During our first encounter he told me he hails from Dutch aristocracy, a trust fund baby who breezes through life flitting from one entertaining moment to another. Although he's somewhere in his mid-forties, his relaxed lifestyle and good bone structure make him seem like a precocious late-twenty-something.

He yanks the dildo from the box and displays it like a trophy. "What do you think?"

I have many thoughts but voice none of them.

"Do you like it? It's for you," he adds.

Is it though? What woman in her right mind wants a four-inch-wide rubber dildo inserted in her—

"It cost four-hundred dollars."

Pleasure to Purpose

My mouth drops. I know he's quirky, but this is downright absurd. "Are you friggin' kidding me? You spent four hundred on *that?* Why didn't you just give me the money? Now that would've been a nice present."

His smile drops as his body sags. I've wounded his sensitive man pride. But seriously, if you want a Porsche and someone gives you a bicycle, it's tough to act grateful.

I take the dildo and gently place it on the table. "I'm sorry. Thank you for thinking of me."

My tongue explores his wide mouth while one hand unbuttons his shirt and the other unzips his pants.

Because Lucas has done a fair amount of cocaine in the past, it often takes time to get him hard. A younger version of me might think I'm doing something wrong, but I've learned not to take anything personally. Besides, the work isn't about me; it's about what the clients need. Most of the time the sessions aren't really about sex at all. It's about connection, trust, release and letting go. People come to me to fulfil their fetishes or fantasies because they're afraid of being judged by their partners, scared their significant others might think them freakish. I'm convinced if there were better communication in relationships, I'd be far less popular.

I fondle his balls and feel him respond. He grinds into me and cups my butt to draw me closer, his signature move when he's really horny. The last time he was here pops into my head. Using a lot of lube, he managed to insert his fist into me. I groaned, feigning pleasure. But even with relatively small hands, a fist inside one's vagina isn't comfortable.

I warily eye the dildo, knowing he wants to try it. It's not that he enjoys inflicting pain, like another client who likes fisting specifically for that purpose. Lucas likes to masturbate while inserting a dildo or peg, imagining he's fucking me. He gets off on the visual, the sounds and the smells. Then I finish him off with a blowjob or regular, vanilla sex.

He steps back suddenly, then removes his shirt and flexes.

"I've been working out. See?"

It's funny he wants me to be impressed. I'm not his girlfriend. Nor has he ever tried taking our arrangement to another level. But clearly my opinion matters, so I stroke his ego.

Pleasure to Purpose

"You look amazing," I lie in a GFE voice, soft with a bit of an edge. In reality, he looks thin, a result of chemotherapy and too much Adderall, his latest drug of choice to keep the cocaine-hungry monster in check.

Severely dilated pupils belie his excitement as he grabs the dildo. "Lay down," he whispers urgently.

I do, but not before grabbing the lube. He angles the dildo toward me as I squeeze a large dollop on the tip, then spread it slowly in a circular motion. He watches me intently, his breath coming faster as I lean back, open my legs and slowly pull my lips open. Using leftover lube, I masturbate while he watches, arching my back and moaning. He thinks the performance is for him, but I want to ensure the lube is evenly spread as the inevitable approaches. He drops his pants, revealing an impressive stiffy, then plays with himself while slowly wiggling the dildo back and forth against my cunt, applying gentle pressure.

After a minute I realize he's under the delusion the dildo is going to slip inside. But no amount of coaxing is going to work because the thing is just too damned big. If he wants entry, we need more manpower. I grab his hand and pull, feeling the massive head breach the edge. As I release my grip to lay back down, suddenly Lucas rises to his knees and forces the dildo inside. Excruciating pain shoots through my abdomen. I scream, certain I've been ripped wide open.

"Get it out! Get it out!" I yell.

He's frantic as he pulls it out it, alternating between "I'm sorry!" and "Are you okay?"

I squeeze my eyes tightly and breathe through the pain while regaining my composure. My teeth are clenched to stop a vile insult that sits just on the tip of my tongue. When I open my eyes, he's staring at the "gift" as if it betrayed him.

"Lucas?"

He looks at me like a dog who's been caught peeing on the carpet. My anger falls away, replaced by pity. How little must he know about the female body to think any woman would want a dildo the size of Canada jammed into her.

"I'm okay… but we're never doing that again. Now I know what it's like to have a baby."

Pleasure to Purpose

We both laugh, me out of relief and him out of nervousness. Staring at the lubed dildo, I shake my head. Four hundred dollars… what a waste. I briefly wonder if he can return it, then realize that people have probably tried that.

"For real, why'd you get this thing, Lucas?"

He shrugs, then mumbles something about his medium-sized penis. *Wow. He really believes he bought it for me.*

"Are you worried I think you're too small?"

He shrugs again, embarrassed. "I thought you'd like it."

That ship sailed and sank, I think as I trace my fingers down his chest, landing squarely on his now-limp dick. "Well, I didn't. But let me say that your size is just fine. It's not the size that matters anyway. It's what you do with it and how you use it. To be clear, you use yours very well."

He laughs, but I'm serious. I've been with men who are massive and men who are small. It truly doesn't matter. I once asked a client why guys are so obsessed with size. He told me that from the age they shower with other boys in the locker room they're comparing size, being made to feel lesser. It saddens me that boys' egos are bombarded with doubt at such an early age.

I kiss his neck and work my way down until I take him in my mouth, twisting my tongue the way he likes. I finish by cupping his balls and sucking him off, leaving him breathless.

Afterwards he smiles down at me, then strokes my hair. His dull eyes tell me his meds are wearing off. I wonder how many pills he pops a day. I consider what he might have been like if his ego had been fostered or if he'd been held responsible for anything instead of being coddled. I avert my gaze, not wanting him to see what I'm thinking. He has a good heart, but he's a total fucking mess. Even though I earn my own money, pay my bills on time and help people in need, society dictates that he's acceptable and I'm not.

I can't be too hard on the Judgy McJudgersons of the world, though, because I held similar views before I became a sex worker. Prostitutes were desperate drug addicts. It was sinful and certainly not a career. After Aaron left, I couldn't cover expenses on my own. As my savings dwindled, I needed a long-term solution. I was scrolling through Craigslist one day when I noticed an ad offering roses in exchange for a date. Curious, I

Pleasure to Purpose

answered the ad, and it quickly became clear that roses were code for money and the ads were about sex.

I remember spending forever getting ready. I was nervous, wondering how I'd feel when the client walked through the door. I had visions from movies in my head where the guy walks in and screams, "On your knees, bitch!" My first was nothing like that. Looking back on his shy, polite and kind behavior, it was probably his first time seeing an escort. After he left, I considered how I felt.

Dirty?

Cheap?

Sinful?

Nope. Powerful. In control.

Energized and relieved to make rent.

That's when I knew I'd found a solution to my money problems.

My body, my choice. Isn't that what women say about reproductive rights? So why do those same women judge what I do with my body?

Lucas begins to snore. I glance at the clock: 6:30. I'm tired after a long day and want to be alone, but he looks so peaceful I decide to let him stay for a little while. Besides, I want to check in on Dad.

I step outside and sit on the top stair, grateful to feel a sense of security again. Although I haven't heard from Stan, I'm confident he will follow through. So when I examine the street, it's to see what's happening in the neighborhood as opposed to scanning for threats. The humid evening presses in on me, a slight breeze kicks up to whisk away the moisture. I inhale deeply, focusing on the goodness in my life, then close my eyes and listen to the sounds of a busy street.

A typical summer night in the city.

Cars rush by.

Hip hop blares from oversized car speakers.

Two men argue over a trash can left in the street too long.

Squeaks from a bicycle with rusty axles.

City sounds, the only ones I've ever known. Maybe that's why I chose to attend college in a quiet, green place where you can hear yourself think. As a child I knew those places existed, places where horses have land on which to roam. I just didn't know how to get there. Now I do. The key is money.

Pleasure to Purpose

Money can't fix stupid or ignorant, but it sure can make life easier.

My gaze falls to Betty, already old when I bought her five years ago. She's seen me through a lot, but it's time to introduce some new car blood. I Google 'used cars near me.' A hot pink Vespa scooter pops up. I stare into the distance, reminiscing about a neighborhood kid who had a scooter while I was growing up. I'd sit on the stair watching him zoom along the street, imagining I was driving with my hair whipping in the breeze. I smile at the memory, then debate the pros and cons of a scooter versus a car.

I'd be at the mercy of the elements. I imagine going on an outcall in the rain, arriving soaking wet with muddy boots. The client looks at me in disbelief, then tells me to go home. I grimace, then chew my lip while looking at some used cars, hoping to find one that fits my budget. It takes only a couple of minutes to decide that, given Franco's situation, I don't want to spend so much. Besides, despite the obvious pitfalls, the little girl in me keeps returning to the scooter. I message the Vespa owner, asking if the price is negotiable. Within seconds he informs me he'll come down $100, so I tell him I'll stop by tomorrow for a test drive.

A scream erupts as two girls race past on bikes with two boys in hot pursuit. Their innocent laughter is infectious, and for a moment I'm wrapped in their exuberance… until I realize I don't remember ever feeling that carefree. I didn't have a lot of friends and although I rode bikes with my brothers, I was always watching and waiting for Tyler to explode. Although we had some happy times, many of my strongest memories are of feeling guarded.

A car rounds the corner slowly. I grab the railing to haul myself up, suddenly convinced Stan didn't do his job. But it's not a Nissan. The driver is an elderly lady who comes dangerously close to hitting Lucas' Tesla. I sit back down, surprised and disappointed at how quickly my brain returned to paranoia.

When my heart settles, I call Dad's cell.

"Hiya, hon." It's Uncle Jay.

"Do you ever leave Dad's side?" I ask.

"Only when Penny's here."

I smile. He likes Penny as much as I do. "How's he doing?"

"Sleeping, but his breathing's much better."

Pleasure to Purpose

A warmth spreads through my core; I recognize it as gratitude that Dad's been given another chance. "And his attitude?"

Uncle Jay barks out a laugh. "Just ducky, as usual."

I can't seem to stop smiling. Then I realize, I don't want to. "I'm so glad he's okay."

"Me too."

I hear a voice in the background asking Jay to get off the phone. "Who's that?"

"Your dad's nurse." Then he whispers, "He's kinda cute."

I hear the nurse laugh.

"Alrighty. I'm going to let you go. Thanks for everything, Uncle Jay."

"My pleasure, hon. Talk soon."

I press the end button and close my eyes, breathing deeply and savoring the quiet moment.

A yawning Lucas emerges. His hair is tousled and he's rubbing his eyes. "Can't believe I fell asleep. I've been off my meds." That's code for *I need some uppers to stay awake.* I nod, then give him a fist bump before he hops down the stairs, settles into his Tesla, and disappears into the evening.

A door slams downstairs. Uncle Steve emerges. "Your dad okay?" he asks.

My mother must have told him, or he was listening by the window. His expression is open, his eyebrows are raised.

"He's gonna be fine."

"Good. Hey, I haven't seen that car you mentioned."

I remember my reaction to the old lady rounding the corner and realize how jumpy and stressed I still am. "Thanks for looking out for it," I answer genuinely. He didn't have to do it, and he certainly didn't have to follow up.

"Who was the guy in the fancy car?" he asks. The softness in his voice has been replaced by something harder.

I turn to face him. "Actually, he's a Dutch prince."

He smirks. "Come to sweep you off your feet?"

Détente was certainly short-lived. I look him up and down, the way some women do when they're trying to figure out my tight leather pants or magenta hair. I suddenly feel sorry for him, having so little in his own life that he needs to be involved in mine.

I smile broadly. "I'm making my own fucking fairy tale. See ya." I open the door and let it slam behind me, then scoop up Don Rickles and plop into a kitchen chair, determining what I want for dinner.

My phone rings again. It's Stan, wondering if we can meet at a Mexican restaurant.

"Do you have news?"

"Can you meet or not?" he asks impatiently.

"Yup. I'll see you there in thirty minutes."

I shower the Dutch prince away while imagining what Stan is going to tell me. The stalker has been arrested and sits in a dingy cell awaiting arraignment after admitting everything. Or, Stan found him sitting outside some other poor girl's apartment and threatened to go public with the story if he didn't cease and desist. Or, worse yet, Stan found him in his suburban home with a wife and two beautiful kids… and what would I like him to do now? I shake the thoughts away and focus on getting ready.

I manage to get Betty to turn over after several tries and arrive at the restaurant to find Stan leaning against his muscle car. Arms are crossed over his wide chest in a bold, cocky stance. He walks with swagger as we make our way toward a corner booth. I tell him I find his confidence sexy, but he responds with a sideways glance, revealing nothing. He clearly has news to share but is toying with me. I play along until I can't stand it anymore.

"Tell me!" I blurt after we order drinks from the hostess.

He offers a sly smile, then asks how much I want to know. I open my mouth to respond, then really consider his question. Is he asking how much detail I want or how much I desire the information? Answering both questions, I decide to put my worry to rest, even if it's bad news for me or makes me complicit.

"Every detail," I respond while drawing my hands to my mouth.

Stan leans in, his eyes drilling into mine, and tells me that after tracking down the stalker using his last cell number, he and an associate waited outside the guy's apartment until he emerged and followed him until he was alone.

"Sounds like a movie," I whisper, completely engrossed.

Stan ignores the comment. "We picked a secluded spot and pulled in front of his shitty, rusty car, cutting him off. The asshole leaned out the

Pleasure to Purpose

window, yelling at us to move. We stayed perfectly still, waiting for him to escalate the situation. Right on cue, he got out of the car, ready for a fight."

Suddenly I don't want to hear any more. I shake my head but Stan's on a roll, his hands gesticulating the action.

"We ambushed him, right there under the fuckin' overpass."

I feel my mouth go slack, the reality of someone being hurt because of me. The stalker is an asshole, but physical retribution seems so... *so what, Scarlett? my brain answers. Draconian? Prehistoric? You knew what you signed up for when you asked Stan for help. Now suck it up! You know if this went on that dickhead might have killed you.*

"So… you beat him up?"

Stan pulls back. "I'm not a freakin' Neanderthal, Scarlett. We gave him a chance. We ordered him to leave our *sister* alone." He winks at his cleverness. "When he said he didn't know what we were talking about, we gave him one more chance to come clean, and…"

My hopes skyrocket. *Now he'll leave me alone. They didn't have to hurt him.*

"When he didn't, that's when we laid into him."

I groan while picturing Stan punching the pathetic excuse for a man. It certainly wasn't a fair fight, especially if Stan had someone helping him.

"Hey, what did you think was gonna happen?" he asks, his arms wide.

I wave a hand. "I don't know, but…"

"There are no buts in this business, Scarlett. Only yesses and nos. Anyway, it didn't take much to get him talking. After a couple of jabs, he admitted to stalking and threatening you, even told us where you live."

I look away, blinking several times as guilt battles with relief.

Stan grabs my hand. "He had it coming, Scarlett. I've seen situations like this before, and this was his fault, not yours. He wasn't going to stop, and honestly, would have escalated. You did the right thing by asking me to get involved."

I think of Shawn the cop, wondering if I should've taken the legal route. It might have ended with me in jail too, but at least I wouldn't carry someone's pain on my conscience.

Stan pats my hand. "Anyway, it's done. He won't be bothering you anymore."

112

I nod slowly, unsure what to say, then I squeeze his fingers in a thank you while finally finding my voice. "When did this happen?"

"Right before I called you." He smirks while looking at me out of the corner of his eye. "But I didn't tell you the best part."

I hold up my hand, then pull it down. I'm already complicit. I may as well hear the rest. I give a small nod.

Stan goes on to say that after the stalker confessed, his associate superglued the guy's balls to his cock.

I stare through Stan at the horrifying image, my head shaking back and forth. "No, no. He already confessed and you beat him. Why would you—"

"It's okay," Stan laughs. "We told him to use acetone to remove the glue."

I close my eyes to erase the visual. Suddenly logic intercedes, and my eyes fly open. Having been a CNA, I know what happens to skin if acetone meets superglue.

I stare in disbelief at Stan. "But that's going to—"

"Burn like a mother!" Stan bursts our laughing, loud and long as I lean back into the soft pleather, amazed that I instigated such terror.

Realizing people are staring, I place my hand on his to quiet him. I suppose I should thank him, but I'm struggling to find the words. I'm pretty sure Hallmark doesn't make a card thanking someone for torturing your stalker.

He reads my look and waves a big hand. "No worries. Happy to help. It was actually kinda fun."

I bury my face in the menu while wrestling with the fact that, on some level, I knew how Stan would handle the situation. I made a choice. But the superglue? I certainly didn't see that coming. I suddenly wonder what Stan's security firm does. I've read about security firms being hired by the government for foreign wet work. I peek at Stan, whose large brown eyes scan the menu while he pulls at his mustache. He's always been tender with me, but clearly there's another side I haven't seen. I perform sex work but it's not who I am. Maybe being an enforcer is what Stan does, but it's not who he is.

Perhaps it's a just a human flaw that we present the personality necessary for the moment. Or, maybe it's how we've survived.

Pleasure to Purpose

I realize another reason I love horses. Franco will always show me exactly who he is and demand I show him my truth as well. Horses mirror our emotions. If we pay attention, they force us to look inward and deal with our own crap. I sigh, wondering if I'll ever meet someone who's exactly what he seems to be. Then I wonder if I want to. *What would I do if I met a man who lives his truth?*

The waiter arrives to deliver our drinks. When I look up to meet his gaze, a bolt of electricity shoots through me.

The waiter grins. "Hey, Scarlett. It's been a minute."

Chapter 16

Memories of Thomas return in flashes. *His fifty-five-year-old wife died of a massive heart attack. He's a semi-retired car enthusiast. He was nervous as hell when we first met. Incredible sex.*

"Good to see you, Thomas." He's gone completely bald, and his mustache/goatee combination is graying, giving him a wise appearance. When he smiles, his clear, green eyes are outlined on each side with deep lines. The hallmark of a man who likes to laugh.

He blushes, the red slowly creeping up his round cheeks. I wonder if he's reading my thoughts.

Although I'm normally in control with men, I'm suddenly lost for words. Instead, I paste on a goofy grin while thinking of something clever to say. "Waiting tables now?" I finally manage. After his wife died, he cashed in her 401K and sold their house. He's living off that money while figuring out what he wants to do next.

He locks onto my gaze, and I'm unable to look away. "I needed to get out, especially after COVID."

Stan clears his throat, waiting to be introduced. I used to find it awkward when clients met one another. Normally they size each other up, then lift a chin or offer a slight nod. An acknowledgement without the commitment of a verbal hello. But not Thomas, who extends a broad hand toward Stan.

"Hi. I'm Thomas. Good to meet you."

Stan tries to stand but the table hampers his efforts. "Stan."

The two very different personalities shake hands as other memories of Thomas come flooding back. He's a golfer who loves all sports. A humble man who bought a trailer-home with a front yard full of lush green grass.

"So… are you ready to order?" he asks.

I'm not but I order anyway, eager to end the awkwardness. As I watch him walk away, I remember he was concerned about his size and I told him he had nothing to worry about.

"Hello. Scarlett?" Stan waves a hand on front of my face.

I shake my head. "Sorry."

"That guy a client?"

I nod, still looking in Thomas' direction.

"Hey, I'm buying you dinner here."

I face Stan and note his irritation. "I'm sorry. You're right," I say, while wondering what the hell is wrong with me. Stan did me a huge favor. I need to focus.

I make it through dinner without further embarrassment, laughing at Stan's witty stories and recounting some of my own. Thomas is an excellent waiter, engaging while maintaining a professional demeanor. When it's time to leave, I tell him I hope to see him soon, and he gives me a polite brush-off by smiling noncommittally. When I try to hug him, he backs away, making me wonder if he's seeing someone or if I did something to put him off. The idea troubles me as I thank Stan for dealing with the stalker and make a date for our next session.

Heavy, dark storm clouds burst open on the drive home. The weather matches my mood. Without an umbrella, I rush up the stairs to find William sitting outside my apartment, his head in his hands.

Panic sends my heart racing. *Did something happen to Dad?* I check my phone to see if I missed a call. Nothing. "What's up, Will?"

He lifts his head. He's been crying. "Remember when Dad took us to the shore? He rented that awesome house and we each had our own bedroom… we swam every day and rented Ski Doos?"

My lips tighten. Of course I remember. Tyler spent a significant amount of time trying to get in my pants. He crept into my bedroom at night or whispered in my ear while the family enjoyed a bonfire. I remember pushing him away and walking down the beach alone. The fire shrank to the size of a lighter flame as I tested the limits of my nerve, on my own in a night so black it could swallow me whole. Out of the void came laughter floating across the breeze, followed by a thundering of hooves as a group of four teenagers flew past me on horseback. In that mental playground of darkness the horses appeared to fly. The riders seemed reckless and dangerous. I stood there staring after them, longing to feel that freedom, until I was approached by a boy named Julian who offered me a toke and asked me to sleep with him. I was fifteen and still a virgin. I liked his hair and sneer of a smile, so I accepted the pot but denied him what he really wanted, which made him angry. It all seems so far away now that I wonder if I imagined the whole thing.

"Do you remember that? Those were good times," William says more to himself than to me.

I remain silent, unwilling to continue down a memory lane riddled with potholes.

He drags a sleeve across his eyes, then wipes his nose. "Dad's dying."

I shake my head. "He's too stubborn to die." I'm terrified William is right, but I won't get sucked into his negativity.

"I don't think he's gonna make it," William says.

A part of me knows I should sit down on the stair and have a good cry, but my feet remain rooted. Although I take care of my family, it often feels more like a responsibility than a desire to help. I question whether I was born this way or whether my trust whittled away each time Tyler came after me or Mom expressed disinterest in my life. I love my family, but I no longer trust them. Without trust, the foundation cracks.

Words fail me as I stare at William, so I repeat what Uncle Jay said. "He'll be alright."

I walk past my brother into the apartment. As I softly close the door, my hoe phone rings. I glance at the screen and suppress a grin as I answer.

"Aren't you still at the restaurant?"

"I guess you still have my number in your phone," Thomas says.

"Of course I do. You're one of the greats." I'm not lying.

Pleasure to Purpose

He laughs. "I told my manager I didn't feel well. I want to see you."

"I'll be ready when you get here. Need my address?"

"Are you kidding?" he asks.

I freshen up, dry my hair and slip into in a sheer red dressing gown, tamping down my rising excitement.

He arrives twenty minutes later, flushed and out of breath. When I ask if he ran over, he answers seriously. "I would've if I had to."

The intensity of his voice is startling and his chest is swollen like a bird vying for a mate. He seems different somehow. More confident. At five eight, he's not a tall man, but he's strong and fit. His warm eyes hold mine as he stands in front of me, droplets running down his bald head. I reach out and snatch a raindrop dangling from his nose.

"I drove here in my '69 Impala," he says.

"Nice car," I say. "My dream is a '69 Ford Mustang Boss."

"I named her Scarlett."

That catches my attention. "Your car?"

He nods.

Inside I feel warm and calm, like I'm wrapped in a heated blanket. I thank him, then ask if he's interested in staying a while.

"How about an overnight?"

I tilt my head, silently asking if he can afford it.

He withdraws a wad of cash. "Fifteen hundred," he announces proudly.

I place the money in a drawer while asking if he'd like me to put something else on. He shakes his head, then pulls me in for a long, slow kiss. Afterwards, he takes my face in his hands.

"Absolutely nothing. I just want you." He stares at me with such earnestness it's almost unsettling. A man pulling no punches. I respect that. Plus, it's sexy as hell.

Thomas is my most unselfish client in that his greatest pleasure is seeing me get off. He prefers vanilla sex to anything BDSM-related and always starts by eating me out followed by ravenous sex. Because I put the client's needs first, I rarely experience multiple orgasms. But Thomas always makes sure I come several times before he satisfies his own needs.

We can't seem to get close enough as we roll around the bed, like we're trying to fill ourselves with the other person. After an insatiable thirty

Pleasure to Purpose

minutes, he rolls onto his back to catch his breath. "You know, every time I'm with you I visualize the pictures on Tryst. They're amazing."

Before deciding to become a career escort I scoured websites to evaluate the "competition." Photos were often blatantly classless, leaving nothing to the imagination. Shouldn't that be part of the experience? The imagining? Sometimes it's not the act itself, but the moments leading up to it that leave me breathless. I planned my photos to the last detail, renting a classic Chevy and beautiful dress that accentuated my curvy figure. Paying homage to Marilyn Monroe; many believe she was an escort prior to acting. I draped myself across the backseat and stared straight into the lens, inviting prospective clients into my fantasy. It was ridiculously expensive, but totally worth it.

"Thanks," I whisper, recreating the backseat pose.

Thomas shakes his head. "You're something. You know, if you ever need anything, just ask. Anything at all. I'll help if I can."

As I often say, talk is cheap, but I'm not. Some men say things like that when they're with me, but then renege. With Thomas, he means it. I wiggle my toes into his crotch and feel him come alive again.

"Have you changed your mind about wanting a boyfriend?" he asks.

I briefly wonder if the question is academic or whether he's talking about himself. Either way, the answer's the same. At least twenty clients have misinterpreted my kindness for something deeper and have received a thoughtful-but-hard no to their marriage proposals.

"I don't think it would work out. How could someone be okay with my job?"

He nods. "You're right. I'd get jealous."

So it wasn't academic! I like Thomas a lot, but I'm not giving up my career. *Unless…*

I look away, shocked I would entertain the idea, especially after mentally scolding Lauren at the last support group meeting.

"I wouldn't mind being a sugar baby for the right guy," I say.

He asks me how much it would cost.

I think about how Lauren wishes she'd asked for more money up front. "Three thousand a week."

His shoulders fall. "I can't swing that."

Pleasure to Purpose

Although I expected that answer, I'm surprised to find a tiny piece of me is disappointed. Either I'm going soft, or I like him more than I thought.

The police have a blue wall, an informal code of silence.

Sex workers have a red wall behind which we hold opinions and emotions. The reason for my disappointment doesn't really matter when considering my financial obligations, so I decide to focus on keeping Mr. Fifteen-Hundred-Dollars happy until morning.

Chapter 17

After spending a relaxing morning in bed, Thomas offers to come with me to check out the Vespa, convinced I'll get a better deal if a man is with me. Unfortunately, he's not wrong. What he doesn't know is that I'm a crack negotiator.

When I bought Betty, I talked the guy down five hundred *and* he fixed the air conditioning. All it takes is engaging in real conversation, having a little patience and telling the salesman I'm an escort. I've read that men think about sex at least nineteen times a day, so when they discover they can pay for my time, the idea stakes out space in the brain, crowding out most other thoughts. They become so eager to please they forget their goal is to fleece me.

We borrow helmets from the owner and take the Vespa for a spin, with me driving and Thomas hugging me from behind. Our bodies fit together like sweet and salty. I enjoy the feel of his arms around my waist as the wind slaps my face. I quickly learn not to open my mouth as a bug launches itself down my throat, culminating in a coughing fit. We return to the seller's house and haggle a bit, then settle on a price. Although I'm sure I could've talked him down more if Thomas weren't with me, the amount I might have gained wouldn't have been worth the blow to Thomas's ego. I arrange to pick up the scooter the following week and we return to my apartment to have sex again before he lingers at my door saying he doesn't want to leave.

"Then don't," I tease.

"I don't have any more money."

I can't deny that I've thoroughly enjoyed spending time with him. Not just the incredible sex, but the way we laugh at the same jokes and how well we worked together buying the Vespa. As I evaluate his open expression, my resolve wavers for a moment. But then I think of Franco. I can't waste time on non-paying clients if I expect to earn enough money for his care. Lifting my chin and cutting my eyes, I smile and slowly close the door, saying I hope to see him soon.

I hear him pause on the other side, then gradually make his way downstairs. He walks to the other Scarlett, whose cherry red paint job glistens in the sunlight.

"She's a beauty," I whisper to the window as my personal phone dings with a text from Uncle Jay.

He's awake if you want to call

I scroll to Dad's number and dial, putting it on speaker. He answers on the third ring, then fumbles with the phone which clatters to the floor. Although Uncle Jay speaks in reassuring tones, Dad's retort is angry. Finally, he comes on the line. "Princess," he growls. "I'm fine!"

"Uh huh."

He clears his throat. "I *will* be fine."

"I know, Dad. But you have to take better care of yourself."

"That's Penny's damn job!"

I listen to Penny crying in the background and I wonder if he truly blames her for his heart attack. Although she's annoying, no one deserves to be spoken to that way. Penny may accept it, but I won't.

"It's *your* job, Dad. No one's responsible for you but you. You make your own choices."

He laughs derisively. "At least I make good choices."

A verbal slap through the phone. I trusted him with my secret, thinking the truth might bring us together. But again, the trust has been breached. Not a straight-on attack. Just a graze, but still... Not to mention that the man just had a second heart attack, and he's taking potshots at *me?*

Pleasure to Purpose

Storm clouds gather at the base of my skull as I compose a response. I gaze at Don Rickles, cleaning himself next to his kibble. Lick a paw and swipe the face. Lick a paw and swipe the face. The sight lowers my ire. I exhale my anger.

"No, Dad. If you'd made good choices, you wouldn't be laying in that hospital bed. Just…" I pause, trying to find a middle ground where conversation lives, not confrontation. "Just try to eat more vegetables, less red meat. Go for a walk once in a while. You can even bring Penny."

He laughs at that, a reedy sound that turns into a coughing jag. When the dust settles, he says, "So… when are you coming down?"

This is my family. They shoot at you, then ask you to reload the gun.

"Do you want me to come?" I can almost feel the shrug.

"Only if you want to."

Now we're playing the game I was born into without knowing the rules. I know them now though and I refuse to engage. "Dad, if you want me to come, I will. Do you?"

A long pause. So long that I think he's fallen asleep. Finally, he says, "That'd be nice."

I can't help but smile. If stubborn were money, he'd be Jeff Bezos. "Okay. I have some responsibilities I need to take care of first though."

Dad asks me what the responsibility's name is.

"Franco."

He grunts. "A foreigner, huh?"

I smirk while placing my rook near his king. "He's from New Zealand actually."

"A kiwi."

"Yup. He's gorgeous and tall with large—"

"I don't need details!" he barks.

Checkmate. "He's a horse, Dad."

It's silent except for a talk show playing quietly in the background. I give him a moment to process, then recount the story of how I came to own a horse. When I express concern over Franco's health, Dad says quietly, "You've always loved horses Princess, ever since you were a little girl, and now you're responsible for one. What is it with you?"

My father isn't known for his philosophical wisdom so I'm curious where he's going.

Pleasure to Purpose

"You take care of people even when they're shitty to you, and now this horse. I mean, why're you so damned nice?"

The comment comes across as a compliment wrapped in barbed wire. Regardless, the question is valid. I cared for my Alzheimer's grandma even though she was nasty to us kids growing up. I live in the same house with a mother who never wanted me. I worry about Dad even though he'll never own a **No. 1 Dad** mug, and for a long time I tried to maintain a relationship with Tyler despite his trying to rape and kill me. I could just leave them behind or push them aside as I make my way through life, but I don't.

"Franco's part of my family, Dad. Some family is given to you while others you gather along the way. I'm responsible for my family, whether I like it or not. It's just who I am."

I recall how physically absent Dad was while I was growing up, how emotionally absent Mom is now, and how messed up my brothers are. Like a river weaving through a muddy ravine arrives at the sea, my love of horses and choice of profession suddenly make sense: In both cases I'm seeking connections I haven't found in biological family. Without meaning to, Dad's hit a large, red button in my psyche. A lump forms in my throat. If it moves a fraction of an inch, a deluge of emotions will crash through, threatening to drown me.

"Well, I'm glad you are the way you are, Princess."

I nod quickly, then swallow hard. "Me too."

My mind wanders to the escorts I've met in the support group and how I feel the need to share my experiences to make theirs easier. Another situation where I'm caring for people without having been asked. Randy pops into my head, the sex worker looking to get out from under a pimp. I dismissed her when she sought help, justifying my actions by summoning my red wall of protection, leaving me responsible only for myself. Maybe that was short-sighted. I make a commitment to seek her out at the next meeting. I'm not going to work with her like she asked, but maybe I can offer some advice that might help. Thinking about the support group reminds me there's a meeting tomorrow and I haven't written my letter.

"I gotta go, Dad. But I'll call soon to let you know when I can make it down there."

124

Pleasure to Purpose

He tells me he loves me, then adds a sentence I've never heard before. One that literally stops my breath.

"Princess?"

"Yeah?"

"I'm proud of you."

Chapter 18

It's funny how time and experience alter your perspective. When I last attended the support group, I felt edgy and unsure what I would find behind the Victorian's heavy mahogany doors. Now I climb the stairs with purpose, the conversation with Dad still fresh in my mind. Not only do I plan to follow up with Randy to discuss ways she might become self-employed, but I carry a hard copy of the letter in my pocket.

Whether she planned it or not, in asking us to outline how we'd like prostitution laws changed, Anne gave me something I didn't know was missing in my life: a sense of community purpose. When I started writing I was representing only myself. As the words poured out, I realized I was speaking for those who can't speak for themselves.

Sex workers don't want special treatment.

We simply want the same rights others are afforded.

Not realizing how much I had to say and how vehemently I hold those beliefs, it took only twenty minutes to write the first draft, then another hour to craft exactly what I want to convey.

The room feels electric when I enter. I wonder if the other girls feel it too, like we're on the cusp of something great. Putting my thoughts on paper has brought them voice, and in coming from the shadows to the light, I feel powerful and capable.

Anne claps her hands to call us to order so I quickly take a seat next to a trans woman with impeccable posture. She's breathtakingly beautiful, with a delicate bone structure any other woman would die to have. She turns suddenly and presents a well-manicured hand.

"Hello. My name's Sunny."

The way her hand is extended palm down doesn't suggest a handshake. Instead, I take her fingers and squeeze them loosely. "Nice to meet you. I'm Scarlett."

She flashes a dazzling smile while glancing at my magenta hair. "Nice touch." She winks, then resumes staring straight ahead.

Anne clears her throat. "Welcome, everyone. I see we have some new faces among the old ones."

"Watch the *old* comments," a sixty-something woman snips.

The group laughs, including Anne, who holds up a hand for forgiveness. "Before we get into our homework, does anyone have something to share?"

I peruse the circle, searching for Randy. Although I see a young, frail woman who resembles her, Randy's not here. This young woman, perhaps a late teen, raises her hand.

"I'm Amber. I don't really know how to ask this, but can anyone share ideas or moves you use?"

Several experienced women laugh derisively. "Where to begin, baby?" one asks.

Amber smiles shyly, embarrassed, but Anne interjects. "Skill sharing. What an excellent idea, Amber. Who wants to start?"

For the next fifteen minutes we take turns highlighting our special moves or skills. Although I don't learn anything new, it's entertaining to hear others' stories. Some of them are sad but most are incredibly funny. Skinny dicks, big dicks, limp dicks, shrimp dicks. It's like a Dr. Seuss book gone wrong.

I share the Dutch prince dildo saga, which leaves half the group cringing and the other half laughing so hard they can't catch their breath.

By the time we're done Amber looks terrified, so Sunny reaches out and pats her leg. "You're gonna be just fine, hon. You keep coming to this

Pleasure to Purpose

group and we'll make sure you head in the right direction. Remember, you have something they want. That means you're in the driver's seat. Got it?"

Two conflicting statements can be concurrently true.

We do have something clients want, but we're not necessarily in the driver's seat.

Despite that fact, Amber's head bobs up and down in agreement. She either truly understands or is going straight from the meeting to McDonald's to find a new job.

By the look on her face, my bet's on McDonald's.

We all turn as the front door opens. A man walks in, a silver badge on his belt reflecting the overhead lights. He's fortyish, tall and lean, with brunette, spiky hair held in place with too much gel. He walks with a hitch in his step, the way gangbangers do to prevent their pants slipping to the floor. His small eyes are tucked under a heavy brow and he has a wicked scar on his forehead.

He strikes me as a street kid from Southie who was lucky to get out alive, much less be in a position of authority. If I had to guess based on his expensive suit, I'd say he's on the take.

I can feel the group's heightened anxiety as lively conversation falls to flat silence. Some girls openly glare, their hostility apparent as they dare the uninvited guest to challenge them. Others shrink in their chairs and avert their eyes, accustomed to becoming invisible around the police.

Anne rises. "Can I help you?"

The cop scans the room, his ferret eyes momentarily stopping on Sunny before darting back to Anne.

"What's going on here?"

Anne places herself between the group and him. Although I admire the moxie, her five-foot-two frame is no match to his six-foot-plus as he gazes over her head.

She lifts her chin. "This is a women's center. We're a group of women gathered for a meeting."

His eyes find Sunny again. He's probably interested but won't waste his hard-earned money. He'll just find her later and demand his "fee" for keeping her out of jail.

"What kind of women?"

Pleasure to Purpose

A tall, skinny beanpole with long red nails jumps up, her blonde-wigged head bobbing back and forth. "The kind of women who'll kick your ass if you don't leave us alone!"

I cough out a laugh as Anne turns slowly, flares her eyes, then motions with her head to sit down. The woman reluctantly retakes her seat, mumbling under her breath.

"Officer—" Anne begins.

"Detective," he corrects her.

"*Detective*, we're gathering lawfully, so who we are and why we're gathering is, respectfully, none of your concern." Anne is supremely confident in her manner and tone, earning major respect points in my book. I also get the sense she's been in this situation before.

The cop holds her stare, then breaks eye contact and holds up a business card.

"I'm here because we found this on an assault victim earlier this evening. She didn't have any ID on her, just this, so I'm hoping you can tell me who she is."

Anne accepts the card, then holds it toward us. It's from the women's center, frayed on the edges like it's been in someone's pocket.

My breath catches.

Only two people accepted business cards after the last meeting. Misty and Randy.

I stare at Misty sitting across from me while reviewing my last conversation with Randy. She had held up the card, telling me she was going to invite her cousin to the next meeting. The next idea comes to me slowly, but hits with the power of an avalanche. *Maybe it was Randy.*

A hot flush runs through me as I spring from the chair.

"Hey, did the girl who was assaulted have blonde hair and blue eyes? Was she little, like this tall?" I hold up my hand to reflect about five feet.

He nods. "Yeah. That fits the description of the victim. Do you know her name?"

"Randy. I don't know her last name, but she works in… wait, is she okay?"

He shakes his head. "She's dead."

The words are so blunt, so matter-of-fact, like he's talking about a mouse caught in a trap. I feel my face contort as I sit down hard.

Pleasure to Purpose

A nothingness overtakes me, tossing me into a black, emotionless void. The most obvious scenario plays on repeat in my mind.

Randy tried to get out from under her pimp and he killed her.

"But… she was so small…" Misty says.

It's a ridiculous statement, the kind people utter when the news is incomprehensible and they're trying to find some logic.

"Sorry about your friend," the detective says while looking at me. Although he's probably done this a lot, his words sound authentic; my opinion of him shifts. I nod while absentmindedly wondering if he knows Shawn.

The room becomes quiet, all of us struggling between sadness for Randy and relief it wasn't us.

Through the silence comes some sniffling from Amber who says, "I bet it's Randy Cirello, my cousin. She told me to meet her here tonight… but she didn't come. Now I know why." She stops talking, a tiny ball of tension and sadness. Girls rise from their seats and surround her, stroking her back and whispering platitudes.

I stand and approach the detective. I came tonight planning to help Randy. Given the circumstances, this is the best I can do. "Listen, Randy was trying to get out from under a pimp. I don't know his name, but I know she worked almost exclusively in Dorchester."

The cop sizes me up, understanding I'm taking a personal risk sharing this information. He knows better than to ask my name, so he simply nods appreciatively, then steps back and clears his throat.

"Thank you, *uh*, ladies. I'll leave my card with—" He glances at Anne, who says her name.

"I'll leave my card with Anne in case you think of anything else that might help. Have a good night." He looks at Sunny again, who holds his stare. Her expression is inscrutable. I wonder if she's inviting him in or daring him to approach. After a moment he breaks the stalemate and leaves the building, gently closing the door behind him.

Anne and I exchange a look, our thoughts in complete alignment. It's time for us to be treated with dignity and respect. I'm impressed the cop was diligent enough to follow up on the business card at all.

130

Pleasure to Purpose

Usually sex worker assaults are ignored or swept under the rug. Our existence just doesn't carry the same importance to cops. If one or two of us are lost, so be it.

It's as if we're not human.

We're understandably subdued while retaking our seats because we've all scraped our way out of risky situations.

When does the luck run out?

As I examine the group, a mixture of guilt and anger coalesce to form a fiery determination. I have to live with the guilt of denying Randy assistance, but I sure as hell can help the rest of us get the protection, respect and rights we're owed.

Yanking the paper from my pocket, I say, "I'd like to read the letter I wrote."

Grateful for the distraction, Anne holds out her hand. "By all means, please."

Conversation dies down as I smooth the crumpled paper, nervous to share my work.

As I look around, I'm bolstered by the defiance I see in my colleagues' faces.

One of our own has been murdered, and in crossing that line, we will no longer stay silent.

I clear my throat and begin…

Dear Senator:

I believe you are a bit misguided on who sex workers are and what needs to be put in place for sex workers. I am a sex worker and I'm not a victim that needs saving. I got into sex work because I was going to be homeless again and thought it was a better alternative. Like you, I believed what society taught me. Society portrays clients as abusive and sex workers on drugs. Though that may be the case for some, in my experience of working in the industry for over five years, I've only had two very brief instances. One was kicked out automatically for trying to stealth (removing a condom without my knowledge), and hurled empty threats of calling the police. Another was a stalker in which I had to get others involved in taking care of him because current laws don't protect me. If you really care about the wellbeing of sex workers, then you should decriminalize it, period, not with ways to go after clients. And by the way, it is consensual with clients. Also, I'm not on drugs. If you really wanted to help the victims in the industry, you should go after pimps. Pimps are one of the main sex traffickers in Massachusetts. They get girls addicted to drugs so that way they can easily give up all their money for the drug the pimp is supplying. You really want to make a difference in the lives of sex workers, make it easier for us to report. Work with us, not for us with misguided information. I'm open to meeting in person.

Best Regards,

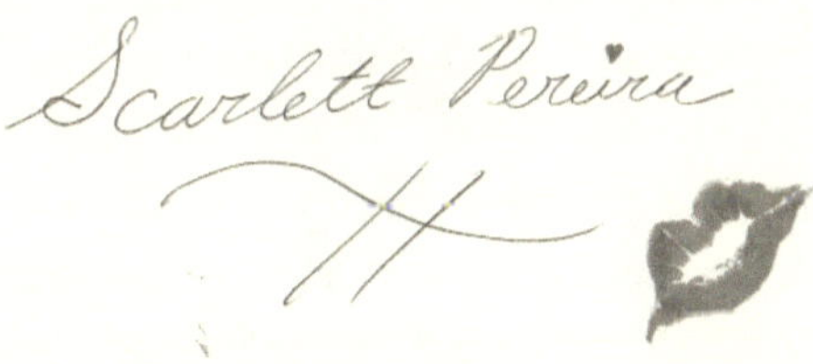

Although I wrote the letter before knowing that Randy was murdered, the words ring true as I look around. Several girls nod approvingly, then raise their hands, eager to read their letters. I retake my seat while replaying my only conversation with Randy. I'm not going to pretend I knew her well, but I'm sad she lived such a short, tough life. The timing of her murder isn't lost on me. It may be the catalyst that unifies our group to drive change. If so, she didn't die in vain. In fact, she'll be a hero.

I carefully fold the letter and replace it in my pocket as Dad's words resonate through my mind.

I'm proud of you.

Chapter 19

The next morning I text Pat to say I'm on my way to the barn. She writes back immediately saying she's under the weather and won't be in. After ensuring it's nothing serious and offering to bring her chicken soup, she tells me not to worry and she'll see me soon. She adds that I should be nice to Serenity because it's her birthday. I tell her I can make no promises, accompanied by a rolling eyes emoji.

I arrive at the barn to find a pissed-off Serenity standing in front of Franco's stall, hands on her hips.

"Nice of you to show up."

"Happy birthday, Serenity."

The goodwill catches her off guard and I enjoy watching her work out how to respond. Finally, she takes a breath, blows it out, and mumbles, "Thanks."

I smile good naturedly, which aggravates her even more.

When she admonishes me for not coming often enough, I apologize and say that Betty barely started this morning and died twice on the way. I add that I'm picking up a scooter in the coming days and will be more reliable after that. I consider adding the stalker, Randy's murder and my dad's health issues to the mix but decide that would invite too many questions about my private life. Besides, looking into Serenity's eyes, I clearly see she doesn't really care.

As if to prove my point, she huffs, "This is a non-profit, not a charity," before stomping away.

Ignoring her, I approach Franco and offer him an apple. "There's my guy." He sniffs it, then turns away, barely acknowledging my presence. I offer it again and he jerks his head to the right. "You love apples. What's going on, buddy?" I ask while stroking his nose.

He steps forward to place his chin on my shoulder. I brace myself to accept the weight. A horse's head comprises approximately ten percent of its body weight. The fact that Franco trusts me enough to comfort him makes supporting the 120 pounds worth it. I tilt my head into his muzzle, place my hands on either side of his neck and gently rock back and forth. As we stand there absorbing each other's love, a foul odor creeps up my nose. I disentangle myself and enter Franco's stall where the stench of ammonia becomes so overpowering, I clamp a hand across my mouth to avoid vomiting.

In addition to cleaning the barn and caring for horses, I pay Serenity a monthly fee to clean Franco's stall and feed him on days I can't make it to the barn. I always text her if I'm not coming and she's supposed to cover in my absence. She clearly hasn't cleaned his stall; she simply threw more bedding on top of the soiled wood shavings underneath, which means that Franco has been lying in his own excrement.

I tamp down my anger so Franco doesn't react, then lead him to the paddock where Xena grazes quietly, still favoring her back leg. The fact that Serenity hasn't called Dr. Styles about Xena's infirmity just adds fuel to my rage. Once Franco is settled, I search for Serenity while allowing my animosity to achieve full velocity. She can shit all over me if she wants, but don't fuck with the horses. I find her painting her nails in the barn, and— asking silent forgiveness from Pat—I want to shove the periwinkle polish right up her ass.

"What the hell were you thinking not cleaning Franco's stall?"

She stops, brush in mid-air. "I put fresh bedding in there."

"But you didn't *clean* the stall first."

She shrugs, then holds her hand up, evaluating the paint job. "We had a deal. You didn't hold up your end, so…"

Pleasure to Purpose

I can literally feel the blood pulsing in my head. "Serenity, I pay you a monthly fee in *addition* to helping you clean."

"I guess I was busy."

I shake my head, truly unable to comprehend what passes for logic in her mind.

"So, you hurt my horse?" I glance at the paddock and point to Xena. "And what about her leg? There's obviously something wrong with it. If I could afford it, I'd get it taken care of myself, but—"

"Well, we both know you can't afford it, don't we?"

I freeze while considering how hard I can hit her and get away with it. Then I remember I don't start fights. I finish them.

"Serenity, all I'm asking is that you do your fucking job."

"Dammit!" She puts the brush down and clears a smudge, then glares at me as if it's my fault.

I sink my nails into my palms, remembering the goal of the conversation. "Please *clean* Franco's stall next time. Also, Xena's leg needs to be—"

"God! Enough already! I know what's wrong with Xena." She glances at her phone. "Besides, the kids are coming any minute, so you may want to get his stall presentable in case they go in there."

My mouth is open to ask about Xena but her last comment derails me. "Kids?"

She sighs dramatically. "I told you we're starting riding lessons with Xena and Franco."

I throw up my hands. "And I told you that Xena's hurt and Franco's unpredictable."

She stands, waving her hands to dry the nails.

"Well, you weren't here to discuss it, were ya?"

She says the last part in my face to emphasize the point. I come achingly close to head butting her. I've only seen it in movies and I imagine it hurts like hell, but the pain might be worth it.

I follow Serenity to the paddock. "So, what's wrong with Xena?"

Serenity attaches a lead to Xena's bridle. "She has Lyme."

I'm absolutely dumbfounded. Stunned speechless. She's going to put a child on the back of a mare whose joints are so affected by Lyme disease

Pleasure to Purpose

that she limps? Not only is it cruel, it could be dangerous. I speak my mind, and she turns on me.

"Fine! Then Franco has to do it because I'm making seventy-five dollars a lesson!"

It's never about the horses. It's always about the money, I think while evaluating her expensive outfit. I turn my back to Serenity and look into Xena's beautiful eyes, knowing I can't subject her to more pain. Franco throws back his head and whinnies, looking very much like a man in charge, then breaks into a trot around the paddock, reminding me of his strength and grace.

"See?" Serenity says. "He wants to do it."

Admiration overtakes me as I watch his muscles ripple under a rich, dark brown coat. He's astonishing as he rounds the curve, his tail and mane bouncing in tandem as a short, yellow bus drives past and parks. Eight excited kids tumble out, pointing and waving at Franco and Xena.

I wince but reluctantly agree. "Don't blame me if something goes wrong. I'll be cleaning his stall if you need me."

As I return to the barn, the happy squeals from the children remind me how much I loved horses when I was little. In spite of my frustration, I smile as they marvel: "He's so big!" and "He's so beautiful!"

The praise straightens my back, reminding me how proud I am of my champion. Although I hate to admit it, maybe Serenity is right. Perhaps interacting with kids will be good for Franco. My good mood is short-lived though.

Anger and bile take turns in my throat as ammonia seeps into my clothes, hair and eyes while mucking out his stall. After removing the offensive bedding, I hose down the stall and search for fresh hay. My Maine hay connection, Manuel, came through with bales stacked against the outside of the barn. I pile bedding into Franco's stall and fill the hayrack, hiding an extra apple as a reward for stepping up today. As I'm reading the note from Manuel, along with a bill for more than I expected … a scream rips through the air.

I run outside to see a girl of about eight on the ground clutching her left leg. She's completely silent as she gazes in wonder at the fractured tibia poking through her skin.

The screaming is coming from Serenity who's thrashing at Franco with a crop.

My feet feel glued to the ground. I look from the shocked little girl to Franco's terrified eyes, then to the crop finding its mark again and again. After several terrifying seconds, Franco rears up and bolts away, narrowly missing crushing three other children as he tries to avoid being whipped.

Suddenly I'm moving, sprinting toward Serenity, both my arms outstretched. I grab the riding crop and slash at her, then realize the kids are watching. I still my hand in mid-strike, recognizing with shock that if they weren't there, I would've continued beating her. Everything stops, for a moment there's complete silence save for the sound of Franco's heavy hooves on the hard-packed earth as he seeks safety.

I glare at Serenity, silently demanding she stand down. Our eyes lock. For a moment, I think she'll come at me. Then she drops her gaze. I tuck the crop in my back pocket taking a deliberate breath before kneeling next to the girl.

Her ashen face betrays her shock, so I smile reassuringly while smoothing some hair from her face. She flinches and I withdraw my hand. I'm embarrassed to realize she's scared of the crazy lady who whipped another grown-up with a riding crop.

"What's your name?"

"Shauniqua," she whimpers.

I smile again, trying to convey warmth.

"Well, Shauniqua, you're going to be just fine, okay?"

She nods, staring at me with huge, trusting eyes. The gaze of a child unused to trauma. No tears yet. I know from experience those will come later when the shock wears off.

The wound is ragged and bloody. I force myself to focus on Shauniqua's beautiful face. Speaking with as much calm as I can muster, I ask Serenity to call 911.

One of the kids begins to cry which quickly unleashes a torrent among the others. Only Shauniqua remains stoic as she stares at them with a look of confusion. I scowl at Serenity as she disconnects. It would be easy to completely blame her for this fiasco, but I'm also at fault. I knew in my gut Franco was too unpredictable for riding and I let myself be convinced in order to cut our disagreement short.

Pleasure to Purpose

Serenity eyes me warily as I approach, her gaze flitting between my face and the crop I now hold in my hand. I offer the crop to her, she accepts it. We're back on neutral territory.

"What happened, Serenity?"

She explains that the kids were just meeting Franco when suddenly his back leg lashed out. "It didn't look intentional," she finishes. She sounds worried as she looks from Shauniqua to me.

I flashback to Franco avoiding the apple I offered.

Two strange behaviors in a very short period.

"I told their teacher to keep the kids in front of Franco, but I guess that kid stepped behind him," Serenity added quickly. The words tumble out. I've never seen her so rattled.

I look around. "Where's the teacher?"

A young woman appears, wiping wet hands on her jeans. "Sorry, I just had to pee—" She stops when she sees Shauniqua on the ground, then pales when she notices the glaringly white, splintered bone and seeping blood.

"Paramedics are on the way," I assure her.

She simply nods, her eyes riveted to the wound. I'm guessing she isn't more than nineteen, a kid who took a camp counselor job because she thought it would be easy and fun. So much for that.

"Um, I'm not real good with blood…"

I grab her arm and whisper, "You need to sit with Shauniqua until the paramedics come. She trusts you, so you need to keep her calm. Can you do that?"

She peers past me at the little girl, who's beginning to tremble.

"Can you do that?" I repeat more urgently.

My tone sobers her. She nods, then kneels next to Shauniqua.

Suddenly Serenity is at my side. "Listen, you need to get Franco off my property."

She no longer sounds remotely contrite or apologetic. I face her. "What? Why?"

She sets her mouth and crosses her arms. "I don't think he intentionally hurt that kid, but it really doesn't matter. Have him outta here by tomorrow."

I gape at her. It's astonishing how quickly she morphed from concerned, caring Serenity to cold, calculating, self-serving bitch. "Where's he supposed to go?"

"Anywhere but here," she answers loudly while looking around to ensure everyone is listening. "I can't have a horse hurting children on my property. If you don't remove him, I'll have to call the authorit—"

"Okay!" I blurt. "I get it!"

I face Franco, who's staring at me intently, his implicit trust boring a hole in my heart. The fact is if Serenity reports the incident, Franco could be euthanized. I made a promise to care for him, and I'm going to keep it. He didn't get this far to die like a rabid dog.

"I'll figure something out," I say.

Serenity purses her lips.

My hand twitches wanting to wipe the smug look off her face. But in the timely, twisted manner fate has of handing you a shit sandwich when you least expect it, my phone dings with a text from Dr. Styles.

I have Franco's lab results. Call me

Chapter 20

I lead Franco to his clean, dry stall while paramedics treat Shauniqua. He stops just short of walking in and sniffs at the fresh bedding and hay. When he catches a whiff of the apple, he enters. He's completely oblivious to the havoc he just caused.

"We're gonna be okay, buddy," I say to reassure myself. I pat his rump before stepping outside to call the vet.

She asks how Franco's doing. I glance at him, replaying the kick that shattered a little girl's leg. Dr. Styles doesn't need details, but she deserves the truth.

"Not so good."

The vet pauses too long and my insides contract.

"Just tell me, Doc. What're we dealing with?"

I hear a chair squeak. I imagine her sitting upright, preparing to deliver somber news. "As you probably know, horses excrete calcium carbonite crystals in their urine. If a horse's gastrointestinal system can't break down the calcium carbonite into small enough crystals to be excreted, they sit in the bladder. Sometimes crystals might also form in the kidneys."

"Like kidney stones?"

"Sort of."

She goes on to tell me that sediment left untreated can cause an infection, which can lead to kidney failure. In Franco's case, because the calcium carbonite wasn't eliminated completely over a significant period, he's suffering from sabulous cystitis. His bladder is very inflamed and no longer empties completely when he urinates, which continues the cycle of infection. She finishes with, "In some cases, neurological symptoms could even appear."

I think back to Serenity's comment about Franco's kick. *It didn't look intentional.* I ask her if neurological symptoms include twitches and involuntary kicks.

"Absolutely."

I tell her about Shauniqua's leg and she exhales heavily.

"If Franco's condition had been treated when it first appeared, I think he would have beaten it," Dr. Styles says.

Two words sting. *Would have.*

"His lab results came back with high levels of creatinine, as well as indications of hyponatremia and hypochloremia, which indicate—"

"That he's a hospice case," I finish her sentence.

Although I don't know what hypo-whatever means, I can read the tone of her voice.

"I'm so sorry. There's really nothing we can do," she says quietly.

With that, Franco's fate is sealed.

I close my eyes, then tilt my head to the sky, the sun warming the tears rolling down my cheeks. I think of everything Franco's endured, enraged that the illness could have been cured if found sooner and disgusted that a champion will die in such a humiliating manner. My mind wanders to my dad, and I feel a rush of gratitude he'll be okay. I'm not sure I could deal with two crises of this magnitude.

"You okay?" Dr. Styles' kind voice reaches me from far away. I wipe my eyes, then ask how long he has.

"It's kind of hard to say. Maybe two to six months, depending on how stress-free you can keep his life."

That's all I need to hear. I thank her and disconnect, then watch the paramedics load the stoic little girl into the ambulance. Shauniqua has a long road ahead—weeks in a cast followed by rehab. She waves to her friends being ushered to the bus. The kids are chatting animatedly about the accident, no doubt recounting their versions to commit them to memory.

I return to my boy, where the half-eaten apple lies at his feet.

"You're not feeling too good, huh, buddy?"

I gaze into his eyes, which now seem lackluster and dull, as if he overheard the terrible news. Knowing horses are intuitive animals, I set my sadness aside and focus on the happiness of the moment. I enter the stall and stroke his side, then grab a brush and give him a good groom, careful to avoid any potential neurological ticks or kicks. He allows the attention for a half-hour before letting me know he's done by turning away when I try to stroke his nose.

"Okay. I hear you. Your body, your choice."

I tell him I'll return tomorrow with a plan, then march to Serenity, who's stowing saddles and tack. I inform her of Franco's prognosis.

She just shrugs. "Still needs to leave. You've put the farm in potential legal trouble with that kid's parents."

I stare for a moment, amazed at her insensitivity, then hold up a finger, asking her to wait. I pull out my phone and text Pat to apologize for what I'm about to do to Serenity on her birthday. She replies with six question marks.

I tuck the phone away and lean in so Serenity hears every word. "I came to tell you something else too. I know you're siphoning money from the rescue. I'd hate to see you go to jail or have your non-profit status yanked because of it. I bet it will even get TV coverage."

I pull back and watch her eyes narrow like a caged animal. I can almost see her hackles standing on end.

"You wouldn't dare."

Now it's my turn to smirk and walk away. I have no plans to use the information; she doesn't know that.

As I round the barn, she calls out. "I know what you are!"

Everything slows as her statement sinks in. I thoroughly enjoy moments like these when someone believes they have you backed into a corner.

What they don't know is that my family has trained me well. I enter the zone where maximum pissed-off meets supreme calm, then return to

142

her, my eyes locked on hers. She doesn't look away. Two alpha females locked in battle.

"What are you gonna do, hit me?" she asks.

I stare into her catlike green eyes, then throw my head back and laugh. The response surprises her and she stumbles backward. I close the gap, then lift my chin and whisper, "Tell me, Serenity, what am I?"

Her eyes dart away, silently betraying her nerves. "I mean… I know what you do for a living."

Successful sex workers learn quickly to spot liars. As I gaze into her perfectly made-up face, I can see she's telling the truth. I briefly wonder how she learned about me, then realize it doesn't matter. This is a battle I can't win, so I break the stalemate and return to Betty. My classical radio station is playing *O Fortuna* from *Carmina Burana,* so I lower the windows and crank it up, the dramatic music matching my brewing fury. Serenity rushes toward me and screams something I can't hear. I respond by maxing out the volume while peeling out, creating a dust cloud that leaves her coughing.

Laughing, I pat Betty's steering wheel while praising the old girl for coming through in the clutch. She may be on her last leg, but like Franco, she's going out kicking.

On the way home I call Pat and tell her about Shauniqua, Franco's diagnosis and Serenity's ultimatum that Franco find a new home.

Pat groans. "Well, bitchin' about that bitch isn't going to help Franco find a new home. Sorry about Franco, by the way."

"Thanks."

"You sure he's a hospice case?"

"That's what the vet said."

"You're not going to believe this, but his diagnosis could helpful."

She tells me about a farm in Rhode Island that specializes in boarding hospice horses.

"It's run by a friend of mine. I help out there from time to time. They're grant-funded, so the monthly fees are pretty low. Plus, he'd be around people who truly understand what he's going through. It's called Custard's Last Stand, named after the first horse who died there, Custard."

Obviously I wish Franco weren't dying. But barring a miracle, the farm sounds ideal for my champion. Pat says she'll call to ask if they have space for Franco.

"Even if they don't, we'll figure something out."

"You said 'we.' You don't have to do this, you know. He's not your responsibility."

"Well, duh! Besides…" She stops speaking for so long I think the call has dropped.

"Pat, you there?"

"Yeah, yeah. It's just that… well… I never had a daughter. And you're special, so…" She trails off again and my hand goes to my heart. *This amazingly kind, joyful, smart woman considers me like a daughter?* I'm not sure how to respond because I've never been in a situation like this before.

"You don't have to say it, Pat. I feel the same."

It takes me a moment to realize the beautiful warmth spreading through me is happiness at being accepted exactly as I am. Then guilt descends to rip away the momentary joy.

Pat is spilling her soul while I continue a dishonest ruse.

"Listen, Pat. You should also know that Serenity told me she knows about my work. I just want to make sure that we're on the same page so there are no surprises."

A pause. "Okay," she says cautiously.

I inhale slowly, steeling myself for the inevitable disappointment I'll hear in Pat's voice. "I think on some level you already know this, but I'm a—"

"Little bit crazy? Yeah, you're right. I already know that. Anything else?"

Her businesslike tone throws me until I realize she absolutely knows my secret and simply doesn't care. Not in the slightest.

Grinning from ear to ear, I release my tense shoulders. Pat's unspoken acceptance relegates Serenity's obnoxious behavior to my mental wastebasket. Plus, if Franco is accepted into Custard's Last Stand, his security will be assured, even though the daily commute from Boston to Rhode Island will be strenuous. As if in response, Betty's engine sputters. I send a prayer upward that she'll survive until I get the Vespa. Not having a

Pleasure to Purpose

vehicle now would send my precarious transportation situation into the abyss.

"I wish we could help Xena too. She's gonna be devastated if Franco leaves," Pat comments.

The calm I felt moments earlier disappears, replaced by worry. Franco won't be happy about leaving Xena, but she's far more reliant on him than he is on her. Having no idea how I'll afford it, I ask Pat to see if she can rent two stalls at Custard's Last Stand.

"But Xena's not a hospice case, is she?" Pat asks.

"She has advanced Lyme."

"I'm not sure that counts."

I bite my lip in thought. "You know how connected she is to Franco. It'll kill her if he leaves. Can you at least ask? Please?"

She clicks her tongue. Finally, she says, "You're a glutton for punishment, but you got a huge heart, girl. Okay. I'll ask."

"Oh, and can I borrow your truck and two horse trailer? After today I know Serenity won't let me use hers."

"My truck's in the shop and I sold my trailer."

I tell her I'll figure it out and thank her for her friendship.

"Hey, don't you let anybody tell you you're too much or not enough. You're perfect the way you are."

"As are you, Pat. Seriously, thanks," I say before disconnecting.

My blood pressure returns to normal as I tap the wheel to a Bach concerto. Warm humid air whips my hair. I laugh out loud when the *Habañera* from *Carmen* comes on the radio. Much like me, Carmen is a strong woman who uses what she's got to survive. But unlike her, my drama will end happily because I'm writing it.

My hoe phone rings. I answer in a husky voice, somewhat relieved to feel in control of something. A regular client named Bryan asks if we can meet this afternoon.

"Can't wait to see you at four," I purr.

Bryan is one of my more interesting clients and will be a good distraction, not to mention the money I'll make on an outcall. After all, I think soon I'm going to be a horse mom times two.

145

I drive for a while, mentally rummaging through who I can contact for a truck and trailer. I've exhausted my ideas when a text from Thomas pops up.

Hope you're having a good day

I pull over to the side of the road and stare at my phone. He's not asking for anything. He must have been thinking about me and sent the text just because. I watch traffic flow while his offer of help replays in my mind.

Although Thomas isn't a horse guy, he knows a lot of people. I quickly text back saying I hope he's having a good day too, then ask if he knows someone with a truck and two-horse trailer. He replies immediately.

On it Give me a half-hour

I pull back onto the road, very pleased with how the day is progressing. Assuming Thomas secures a truck and trailer, I need to make only one more call to close the loop. I call Serenity to ask if I can take Xena off her hands, certain she'll jump at the opportunity to lower her monthly expenses.

"You want to move Xena?" she asks.

"Yes. So she can stay with Franco." I omit the fact that she'll also receive far better care.

"Um, let me think about it… no."

I give the phone a *what the fuck* look. "Why not?"

"Simple. Because you want her." Her voice is sing-songy.

Serenity knows Xena will be crushed when Franco leaves. She's using the poor horse to punish me, a small person's reaction to feeling wronged. I appeal to her sense of morality, but she's adamant.

"In fact," she adds, "when you come back to get Franco, Xena might not be here."

Several scenarios skip across my mind. None of them are good, so I ask what she means.

"I told you she has Lyme and isn't getting better."

I shiver in the warm car, shocked by her cruelty. "Why put her down when she still has life left in her? Why not let me take her so she can be with Franco in her last days?"

Silence. She's hung up. It doesn't matter. I already know the answer. My blood runs cold as I realize she's not bluffing.

146

Pleasure to Purpose

Chapter 21

I push aside my frustration to concentrate on preparing for Bryan, a true BDSM junkie. It's imperative to enter these sessions in a balanced emotional state since it's easy to get carried away and miss important warning signs. Clients who engage in domination are often not cognizant of their own body's limitations, like Mike with the riding crop. If I don't pay attention, I could cause irreparable harm. Not only does my conscience not allow that, but it's bad business.

I stop at home to shower and collect the tools I'll need: nipple clamps, a studded dog collar and leash, and a riding crop.

I mentally prepare on the drive, knowing I'll be causing Bryan great pain. I used to feel physically ill at the sight of welts, but I'm past that. Although I don't understand the desire to be beaten or humiliated to become sexually aroused, I accept and respect the great number of people who own their fetishes.

Bryan is a married, six-foot four former professional linebacker who's so afraid of being seen in public that we meet in a heavily wooded area where animals are abundant, people scarce. I park behind his BMW on the side of the road and hike several minutes to our designated rendezvous to find him with his shirt unbuttoned and a massive erection pressing against the fly of his jeans. He's gained some weight since I last saw him, making him even more physically intimidating. If I didn't know what a sweetheart he is, his size, bald head and long beard would have me running. He shifts impatiently and rubs at his crotch while I approach, already in dominatrix mode.

"Can we—"

"Silence!" I command.

His eyes drop to the ground while he holds out my payment.

I stuff it in the pocket of my overcoat while shaking my head, feigning disappointment. "Did I ask you to speak?"

He shakes his head. I whip a nearby tree with the crop. The *thwack!* resonates through the woods.

"Answer me!" I bark.

"You didn't ask me to speak."

"You're disgusting," I whisper in his ear, then bite the lobe hard enough to draw a gasp. I step back. "Look at me!"

His eyes are glassy with arousal as I shrug out of my coat to reveal a black leather bodysuit with the breasts and crotch cut out. I give him a wicked half-smile, then approach and slowly run my tongue from his navel to his throat, listening as he pants like a dog. When he reaches for me, I smack his hand away, then unfasten his jeans and reach inside to grab his hard-on. I rub it until he groans, then order him to undress, watching to ensure he follows my rules exactly.

"Shirt."

Once his shirt is on the ground, I pinch his nipples to get them hard, then attach the clamps. They're made of stainless steel with red pom-poms hanging from the ends. I twirl the pom-poms, laughing derisively to increase his excitement.

"You're a fuckin' pussy, you know that?" I ask.

He doesn't answer. He doesn't need to. It's all part of his favorite game.

"Pants," I order.

"But I—"

The riding crop lands hard on his ass.

"I said *pants!*"

Pleasure to Purpose

He whimpers while quickly pulling down his pants and underwear, revealing a red line where the crop landed. He stands completely naked and vulnerable as I walk around him, evaluating from every angle. After completing the circle, I shift my gaze to focus on one of the longest cocks I've seen in the business. When we first met, he told me his fraternity nickname was Horse. I told him to prove it and he dropped his pants on the spot.

I grab him, rubbing slowly back and forth while squeezing a little too hard. He stops breathing, then takes staccato breaths until I loosen my grip.

I pick up the dog collar and leash. "I think someone's watching us," I whisper while securing the collar. I tug hard, almost causing him to fall. "You like it when people watch, don't you?" I taunt.

He whips his head around. Being outed is his greatest fear, but it also gets him rock hard.

"Walk!" I order.

When he stumbles, I crack the crop on the ground behind him, threatening to hit him if he slips again. The image of Serenity whipping Franco flashes across my vision. I pause to shove it back into the box where emotion lives.

Bryan suddenly slows, ready for the next step in the game. After showering him with verbal abuse, he stops and refuses to continue.

"You know what happens if you don't listen," I warn.

"Yes." His voice is barely audible as he bends over.

I pull the crop back and deliver a solid blow across his butt. He howls and arches his back. I pause, afraid I've overstepped. But a second later, he resumes the position.

"Do it again."

Several thrashes later, he tells me I'm being too intense. I immediately relent, but he then says I'm not into it enough.

Oxymoron is the nature of BDSM. Powerful people request humiliation. They say it hurts but ask for more. They tell me to relax, then want me to be "into it more." Some clients like to dress up as women and imagine they're having lesbian sex. I've lost count of the number of guys I've bound with rope, tape, wire and chains, always with a safe word because the submissive must always have true control. To do otherwise would be torture, and that's not what BDSM is about.

Pleasure to Purpose

Once Bryan has satiated his need to be dominated, he jams me against a tree and lifts me off the ground as he pounds into me. When he's done, he completes the ritual by removing the condom and pouring the cum into his mouth. Bryan is a complicated guy, but he's been a consistent client for several years and has always been respectful. I treat him in the same manner, choosing to judge him only by how he treats me as a person.

Once the act is complete, we return to where we left his clothes. He removes the nipple clamps and drops them into my outstretched hand, then gets dressed and holds my coat open for me. We return to our cars, chatting along the way before Bryan kindly ensures Betty starts before getting into his own car.

On the way home I read a text from Pat saying Franco has been accepted into Custard's Last Stand but Xena has not. Pat doesn't know that Serenity declined my offer to take Xena and before I can tell her, my phone dings again with a text from Thomas.

I got a pick-up and 2 horse trailer

Marveling at his ingenuity, I decide to call. "Hey," I say.

"We're all set for tomorrow."

I can hear the grin in his voice as I ask him what he means by *we*.

"We, as in you and me," he answers. "You can't move two horses by yourself."

It's not two horses, unfortunately, and… of course I can, I think, while politely declining his offer.

"What if I want to come?" he asks.

I ask him if he even likes horses.

"Nope. But I like you."

Never have my two distinct worlds so perilously intersected. Test driving the scooter was one thing. Having a client escort me on such a personal, horse-related errand feels almost too intimate. He did arrange the truck and trailer though, so I thank him and reluctantly agree to meet tomorrow morning at nine at my apartment.

I arrive home, feed Don Rickles then call Dad to check in. The call goes to voicemail. I leave a message. As I disconnect, a text from William comes through.

Come downstairs for dinner

Pleasure to Purpose

The last time I ate a meal with my family was on Mom's birthday. We went to Cheesecake Factory, had too many margaritas, and ended the evening in a knock-down-drag-out over football. If arguing were an Olympic sport, my family would win the gold, then be disqualified on a technicality. Not having a better alternative, I shower, slip into jeans and a light blue, cotton sweater and go downstairs. As I descend, I realize I'm looking forward to it. Despite our challenges, I genuinely love them and want the past to be water under the bridge. I can only hope the brackish, muddy water doesn't rise until it swallows the bridge with me standing on it.

I enter the apartment to a mouth-watering aroma of butter and garlic. My stomach responds, registering the fact that I haven't eaten since morning. Neither William nor my mother cook, so either they ordered from a local Italian restaurant or Uncle Steve prepared the meal.

I have my answer when Uncle Steve uses his butt to open the swinging door between the kitchen and dining room. In his hands is a glass dish filled with steaming lasagna, the cheese still bubbling. Mom follows with a hearty hello, a basket of garlic bread in one hand and a large salad bowl in the other. I comment on the table settings and flowered tablecloth, wondering why so much care has been taken. Mom shrugs, then smiles as Steve takes a seat at the head of the well-appointed table. The tableau is complete when William delivers glasses of ice water and takes a seat to Mom's left. The ambiance is jovial, and although I want to believe, history has taught me caution.

I ask why we're eating together.

Mom looks at me as if I've brought home an F on a report card. "We're family, that's why."

We've been family forever and I don't remember the last time we enjoyed a home-cooked meal together at Mom's table. As I lean back in the chair watching everyone load their plates, I wonder if I need to release some of the emotional burden I've been carrying for so long.

I glance at William, who grins while dumping a massive chunk of lasagna on his plate. I smile back, for the first time in a while feeling like I'm looking at my brother. I peek at Steve who gazes steadily at me with a funny look on his face. Caution returns as I wonder if he plans to "out" me. But he breaks into a grin and asks why I'm not eating his masterpiece.

Pleasure to Purpose

I fill my plate and dig in, the gooey cheese warming my belly and soul. I look around the table as the group chats good-naturedly. I always wanted a family like this. The kind that gathers for Sunday dinners and makes it through a holiday without a war. I can't put all the blame on them. Maybe it's time for me to open up and allow it to happen.

After the obligatory discussion about weather, Mom asks about my day. I put down my fork, gauging her sincerity through my cautiously-open heart, then tell her about Franco, Serenity and Xena.

"Aren't horses expensive?" Mom asks.

My eyes flit to Steve again. If he's going to do it, now would be the time. He smirks but keeps his gaze on the plate.

"Don't worry about it, Mom. I can cover the cost," I say.

She sniffles, then uses a napkin to wipe her nose.

Is she crying? "What's wrong?" I ask.

She shakes her head as glances fly across the table. I'm not the only one in the dark. "Family really is everything." Her voice is shaky making me think the family dinner is legit. Maybe Dad's health scare is really affecting her. I take her hand, feeling an unusual sense of quiet peace as she looks from William to me with a strange expression.

Mom withdraws a letter from her pocket and places it on the table.

William looks confused as I stare at the return address in Delaware: **Greenhaven Mental Hospital.**

"He asked me to make sure you read it, Princess."

I wince at the use of Dad's nickname for me because she uses it only when she's trying to manipulate. That's when it hits me. She wasn't referring to my father when she said family is important. She was referring to Tyler.

The letter is addressed to me in Tyler's messy, tiny writing. I won't read it because I won't allow him back into my life. I can't. I've forgiven him, but I haven't—nor will I ever—forget. I evaluate the beautiful table display and shake my head. The entire dinner is a ploy to suck me back into the washing machine of tumultuous co-dependency. I stand but she grabs my wrist.

"Tyler loves you."

I choke out an ugly laugh while my mind takes a walk through time, ending with Tyler's hands around my throat while Mom watches.

"Yeah. Perhaps a little too much."

Pleasure to Purpose

I jerk my wrist from her hand. She pouts and changes tack, saying she's been thinking about Dad and how none of us knows when our time is up. I've gone numb. My emotions are safely tucked away where they can't be twisted or stomped on. A reflexive safety valve I initiated when I was a child. I look at William, silently asking if he knows where this is headed. He peers back, no expression. Either he doesn't know or isn't telling.

Mom looks like she's going to cry. I settle back into my seat, staring at her from the corner of my eye.

"Eventually I'm going to die too, of course, so I wanted to let you know that you'll inherit part of this house."

She caresses William's cheek, a loving gesture I've seen very few times. His incredulous look is almost comical. He clearly didn't know this was coming.

I feel the tide shifting, drawing away the rising water from under the bridge on which I stand. I scold myself for being so cynical and not giving her the benefit of the doubt. Clearly Dad's health scare has her thinking about what will happen after she's gone. She doesn't have to leave her belongings to us. She could will them to Uncle Steve. Perhaps her attempt to reconcile Tyler and me is because we'll have to get along if we own the house together.

I feel foolish and selfish as I pick up Tyler's letter, deciding to give him another chance. I don't want to, but it's the right thing to do for family. "Thanks, Mom," I say.

"For what?" Her face is open. Almost pleasant. A regular family conversation.

I glance at William. "For giving us the house."

She stares at me as if she doesn't understand my confusion. "No, no. You got it wrong. I'm giving William half of the house. You can purchase the other half if you like when the time comes."

Chapter 22

Although I heard what Mom said, it took a restless night's sleep to fully process. There's no point in asking why she's gifting the house only to William. Based on experience she wouldn't answer me if I asked. I feel like I'm wallowing in quicksand, grasping onto warmth or kindness, only to have it yanked away, plunging me deeper into the muck.

As I sit on the curb waiting for Thomas, I wonder about my maternal grandmother and what it must've been like for Mom growing up with someone who'd push her own granddaughter down the stairs. It couldn't have been easy. That knowledge is the only thing standing between hating Mom's behavior and hating her. I assume she's simply paying the distrust and anger forward to the next female descendant. So it will continue until someone breaks the cycle. That's my self-appointed job, breaking cycles and barriers and anything else that stands between me and happiness.

Thomas pulls up in a shiny Ford F-150 with a horse trailer attached. He jumps out and rubs his hands together. "This is going to be fun!"

The look on my face says otherwise.

"Or not," he mumbles.

I'm quiet during the drive as he talks about his two daughters, his granddaughter, nursing his wife through her illness and his personal reinvention. "After my wife died, I cashed in her 401K and sold the house because it reminded me of her. I've been living off that money while figuring out what I want to do next. Then you came back into my life." He smiles broadly, trying to carry the weight of conversation.

I smile at the right times and nod my head, but the fact is I'm still reeling from last night. I'm also terrified Serenity has already euthanized Xena.

I explode in happy tears when we make the turn down the barn's driveway and I see her grazing in the paddock. I explain the entire situation to Thomas who falls silent as he graciously allows me room to work through my grief.

As I get out of the truck, I note that Xena is limping worse than yesterday. I offer half an apple, which she crunches gratefully before leaning her head into me, as if to say goodbye. My heart literally aches, the pain radiating into my abdomen. Xena is a smart, kind horse who's been a good friend to Franco. I hope she doesn't absorb my sadness as tears fall on her warm fur.

Sensing a presence behind me, I turn to find Serenity and Dr. Styles. I glower at Serenity, who blurts, "I swear I didn't plan it like this, for you to be here… I mean…" She trails off, knowing she's gone too far.

Dr. Styles' eyes dance between us, ignorant of the backstory in the macabre play unfolding. Serenity asks her to give us a minute. When the vet is out of earshot, she says, "Listen, after you left, I called Dr. Styles and asked her to take a look at Xena." She glances at the vet, who's stroking Xena's side. "Xena does have Lyme, but she also has intestinal lymphoma. Even Dr. Styles agrees it's time."

Looking into Serenity's eyes, I can see she's telling the truth. Her tone is urgent, like she needs me to understand.

Seeing an opening, I grab Serenity's hand. "Give Xena to me. If she's dying, maybe I can get her into the place I'm taking Franco. Don't euthanize her. Please." My voice cracks as I realize I'm asking Serenity to complete a gargantuan task—to set aside her own ego.

She crinkles her nose and bobs her head back and forth. Finally, she huffs, "Fine! You have two days to find her a new home."

"Two days?"

"I kinda already promised her stall to another horse."

Pleasure to Purpose

I close my eyes, resisting the urge to yell. She reads the look and crosses her arms. "Or do you want me to tell Dr. Styles to—"

"No! Two days it is. Thanks."

She waves a hand. "Whatever. I'm not a complete monster, ya know."

I smile tightly. "Now I know, yeah."

Serenity gives a low-lidded stare before returning to Dr. Styles.

I cross to Xena and stroke her neck, enjoying the warmth and softness. When she pulls away, I whisper, "We both live to see another day, huh, girl? I'll figure something out."

Momentarily relieved, I turn to find Thomas looking perplexed as his gaze travels from Xena to me to Serenity. I walk back to him and he asks, "Are you okay?"

I smile and pat his cheek. "I'm good." He points to Serenity. "Is she good?" I shrug. He nods dumbly, then points to Xena. "And her?" I smile again, wondering if he regrets tagging along.

I leave him standing there and enter the barn to find Franco straining to see past me. I follow his gaze to discover he's focused on Xena. Even now, he's worried about his friend. *Humans should show such loyalty.*

"Time to go to your new home, buddy."

Although I try to sound upbeat, my heart just isn't in it. As I guide him to the trailer he pulls hard on the lead, then breaks away.

"Franco!" I yell.

But he's off, galloping toward the paddock. I watch in horror as he nears the fence, terrified he's going to try to jump it and break a leg. But at the last possible second, he skids to a stop, a dust cloud enveloping him.

His chest lightly touches the rail as Xena walks over, favoring her back leg. She leans into him and rubs her head against his broad neck, as if she knows my plan could fail and they might never see each other again. My tears come freely now as I watch these two magnificent animals support and love each other with more empathy and compassion than many humans will ever share. I glance at Thomas, who watches in stunned silence, his mouth dropped in awe, his gaze laser-focused. A lone tear runs down his ruddy cheek. He self-consciously swipes at it, then clears his throat.

I don't know how long we stand there, but eventually I trudge over to Franco and gently grab his lead. He allows me to guide him, resisting only slightly as we turn away. When we're almost to the trailer, a long, high-pitched scream pierces the air.

Franco and I whip around to see Xena throwing her head and trying to rear up, reacting in terror to Franco being taken away. Her eyes are wild as she writhes, trying to find a way to get to him. He stomps and whinnies loudly, then suddenly deflates, falling silent with his head hanging low. Guilt lands heavily across my shoulders as I realize he's given up. The champion has been broken.

I turn to Franco and lift his massive head, then place my forehead against his, willing him to understand I'm doing my best. When I pull away, he's looking at me with such frank honesty that my heart stops for a moment.

"I promise I'll bring her to you, Franco! I promise!" *But what if you can't?* a little voice whispers in my head. I whip out my phone and text Pat.

Long story short, Xena has cancer. Please get her into Custard's!! We've got two days!!

At this point I can't get away from the barn quickly enough, so I secure Franco in the trailer and drag myself into the passenger seat. Thomas reaches over to squeeze my hand, but I pull away, a sob barely contained behind lips set in a tight, thin line. The reality is I'm afraid his kindness will break me open to reveal a blubbering mess.

As we leave, I look back to see Dr. Styles and Serenity huddled together, no doubt discussing Xena's euthanasia if I can't follow through on the commitment I made. I'm worried. I lean my flushed cheek against the cool glass window.

We drive in silence until I thank Thomas for coming with me.

"I didn't do anything," he says.

I examine him while wiping my eyes and blowing my nose on an old tissue I find in a pocket. Strong forearms and a solid torso. Deep smile lines and a kind, open expression as he looks at me with genuine concern. He's truly one of a kind.

"Yeah, you did. More than you know."

An hour later we arrive at Custard's Last Stand where Pat waits with a huge grin.

Pleasure to Purpose

"I had to be here for Franco's arrival," she says as I tumble out of the truck. Seeing my face, she waves me toward her and envelopes me in a bear hug. "It's gonna be okay," she whispers.

I close my eyes, absorbing her kindness. Somehow, in that moment, I know Pat is right. It might not be easy, and I may not like the result, but it's going to work out as it should.

She pushes me away and looks suddenly serious. "You look like you could use a beer."

I raise an eyebrow. "Something like that."

She catches sight of Thomas and whistles. "Well, who's this tall, handsome drink of water?"

Thomas bursts out laughing while shaking her hand. "The name's Thomas. I'm not tall, but I'll give you the handsome."

He winks at me, and for the first time, I find myself seeing him with an open heart. Fear and confusion muddling my emotions.

Pat hooks a thumb toward Thomas. "I like this guy. C'mon, let's show Franco his new home." She opens the trailer. "Hey, Franco. Welcome home, my friend. God willing, Xena will be here soon too."

I nod hopefully.

She grabs his lead. Franco doesn't hesitate, acquiescing to her trained hands. She shows us to a roomy stall, freshly stocked with everything a horse could ever need. I'm overwhelmed that she has gone to such lengths. When I thank her, she waves a hand.

"You're family," she says.

You're family.

People who say things like that grew up in safe, loving, supportive homes where they go out of their way to help one another. I imagine that it's in this core of love they learn life isn't a competition, but a collaboration. If one wins, we all win.

In my experience, family is a tricky word often filled with booby traps and false starts. I regard Pat and Thomas, two relative strangers who've done more for me than my biological family, reminding me that the family you choose stays with you 'til the end.

Overwhelmed by gratitude, I quickly close the distance and wrap Pat in a huge hug. "Thank you," I whisper. It's all I can manage without completely breaking down.

Pleasure to Purpose

"My pleasure, hon," she says rubbing my back.

Composing myself, I count out seven hundred dollars to cover the first month's rent, then tell her I'll come every day.

"No need. I'm here a lot these days seeing as I can't stand being around Serenity anymore." She rolls her eyes. "If you can't come, I'll make sure Franco's good. Just let me know. Oh, by the way, I know a vet at Tufts who might have some ideas regarding his condition. Want me to have her call you?"

"That would be great. Thanks so much."

My eyes linger on Pat, admiring her selflessness, then turn to Thomas, who's tentatively brushing Franco's side. I watch Pat guide Thomas' hand in long, slow strokes as Franco stands perfectly still, enjoying the attention. My heart calms as I watch him settle in, my almost-perfect world unfolding before me.

I look at Thomas again, a man who likes me for me and went out of his way to help when no one else would. He's seen me at my emotional worst and is still here, seemingly eager to learn about the horse I love so much.

He asked me if I want a boyfriend, and I told him it wouldn't work. Perhaps I was too hasty. Logic dictates it shouldn't work. Sometimes logic is overrated.

Sometimes we have to let the heart lead.

Chapter 23

Several days later Don Rickles and I hold a funeral for Betty, watching from the upstairs window as a driver loads her onto a tow truck. Although I'm excited about the scooter's impending arrival, I chew on my lip while thinking about Dad.

After receiving no response to my voicemail, I called him again yesterday. No answer. Troubled, I reached out to Uncle Jay, who seemed evasive.

"Hiya, hon. Your dad's recovering well but still sleeps a lot."

"That's pretty normal, right? The man just had major surgery."

"Yeah…" He sounded tentative, like there was more to say but he didn't want to say it.

"What aren't you telling me?"

"I don't want you to worry."

I rolled my eyes. "C'mon, Uncle Jay!"

"They're doing more tests."

"Okay. What are they looking for?"

He sighed deeply. "Honestly, I'm not sure they know."

"Tell him I'll come as soon as I can."

"I will."

"And tell him I love him."

Uncle Jay paused. "He knows, hon. But I'll tell him."

Although the call left a pit in my stomach, it also motivated me to stabilize Franco's health as quickly as possible so I could get down to Delaware.

The metallic sound of the truck bed lowering draws my attention, and I scoop up Don Rickles. "The end of an era, Don." I blow raspberries in his fur; he wriggles out of my arms and thumps to the ground. "Don't worry though. The Vespa's coming today."

Perhaps sensing a crack in my romantic armor, Thomas offered to pick up the scooter and deliver it if I would go to dinner and a movie with him.

"But there will be no sex," he finished.

"Hey, that's my line."

He laughs. "I'm serious. I want to take you out."

"Like… a date?" I asked.

"No, no. Not a date. That would imply a romantic intent. I'm only interested in getting to know you better because I like you. That's all." He smiled sweetly while batting his eyes.

Marveling that I keep blurring business with personal, I paused only a second before agreeing.

"What shall we name the scooter?" I ask Don Rickles, who lifts his tail and sashays away in the manner cats have of looking like they're parading on a… well, a catwalk.

The name comes to me almost immediately: Velma, after the smart girl in Scooby Doo. I nod, cementing the idea.

My mind wanders to Pat, who has been unsuccessful in getting Xena into Custard's Last Stand. In a remarkable twist reminiscent of a miracle, Serenity decided Xena could stay at the rescue until she passes. I can only assume the reprieve is thanks to Pat's handiwork, perhaps convincing Serenity how little time Xena has or threatening to tell Serenity's parents about the stolen money. However it happened, I called Serenity to thank her, to which I received a "Yeah. Whatever," before she hung up. Although I feel regret that Xena won't spend her last days with Franco, the guilt is outweighed by the fact that her life will end naturally. I couldn't keep my promise, but at least Xena can go out on her own terms.

I've visited Franco every day for the last week, thoroughly enjoying mucking his stall and chatting with Pat. Franco was subdued the first few days, perhaps missing Xena. Gradually he regained his haughty-but-loveable demeanor and developed some horse friendships on the farm.

The Tufts vet Pat mentioned is examining him today, so I had his medical records sent ahead so Dr. Martin has a full picture of his past as we discuss future options. Given Dr. Styles' prognosis I'm not holding out much hope, but I have to try.

I watch from the window as Thomas pulls up to the curb, opens the trailer, and walks out with Velma in all her hot pink glory. My inner little girl giggles as I run down the two flights of stairs and straddle her.

"You look like CEO Barbie going to work," Thomas quips.

"More like horse mom Scarlett going to the vet." I grin, unable to contain my building excitement at realizing a childhood dream.

He asks if we can have our dinner tonight. I explain that I have the Tufts vet appointment followed by a callout client in the evening. Though he tries to hide it, his eyebrows knit and he pouts. I gently remind him that he *offered* to drop off the scooter. An intuitive man, he takes the hint and holds up his hands.

"You're right. You'll tell me a good time for our dinner?"

I promise, somewhat surprised that I mean it. It's not that I don't enjoy spending time with clients outside of the bedroom, but I'm finding I genuinely care for Thomas. He makes me laugh. He cares about people. He's kind and real.

As I guide the scooter to the side of the house, Thomas says, "Oh! I almost forgot. One more thing."

I turn to find him holding a white helmet that has Scarlett on each side in hot pink cursive lettering. It's a solid piece of protection meant to complement the scooter.

I shake my head at his thoughtfulness, then approach him. Placing the helmet carefully on the ground, I kiss him deeply.

"You're my hero," I whisper before retrieving the helmet and walking away, my BBW ass swinging like Don Rickles.

I feel his eyes on me as I run upstairs with a lightness in my step, like a teenager returning from a date with someone she really likes. Trying not to overthink it, I simply enjoy the feeling while dressing for the barn and preparing a backpack for the evening outcall. I don't need much for tonight's client. Just a whip and some butt plugs. I fill Don Rickles' food bowl, tell him I'll be home late, then bound down the stairs, elated about my maiden voyage.

The thrill lasts about five minutes before I realize that although Velma's speedometer goes to eighty, she can't go past forty-five without shuddering. I think back to the test drive around the previous owner's neighborhood in which I never exceeded thirty-five. Frustrated, I try again, only to find the vibration so jarring I almost lose my grip. I ride in the breakdown lane of the highway, magenta hair flying free from the edge of the helmet as cars whiz by. Several honk to say hello or perhaps voice their opinion that I shouldn't be on the highway at all, a sentiment with which I'm beginning to agree.

An hour and twenty nerve-wracking minutes later I arrive at Custard's, only to have Pat double over in laughter and say I look like I went through a clothes dryer. "Also, the vet's been here for an hour, and there's a bee in your hair."

After relocating a very pissed-off bee, I find Dr. Brooke Martin reviewing medical records by Franco's stall. A tall, lean woman with clear blue eyes and a ready smile, she starts talking without introducing herself.

"Are you Franco's mom?"

I nod.

"I hope it's okay I examined Franco before you got here. I don't have a tech today and have a full patient schedule, so I wanted to get going. Plus, I wanted to draw my own conclusions before reading Dr. Styles' notes."

Some people might be put off by Dr. Martin's efficiency and frankness, but I'm all for getting right to the point.

"And?" I prompt.

"I completely agree with her diagnoses and prognoses… with one exception."

"What's that?"

"He also has osteoarthritis. His body is attacking itself."

My entire body sags. I thought I was prepared for the worst, but I now realize how much emphasis I'd placed on a miracle. I fight against the looming depression just waiting for me to lower my guard.

"There is one thing I could try…"

Pleasure to Purpose

My emotions flip flop as Dr. Martin describes a procedure in which high-pressure water is inserted quickly into the bladder to create a tsunami that dislodges sediment. The water is then quickly vacuumed out, not allowing any remaining sediment to settle to the bottom.

I respond without hesitation. "Let's do it."

"I'll need to take him with me and keep him for day or so to monitor him. Between my time, the tech's time, the procedure, sedative and boarding, it'll cost several thousand."

Although my breath catches, I try not to let the shock show. The result is silence with a lot of blinking. Dr. Martin grimaces, then starts to apologize, but I interrupt her.

"Money is only paper, and paper is replaceable. There's only one Franco. Let's do it."

While Dr. Martin calls her office to prepare them for Franco's arrival, I spend some quality time brushing him and explaining what's coming, then help Dr. Martin load him into her trailer. He seems oblivious to the drama unfolding around him, happily munching on a carrot as I close the trailer door. I try to emulate his nonchalance. But as Dr. Martin pulls away, the memory of Tyler disappearing from our home pops into my head, followed by a happy memory of Dad taking us kids to feed the ducks and ride the swan boats in Boston Garden.

The two opposing memories bang against each other, resulting in a raging headache.

After saying goodbye to Pat, I drink a bottle of water to prepare for my client, then start the drive. Instead of lamenting Velma's speed limitations, I decide to enjoy the slower pace. Choosing back roads instead of the highway, I relax into the drive, the warm wind slapping my face as my mind wanders.

Richard is a fifty-three-year-old accountant who has erectile dysfunction but won't go to the doctor because he's afraid of two things: his wife will somehow find out he visited a doctor for ED meds and, therefore, he'll have to sleep with her. He told me that in his world it's easier to skulk around with me than deal with his wife.

His version of married guy logic, I suppose. He enjoys sensual domination: being controlled sexually without verbal or physical abuse. For example, he likes water games involving various bodily fluids, being stroked with a feather while blindfolded or having plugs inserted in his ass. In the end, he usually wants to finish with a blow job. During one of our sessions he told me he and his wife haven't had sex in years and that he's dreadfully unhappy. When I asked him why he doesn't file for divorce, he looked at me like I was crazy.

"Because my wife would kill me."

I arrive at the hotel and enter our regular room to find him laying nude on the bed while watching CNN. Unlike other clients who chat about their lives or prefer to be worked up slowly through foreplay, Richard is all business, every time.

When I walk through the door, he turns off the TV and assumes a spread-eagled position. I freshen up, brushing out my hair and applying bright red lipstick, then exit the bathroom completely naked except for a towel in one hand and a large feather in the other.

Placing the feather in my teeth, I straddle him and lean over, brushing the feather along his concave chest and flat abdomen. He groans and closes his eyes, then opens his mouth, silently asking to play a water game. The bottle of water I chugged earlier has worked its way through and, although this is a fetish I don't enjoy, I oblige by squatting over his torso, then moving slowly up toward his face until I'm peeing in his mouth. By the time I'm done, his relatively large cock is rock hard. He turns on his side for the next step.

An interesting fact about the rectum is that it acts like a vacuum, sucking in anything that's inserted. Early in my career I learned to use plugs with a flared base and extraction ring after one of my clients ended up in the emergency room with a plug we couldn't remove.

Richard can't achieve orgasm without anal stimulation, so I start with a small, lubricated silicone plug, working it in gently while he masturbates. I repeat the process with incrementally larger plugs until we get to Big Momma, a stainless steel, one-inch-wide plug that makes him gasp as he brings himself to the edge. His breath comes faster until he stops suddenly, rolls onto his back and spreads his legs for the grand finale.

While gently tugging on the plug's extraction ring to stimulate the anal nerves, I take my time with the bareback, withdrawing when he's close to climax, waiting a few seconds, then starting again. After ten minutes he grabs my hair to keep me on him and comes really hard, thrusting his hips

Pleasure to Purpose

upward for maximum impact. Richard is one of those men who might be physically small in stature but becomes a lion in bed. And next to horses, lions are my favorite animal.

Afterward, I dress while Richard showers, then pack my things and collect the money from the dresser. We make an appointment for the following month. Fifty-five minutes after arriving at the hotel, I'm back on Velma, three-hundred-fifty dollars richer.

The evening sky is ablaze with vibrant hues that fade quickly to a dusty pink, then misty blue, and finally to black as the sun dips below the horizon. The back roads aren't well-lit, but Velma's bright headlamp meets the challenge, illuminating the asphalt in a cone shape that stretches into the shadows that line the road.

To avoid road hypnosis settling in, I review my last conversation with Uncle Jay. Although I run through a list of tests the doctors might be performing, until I can get to Delaware I have to trust that Uncle Jay is doing all he can.

Sudden movement in my peripheral vision draws my attention. It starts as slow recognition that an object is hurtling toward me, quickly followed by the realization that its trajectory will place it squarely in my path. As these thoughts coalesce in a split second, I calculate the best way to avoid the collision and jerk Velma's handlebars to the right.

Unable to alter its direction, the deer moves in tandem with the scooter. We smash together as one mass of flesh, metal and fur. This is only for an instant, before the doe's large torso bounces off Velma's faceplate, which crumples like aluminum foil.

Fight or flight chemicals release making me stunningly alert. I understand that if I hadn't veered slightly right, the deer would've hit me directly; I would be dead.

I manage to keep control while skidding to a stop, adrenaline infecting my trembling body. My hands are frozen in a vise grip around the handlebars as I force deep breaths and replay the crash in my mind. Terrified I've wounded the doe beyond repair, I walk back to the site of impact. She's gone, vanished into the brush lining the road.

It sickens me to think I might have killed such a gentle, graceful creature. I once read that colliding with a deer signifies transitions in your life, serving as a reminder to be more present and seek balance.

166

That interpretation certainly could apply to me.

I catch my breath while evaluating Velma. The face plate is gone and her handlebars are crooked. But she's drivable, and I'm alive. I close my eyes, willing my body to stop shaking while sending a quick thanks skyward.

I'm alive. Franco's alive. Dad's alive.

Three things for which I'm incredibly grateful.

Chapter 24

After reliving the accident repeatedly in my dreams, I awake the next morning to the buzzing of my personal phone. It's Dad, who is wheezing due to a lung infection contracted in the hospital. I rub sleep out of my eyes while absorbing the fact that a place of supposed healing has made him sicker.

"Any word about the other tests?" I ask.

He avoids the question by telling me not to worry.

Telling a concerned person not to worry is akin to ordering a stressed person to calm down. It's pointless and infuriating.

"I'm going home tomorrow."

"Who says?"

"Me."

Taking a page from his book, I grunt. Based on his wheezing, he's not going anywhere.

"Penny's driving me crazy."

No surprise there. Then I remember the spiritual significance of last night's deer collision and the need to find balance.

"I'm sorry to hear that, Dad. No word on the tests then?"

He ignores me again and says that he finds his nurse offensive. The comment catches me off guard, making me laugh. "What's wrong with your nurse?"

He laments that he has a male nurse with an attitude instead of a young, pretty woman. Although I love that he's maintaining his sarcastic attitude, my response is swift. "One word, Dad. Karma."

He chuckles, appreciating the joke. A strong sense of humor is something Dad and I have always had in common. When I was five I told him a joke he stills says is the best he's ever heard:

Knock knock.

Who's there?

Impatient cow.

Impatient cow wh—

MOO!

"So, how's things, Princess?"

He obviously doesn't want to discuss his health, so I lean back into the sex couch that arrived last week and wind one of the restraints around my finger. Although I haven't had a chance to take it for a test drive, I'm thinking Thomas might be the guinea pig to inaugurate my purple velour goddess. Regardless, I'm pleased she adds a pop of color to an otherwise understated room.

I update Dad on Franco's illness, Betty's death and Velma's purchase and subsequent partial demise. When I tell him about Thomas' desire to become more than a client, he grunts.

"Something to say about that?"

He coughs, snorts, then spits. I imagine Dad's nurse starting his shift to find a loogie on the floor. I'd have an attitude too.

"I think you should settle down with this Thomas guy."

At first I'm speechless, then I choke out a laugh. The irony of my absent, thrice-married father offering relationship advice is beyond comprehension.

"You've never even met him. I know you mean well, but—"

"I'm worried about you, Princess. That's all."

Pleasure to Purpose

His words come out as a whisper. I hear genuine concern in his tone. It's not that I haven't heard it before, but the sentiment feels declarative and final, like he's trying to put everything in order before he—

"What happened with the extra tests, Dad? Are you okay?"

He coughs again, longer this time, then returns to his brusque self. "I'm fine!"

Dad believes saying something really loudly makes it true. As he lapses into another coughing fit, my hoe phone dings with a text from Anne.

Coming today? Have good news

I check the time. Eleven-thirty. If I shower quickly, I'll just make the noon support group meeting. I tell Dad about the group and he peppers me with questions I don't have time to answer.

"I promise I'll tell you more next time. Okay?"

Right before I disconnect, he says, "Hey, Princess?"

"Yeah?"

"I, uh, love you."

I tell him I love him too, but he's already hung up.

Dad grew up in a family that didn't openly express love, so he rarely shows a vulnerable side. After finally learning how to say I love you, he still has a hard time accepting the sentiment in return.

I hurriedly shower, then slip into jeans and a black sweatshirt. Grabbing my helmet, I run downstairs where Velma sits proudly in the space Betty used to occupy. Before I fell asleep last night, I texted my mechanic, Kamil, asking if he'd stop by to evaluate the damage. He must have come this morning while I was sleeping, because although the paint is scratched on the motor casing where a hoof dragged across it, the handlebars are perfectly straight and there's a new faceplate. I hop aboard to make the short trip, setting a mental reminder to follow up with Kamil about the bill.

I arrive at the Victorian to find the meeting has started. The only available seat is next to Misty… and after a beat I understand why the seat is vacant. Misty's cracked, yellow nails advertise the stifling aroma that wafts toward me, making me wonder how many packs she smokes a day and if her habit impacts her work.

Pleasure to Purpose

Anne requests our attention, then offers an update on Randy's murder investigation.

"Randy's pimp was arrested. Apparently, he bragged about strangling her, so hopefully he'll go away for a while." The newbies gasp when they hear the cause of death. The rest of us sit quietly, imagining the young girl's terror as her life drained away. Having lived Randy's nightmare through my experience with Tyler, I can only hope she felt the same sense of peace toward the end.

Anne brings the conversation back around to the living, reminding us that when police round-ups occur, it's the workers, not the pimps, who spend an uncomfortable night in lock-up.

"But this time…" Anne holds up a finger, "the pimp is going down. In fact, several girls plan to testify against him in honor of Randy."

The veterans exchange looks, silently expressing incredulity. Even if the pimp goes to jail, he has connections on the outside that'll keep his enterprise running, including the punishment side of the business. Those girls are either really brave or really stupid because they're signing their death warrants by testifying. Or perhaps they're just fed up with a system that's rigged against them and are willing to pay with their lives to see justice served.

"One of the girls is with us today. Stella, please stand," Anne finishes.

All of us turn toward a tall, strong woman in her early forties with a lean face, a platinum crew cut and too many teeth. Her size, strength and crooked nose give the impression of a lightweight boxer turned sex pro. Large, puffy green eyes against impossibly pale skin belie a life filled with heartbreak. Lip, tongue and nose piercings make the imagination fly regarding where other piercings might lie.

We break into respectful applause. Stella's fair cheeks blush bright pink. Although I respect and admire her decision, if being singled out in our little group causes her stress, I wonder how she'll fare on a witness stand with a high-priced attorney badgering her, not to mention the defendant's hate-filled glare.

Anne abruptly changes the subject, saying that the state representative is impressed with our letters. "There's something else. She was really affected by one particular statement."

I look up from my lap to find everyone staring.

"Scarlett, she'd like you to testify before the committee and potentially join the task force."

I feel my eyebrows shoot up as my mouth drops open. I blink several times and look around. Scarlett Pereira, the once-homeless, college dropout from a broken home is being asked to speak before the Massachusetts House of Representatives and potentially join their... *task force?* As a member of a group that represents sex workers, I'd have a hand in sculpting our future. It's unthinkable. Literally almost unbelievable. I can't change the fact that I didn't help Randy, but I sure as hell can make a difference moving forward. I feel like I'm going to float right out of my seat and can't wait to tell my dad.

"Well?" Anne prods.

I realize with embarrassment that I haven't said a word.

"Yes!" I blurt to laughter and applause.

My right leg bounces with excitement for another excruciating forty minutes before Anne closes the meeting. I drive home as fast as Velma can take me, bound up the stairs, and plop onto my bed to dial Dad.

"Prinshess?" he answers.

His speech is somewhat slurred, so I apologize for waking him, then tell him that my letter was singled out in the support group. He doesn't respond, so I cap the story with the fact that his only daughter will be speaking before the Massachusetts House.

"Can you freakin' believe it, Dad? They chose *me!*"

Heavy wheezing comes across the line. When I ask him if he's alright, his response is slow. "I... okay."

The hairs on my neck stiffen as nausea creeps into my gut. "Hey, Dad. Can I talk to your nurse for a sec?"

The phone becomes muffled as I imagine it falls to the bed, followed by a scratching sound, then Penny's voice.

"Hiya, hon." She's uncharacteristically reserved, which unnerves me even more. I ask if Uncle Jay's around.

"No, just your dad and me."

"Why does Dad's voice sound weird?"

"He had a stroke."

Pleasure to Purpose

She says it so matter-of-factly that the breath expels from my lungs like I've been sucker-punched. The world rocks as I process that she's calm and I'm not.

"Is he gonna be okay?"

"Because of the stroke? Probably."

Her answer makes me wonder if she's losing it. She's never done well under stress.

"The doctors think he might have had two strokes actually," she continues in a low, even tone.

She's cracking under the pressure. I ask to speak with Dad's doctor. When she says no, I request a nurse. She answers negatively again. "Are you okay, Penny?" I finally ask.

"Since when do you care?"

Penny's always tried to make me like her, so the drastic turn has me genuinely concerned. I tell her I'll call back, then dial Uncle Jay, who answers immediately.

"What the hell is going on with my dad? Penny *isn't* freaking out so I'm kind of freaking out."

Although Uncle Jay has marched in Washington, been the victim of an anti-gay hate crime and has generally been discriminated against since he came out, I've never heard or seen him cry. So when I hear him sniffling, my arms go numb.

Suddenly I don't want to know. I want to remain in Schrödinger's Box, that hopeful place that separates ignorance and knowledge. But he knows me well and hits me head-on with the news.

"There's been another diagnosis. Your dad has leukemia."

I drop the phone as my brain flies away to somewhere safe. Uncle Jay's voice reaches me, but from very far away. "Sorry, hon, but… he doesn't have much time left."

Chapter 25

After hearing the news from Uncle Jay, I take a few minutes to have a good cry, then call Dad back to tell him I'm coming down. He tries to argue with me, saying he's fine, but I tell him he doesn't have a choice. I then text Thomas, who promises to care for Don Rickles and finish by calling Pat, who tells me Franco has become quite a Casanova since returning from the vet. The vision makes me smile.

"Don't worry, honey. I'll take care of the big guy while you're gone. Hey, has Dr. Martin called you with Franco's results?" Pat asks.

"No, why?"

"No reason. Just thought she might've by now."

Pat's comment rattles me, so I leave a message at Dr. Martin's office asking her to return my call.

The next day I'm on the train from Boston to Wilmington, Delaware, each passing mile multiplying my dread. Throughout the trip I check my phone incessantly, simultaneously relieved and stressed the vet hasn't called.

Five hours later Uncle Jay wraps me in the kind of hug you want to inhabit forever. "How's my favorite niece?"

I'm his only niece.

"How's Dad doing?"

Uncle Jay's smile drops. "I'm not going to lie. He's not good." His face brightens. "But you're here now so I'm sure he'll feel better."

I ask about hospital visiting hours and he seems confused.

"He's home, hon."

I shake my head. "The man had two strokes and has a lung infection and he's home already? Seriously?"

Uncle Jay takes my face in his large, rough hands, calloused by years of woodworking. "Honeypie, your dad's under hospice care. The leukemia diagnosis was made too late for him to undergo chemo. It's about keeping him comfortable now."

I stare through Uncle Jay as an emptiness hollows out my core.

Uncle Jay reads me well. "This isn't about you, hon. It's about your father."

I gaze into his warm brown eyes, hating that he's right. Dad is a recipient of the Parachutist Badge and the Good Conduct medal, as well as the National Defense Service Medal for time spent as a POW in Vietnam. He still deals with PTSD and is one of the toughest guys I know. As hard as it is to let him go, he deserves to die with dignity.

I nod and Uncle Jay smiles sadly. "That's my girl."

He squeezes my shoulder and then we're in the car, weaving through the inner city toward the outskirts. We arrive at Dad's house and the first thing I notice is the overgrown lawn infested with weeds.

"Yeah, I need to mow," Uncle Jay comments.

Upon entering the one-level brick ranch I'm hit with the smell of bleach and wood soap. I turn questioningly to Uncle Jay, who grimaces.

"Penny did some cleaning before your dad came home."

The fumes burn my eyes. I blink away tears, wondering if my lungs will survive the visit. I open a window.

Penny rushes in. She slams it shut, then turns on me. "You think you can come in here and take over?"

I hold up my hands in surrender while exchanging a look with Uncle Jay, whose expression falls between surprise and confusion. Penny stomps away, her dyed blonde ponytail bouncing as she goes. Jay and I follow to the living room, where the TV is tuned to a soap.

My sleeping father lies prone in a hospital bed in the middle of the room, his head propped on two pillows. His thinning gray hair is

Pleasure to Purpose

unbrushed, his beard stubble is at least a week old. He's lost a lot of weight, leaving his body wan and frail under the white sheet. His forearms, always a hallmark of strength, seem thinner, with multiple bruises from IVs and blood draws. My overall impression is that he's already started the process of leaving.

Suddenly his eyes open and he grins. "Princess!"

For a moment he's his old self and I question whether what I've been told is true. But then his smile falters while his eyes snap shut.

A high-pitched squeak draws my attention. I turn to find Penny crying quietly on a light pink, overstuffed chair in the corner. Steeling myself, I approach slowly. She's annoying, but Dad loves her, so I need to try.

"Listen, Penny, I know we haven't always gotten along, but I want you to know I plan on staying for as—"

Her hand flies up, fending me off. "Don't waste your breath. I've managed this far on my own."

Although her vehemence is surprising, I'm a little impressed she's found a backbone. Maybe there's more to her than I thought.

Their cat, Sparkles, limps by, dragging a back leg. The cat was ancient when I was here three years ago. I track his slow progress, then turn back to Penny with a questioning look.

"Oh, he's diabetic. He's fine though."

I watch the poor animal, who struggles to negotiate a turn around the door jamb. I comment on his obvious pain.

"I've been a little busy with your dying father for the last few weeks! The damned cat can wait!"

Although my first reaction is to strike back, I know it would do more harm than good. I literally bite my tongue to stifle a retort, then offer to take Sparkles to the vet. I can't help Dad right now, but I can at least alleviate the cat's pain. Penny waves a hand dismissively.

"Do whatever you want. I don't care."

When she turns her attention to the TV, I return to Dad and pull a chair close to the bed as Uncle Jay falls into a ripped, faded leather recliner whose footrest is stuck halfway up.

"I wish he'd dealt with the illness earlier," Jay mutters.

"What do you mean?" I ask.

Pleasure to Purpose

Uncle Jay tells me that Dad knew something was seriously wrong for weeks before seeing a doctor. When he finally went and was given the anemia diagnosis, Jay suggested he seek another opinion. But Dad is stubborn and was against the idea.

He let it happen. He either thought he was invincible or didn't want to face reality. Either way, my father is dying.

I stare at Dad's wasting body, absorbing my role in the fiasco. Too enmeshed in my own dramas, I didn't take his illness as seriously as I should've. If I had, I might've been able to convince him to seek treatment earlier.

If and **might.** Two words that are useless if not downright dangerous. **If** usually leads to what **might** have happened, and I could play that game all day… no, for a lifetime. If I had stayed in college, I might have become a vet. If Sonya hadn't died, we might have started a horse rescue together. If my fiancé, hadn't absconded with my life savings, I might be happily married with two kids. If I'd been born into a functional family, I might not have become a sex worker.

Then I consider other ifs and mights. If I weren't a sex worker, I might not be presenting before the Massachusetts House. If I hadn't had a stalker, I might not have been at the restaurant to see Thomas. If I didn't have Pat as a friend, I might not have Franco in my life.

I look at my dad again, thinking that if he weren't sick, we might not have become closer and I might not be sitting here. One thing leads to another, guiding us down a life path. The road isn't smooth. God knows mine is full of potholes. But it's my road to own, and I'm beginning to realize how much I like where I am and who I'm becoming. I take Dad's hand, his long slender fingers melting gracefully around mine. The hands of a father who, like all of us, is doing the best he can.

Penny appears, holding a small, brown, plastic bottle. She removes some pills and places the vial on a table.

"What's this?" I ask, picking up the bottle.

"It's nitroglycerin for his heart."

"This is only supposed to be used for angina attacks."

She looks at me like I'm an idiot. "That's what he has."

I try again. "It should be used only for *sudden* attacks, not…"

Pleasure to Purpose

She waves me off and rouses Dad, who swallows the pills before I can stop him.

"How many pills did you give him?"

She stares into the distance. "Two."

I hold the vial toward her. "The directions say 'only as needed.' You could literally kill him with these."

Her face crumples in confusion before holding up shaking hands. "My hands… aren't working right."

"What?"

She continues to stare straight ahead.

I look to Uncle Jay for guidance, but he seems as lost as I am. It occurs to me that the prolonged anxiety of Dad's health has affected her thinking, or perhaps she might be in early-stage dementia. I ask for the written directions the hospice nurse left. Penny searches for several minutes before handing me a scrap of wadded paper from her pocket. The handwriting is shaky and barely legible.

"Did you write this, Penny?"

She nods.

"I think we should get you some help."

"No!" Dad roars.

Uncle Jay and I jump while Penny clamps her hands over her ears like a child. Suddenly awake and completely coherent, Dad continues in a calm, kind tone. "Princess, when did you get here?"

I close my eyes, trying to re-center. My instinct to get angry at Dad's outburst might make things worse. I ask Penny to get Dad some tea, then take the opportunity during her absence to have a blunt conversation about his care.

"Dad, Penny can't handle you on her own, and Uncle Jay and I can only stay a little while. If we get some help in here—"

"No!"

I understand the impulse to want to hide his infirmity. He's a proud man who doesn't want to rely on strangers. I have to make him understand that the current situation is simply untenable. Sparkles limps by, then collapses on the hardwood floor where the sun pours through a window. His breath is labored from dragging an atrophied leg.

"I'm going to take Sparkles to the vet."

"Fine, George."

I look at Uncle Jay and mouth, *Who's George?*

He shrugs.

Gently placing my hand on Dad's, I remind him who I am.

"Get the hell outta my way or I'll fuck you up!" he screams, then closes his eyes, shunning me.

All ego is stripped away as I realize I'm losing my father a piece at a time. A pressure settles in my chest that feels like my heart is about to explode. I look to Uncle Jay, desperate to find a touchstone. He shakes his head slowly, his anguish palpable without tears or words.

"I have to get out of here," I say, suddenly wanting to be anywhere else. My eyes fall to the obese cat licking his leg.

"Can I borrow your car, Uncle Jay?"

Without waiting for an answer, I scoop up the car fob and the cat. I place Sparkles on the passenger seat of the Mini Cooper and we drive to the vet.

The tech draws some blood for analysis while I sit numbly on a hard wooden bench. Sparkles manically licks his useless leg, obviously trying to rid himself of the burden. After thirty minutes, the vet walks in reviewing a piece of paper. He introduces himself, then gets right to the point.

"Sparkles isn't well, but I think you know that. He's severely diabetic. Not to mention he's seventeen years old. Having said that, you have two choices. His leg is becoming necrotic. If it's removed, he might have another year at most."

I hold up my hand, not needing to hear the other choice. If he survived the surgery, Sparkles would be reliant on Penny for his care, and she's already over her head with my dad.

I authorize the euthanasia. The vet tells me he can do it tomorrow or later today. I look at the immobile ball of fur and can't find the heart to let the poor cat suffer one more day. I say I'll wait, and after two hours of playing games on my phone (interrupted only by client calls and a text from Thomas with a picture of him holding Don Rickles) the vet returns with two syringes and a tech.

I cradle Sparkles as the sedative is injected and whisper sweetness in his ear as he fades away. The vet asks if I want to bring his body home. I pause, wondering what my dad would want. When I imagine Penny's

Pleasure to Purpose

histrionic response upon seeing Sparkles' body, I request cremation be done by the office.

Being witness to the death of an innocent soul is overwhelming. I weep openly on the return drive, knowing the tears aren't for a cat I barely knew, but for Franco's illness and my dad's impending death. Grief has settled into my joints, making them tender and swollen. I wonder when life might look bright again. I feel like I'm on a treadmill trudging in darkness, even as I understand it's part of the grief journey. I can't walk around it. I have to go straight through.

I pull in the driveway to find Uncle Jay taking a second pass at mowing the lawn. The first cut left mounds of grass that are now being eaten again by the mower, ground up into tinier pieces. I wave, then enter the house to a stench of diarrhea so overpowering I gag.

Covering my nose and mouth, I walk into the living room to find Dad sleeping soundly as Penny scrolls through her phone. She doesn't look up as I lift Dad's midsection and liquid feces spills from his diaper onto the sheets.

I've been gone four hours. Uncle Jay's been outside for at least an hour working on the lawn.

"How long as he been sitting in his own shit?"

Any earlier kindness related to her fragile mental state shatters as she looks up and begins to cry. I ignore her and allow my medical training to kick in. I carefully wake Dad and help him to a plastic chair in the shower, then order Penny to undress him and wash him thoroughly. While she's doing that, I strip the bed and remake it, then throw the soiled sheets into the washer. By the time I return to check in, Dad is clean and partially dressed, sitting precariously on the edge of the bed.

Seeing me, he raises his hand in greeting. "Sharon, great to see you!"

I stop mid-stride. His face sags suddenly as clarity returns, the expression falling somewhere between confusion and fear. I watch in helplessness as this mountain of a man crumbles into disorientation and panic.

"It's okay, Dad. Let's get you back to bed."

Penny snaps, "That's your problem. You're never letting him walk on his own. That's why he's so unstable. He needs to walk on his own to build strength."

Pleasure to Purpose

I know from experience that patients in Dad's state shouldn't walk independently. I tell her that and she pushes me out of the way to drag Dad from the bed. Before I can stop him, he takes a step and falls heavily to the carpeted floor.

Penny throws up her hands. "See? I told you! He needs to walk more!"

I set my jaw. "No. He needs to use a walker or not walk at all!"

"You're never letting him walk. It's ridiculous!" she rants.

The room starts spinning. I feel like Alice falling through the looking glass. Death is everywhere and nothing is logical.

For a person used to being in control, the last few days have been a nightmare. I steady myself, then return Dad to the bed, Penny trailing behind while grumbling under her breath. I smooth his hair.

His eyes suddenly brighten as he becomes fully alert.

"Hey, Princess, you came!"

I take a shuddering breath and force a smile. "Yeah, Dad. It's great to see you too."

Pleasure to Purpose

Chapter 26

After a week at Dad's house, I'm convinced of three things: Uncle Jay should be nominated for sainthood, Penny is legitimately starting to lose her mind and the hospice nurse who attends my father thinks I'm a jerk.

When Penny and I disagree, which is often, the hospice nurse usually agrees with my clinical assessment but asks me to speak with more patience and kindness to my stepmother, a moniker I find challenging as she's never acted in that capacity. Uncle Jay usually intervenes at this point, astutely pointing out that our bickering helps no one, especially Dad.

On the second day I received a call from Dr. Martin, presumably with Franco's test results. Not wanting to hear more bad news, I let it go to voicemail. When Penny runs to the store, Dad and I share a wonderful conversation about horses, which sparks memories of my childhood.

He recounts various stories, always ending with him laughing and saying how much fun we all had. Most of the stories are new to me. I wonder if they're real or if his brain has manufactured a history that's more pleasing than reality. Or, more troubling, perhaps it's my wounded view of the world that no longer allows me to remember the good. In the end, I decide it doesn't matter because he's happy and we're enjoying each other's company.

After Dad's favorite lunch of peanut butter and jelly sandwiches, he asks, "Hey, where's that damned cat? I used to see him all the time around here!"

Uncle Jay and I exchange a look, then tell him about the euthanasia. A gut-wrenching pain crosses his face; his eyes swell with tears. He retreats into himself, not speaking to me for two days. I can't blame him. Perhaps he fears he'll share Sparkles' fate. His world is upside down and he has absolutely no control over his physical state or mind. I'd be pissed off too.

On the fourth day a navy-blue, leather recliner arrives, courtesy of me, who almost broke a hip trying to climb out of the previous one. When she sees it, Penny's only comment is that she detests navy blue, even as Dad relaxes with his feet up, the happiest I've seen him since my arrival. I relax a little when we watch TV shows together and debate politics, proving that the old Dad is still in there somewhere.

On the fifth day I decide to listen to Dr. Martin's voicemail. In it she explains that the pressure washing procedure removed a lot of dark orange sediment, but now we need to see if Franco's kidneys function well enough to keep additional sediment out of his bladder. She also performed an endoscopy in which she found a large ulcer in his stomach lining and evidence of a tieback, a procedure sometimes done on racehorses to maximize the airway. "I'm prescribing medicine for the ulcer and recommend soaking hay pellets before feeding him to minimize any choking hazard. You should also add beet pulp to his diet and wean him from grain." She ends by saying she emailed me the bill and will follow up in a week to see how Franco's doing.

Feeling lighter than I have in a week, I let out a long sigh. Dr. Martin's voice sounds tentatively optimistic in the message. That's enough to make me want to dance across the room. *Franco's going to be okay.* Well, not okay. But not in imminent danger.

I call Pat to share the news, and she tells me not to worry about Franco because he doesn't miss me at all and has become BHOC, big horse on campus. I don't know if it's true or if she's trying to make me feel better, but it works. I laugh, surprised by the light-hearted sound. I check in with Thomas who says Don Rickles misses me, as does he. The sentiment brings a smile to my face. I realize how few times I've smiled or laughed since coming to Delaware. I reply with a red heart emoji, for once not caring how it's perceived.

I pull out my hoe phone to find numerous text and voicemail messages from clients. I respond to each one, saying I'm out of town on family business and will let them know when I'm available again. I also listen to a voicemail from Anne who reiterates how quickly the committee meeting is approaching, ending with, "Do you feel ready?"

That reminder lands hard on my buoyant mood, weighing it down with an anchor. Although I'm proud to have been asked to speak, I have no idea how quickly Dad's illness will progress and am not sure I have the bandwidth to tackle such a massive project. I picture Randy's innocent, wide-eyed gaze, followed by Dad's words, *I'm proud of you.* I close my eyes and nod, responding to an unseen spiritual directive.

"Okay. I'll do it," I say aloud.

* * *

On the sixth day, Penny and I have a blowout in which she tells me I'm ungrateful and nothing like her two grown children. Responding to a pleading look from Uncle Jay, I hold my tongue. But as her relentless needling continues, I ask where her perfect kids are and why I haven't met them in the thirty years she and Dad have been married. Penny dissolves into tears and runs from the room while a crushing need to return home overtakes me.

I spend the last evening with Dad holding his hand and whispering how much I love him as he sleeps. The fatigue has worsened in the short time I've been here. It's excruciating to see him wasting away right in front of me.

The next day I hug him goodbye and promise to return soon. He waves jovially, seemingly unaware of our relationship or his failing health. "Thanks for coming! Happy trails!"

For some reason his ignorance pains me more than if he whispered goodbye, knowing he might not see me again. I know it's selfish to want a partner in grief. It's so much better for him that he doesn't know the truth.

The dilemma is that the man he used to be would want to know. When I voice that, Uncle Jay takes my hand and pulls me away from Dad.

"Hon, he's not the man he once was. He's a new version of himself, removed from his own reality. It's better he doesn't know."

I dissolve into tears before returning to kiss Dad on the cheek. Struggling to maintain an even voice, I whisper in his ear. "I love you, Dad. I'm going to continue to make you proud."

I face the window as Uncle Jay drives to the train station, trying but failing to fend off a deep, throbbing melancholy.

"I know it's hard, hon. It's tough for me too, to see my big brother reduced to a diapered mess. I mean, he used to beat me up. Then, when we were older, he'd beat up the kids who picked on me." He pauses, nodding at memories only he can see. "He was my hero."

I keep my head turned away because I'm embarrassed I haven't considered Uncle Jay's feelings.

"You gonna be okay?" he asks.

I look at him sideways, wanting to tell him I haven't worked in a week and Dr. Martin's vet bill came to six thousand dollars. I don't have a car, only a beat-up Vespa that can barely drive straight, and my mother is emotionally blackmailing me. But I don't. Although I love and trust Uncle Jay more than anyone else in my family, I just can't show that vulnerability. Maybe I've been hurt too many times. Maybe I'm just broken.

Instead, I say, "Penny's a twat."

He smiles and nods, seeming to understand me on many levels.

We arrive at the station where Uncle Jay insists on sitting quietly together on the platform, each of us lost in thought until the train pulls up. I sling my bag over my shoulder and reach up for a hug.

"Thanks for everything, Uncle Jay. I'm really sorry you're bearing the brunt of this," I say into his chest.

He rocks me back and forth; our sadness made a little lighter by sharing the load.

Hours later I arrive home to find William sitting on the top stair. He asks me how Dad is, so I recount the entire week, then urge him to go down.

"It could be the last time, Will."

Pleasure to Purpose

"I'm not sure I have time. I don't think I..." His voice trails off as if he forgot what he was saying. Of the three kids, William has always been the holdout with Dad, as if he never got over how he treated Mom. I'm sure he loves our father, but he struggles to be in the same room with him.

When William looks at me again, I see guilt colliding with sadness creating a cacophony of emotion that's rocking him to the core. He holds my stare a moment, then walks slowly down the stairs, leaving each of us alone with our grief. I ponder what my family would've been like if we shared our highs and lows and talked through challenges. I quickly realize that's wishful thinking, the kind of idea I tried to put in practice as a child. Each of us has become a silo, stoic and unyielding in both love and distrust.

When my hoe phone rings, I answer eagerly. A new client named Greg, he was referred by Steph, who I haven't seen since the Jared incident. He asks for an outcall, and after providing the prerequisite piece of mail, I tell him I'll see him in an hour. I run upstairs, give Don Rickles a squeeze and some dry food, then check the litter box.

Thomas was true to his word. Don looks well-fed, loved and the litter is fresh. I send Thomas a quick text of thanks, then jump in the shower, throw some toys into a backpack and hop onto Velma, excited to be back in the proverbial saddle.

I enter the address in Wayz and arrive forty minutes later at a forest-green house in need of new paint and some bush trimming. Greg meets me at the front door with a finger to his lips, then motions me to follow. He's skinny and young, maybe mid-twenties, with curly brown hair that flops onto his forehead. As he leads me down a shag-carpeted hallway, I notice a dramatic limp and look down to see that his bare, right foot is severely swollen. I follow him through a door and down a set of wooden stairs to the basement where he turns and spreads his sticklike arms.

"Welcome!"

Greg seems nervous, making me wonder if he's done this before. I quickly scan the room as he limps over to turn on a lava lamp. Surprisingly lush, navy blue carpet covers most of the floor. At one corner is a small kitchenette. A queen bed sits in the northwest corner, a cream duvet partially covering light blue, wrinkled sheets. Completing the motif is a strobe light on the bedstand, splashing color haphazardly across the ceiling. All that's missing is a mirrored disco ball.

"Can I get you something?" he asks.

Now I know he hasn't done this before. Most clients aren't rude, but they know I'm there for one reason only. This guy is acting like we're on a date. I politely decline while glancing at his swollen foot.

"Diabetes," he says.

I picture Sparkles dragging his leg across the floor.

"I have neuropathy. Sometimes the numbness means I can't feel things, like a needle going into my heel."

I have several questions but remain silent. I've been doing this long enough to know that clients will share if they feel inclined. It gives them a sense of control if they volunteer information rather than my asking.

"I accidentally stepped on one of my insulin syringes and didn't feel it. The tip broke off inside my foot, but I didn't know until an infection developed. They did surgery to remove the needle, and I almost died from the infection."

Nothing like bacteria to get a girl going, I think. But I'm a professional, so I turn up the heat. "I think your swollen foot is sexy," I say. "Let's see if something else is swollen."

I approach and fondle his erection, then unbuckle his jeans and reach inside. I pull him out and drop to my knees, then work my tongue to find his G spot. He grabs my hair and throws his head back, moaning loudly. That's my cue.

"I just need the money first."

He almost falls over trying to scramble the bills from his front pocket. I feel the wad for accuracy while pushing him slowly back toward the bed.

"What do you like, Greg? I brought everything with me. Just say the word."

"I… um… I…"

The way he mauls my breasts makes me think he's a virgin. He's living in the basement of a house that saw its prime in the seventies, so he's probably renting space from his grandma until he "saves enough for his own place." I've heard it so many times I can recite it by heart.

I push him down on the bed and turn my back to him, then sway my hips while undressing slowly. Once I'm nude, I bend over so he can get a full view.

Pleasure to Purpose

Thinking he's had enough foreplay, I turn to face him. "What do you want to—"

Greg is lying spread-eagled, his swollen cock on full display. In his right hand he holds a can of whipped cream, which he bobbles back and forth. He is beaming like a teenager who's hit the sex lottery.

He squirts a dollop on the tip of his penis. I cover my mouth, trying not to laugh. In all the years I've been doing this, no one has wanted whipped cream. I know it's a fantasy to suck anything—liquor, fruit, chocolate or whipped cream—from a woman's nipple, belly or pussy, but it took meeting Greg to check this particular fetish off my list.

We spend the next fifty sticky, uncomfortable minutes eating whipped cream from all orifices before finishing with vanilla sex. It's only when he falls back onto the bed, completely satiated, that I realize there's no shower in the apartment. Only a large laundry sink.

I perform a quick clean-up to ensure bugs don't stick to my skin on the way home, then ask Greg about the house. He tells me his mother passed away, leaving it to his sister and him.

"Sissy lives upstairs, and I live down here."

Although Sissy clearly got the better end of that deal, I certainly can commiserate given my mother's recent declaration. At least Greg owns part of the house, even if it is the basement.

I watch him spray the last of the whipped cream into his mouth. Then it occurs to me. "Hey, aren't you diabetic? I don't think you should be eating that stuff."

He smiles, his teeth covered in white cream.

"That's nothing. I'm also lactose intolerant."

Chapter 27

For the next three weeks I visit Franco every day and follow Dr. Martin's advice regarding his diet. It works for about two weeks until he seems to have trouble swallowing, so I grind his hay into tiny pieces. I spoil him as much as he'll allow with apple slices and sugar cubes, but eventually even those end up on the floor of his stall. His haughtiness has disappeared, replaced by a somber serenity reminiscent of a senior statesman stoically accepting his fate.

Franco's attitude reminds me of Sonya's last days, how she insisted I maintain a positive outlook. Following her lead, I ball up my anxiety and tuck it away before seeing Franco, choosing to send him only constructive thoughts and vibes. Despite his failing health, he's always happy to see me, greeting me with a head nod and shared breath as I hold my nose to his.

During one of my visits, Pat praises my commitment to a horse who's brought only expense and pain. I return home that evening pondering her words.

What many people don't understand is that animals represent all that's good in the world.

They don't hold an agenda or grudges.

They don't try to change or refine us.

They give loyalty and love freely, expecting nothing in return.

Even a kicked dog will come when its master calls—not because it's weak, because it's loyal. Horses enjoy these wonderful qualities, they also embody grace, dignity, strength and even empathy. They represent all humans can achieve when we strive to be our best. Franco is the puzzle piece I've been missing my entire life. He deserves to be loved the way he loves, unconditionally. I find courage in his tenacity, comfort in his touch and humanity in his gentleness.

If only humans could honor the greatness in one another without judgment, we might begin to heal from within and build a stronger, more united world.

On the way home from the barn I check in with Uncle Jay, who reports that Dad has weakened and will soon require a nursing home. Penny can no longer provide the care he needs and seems to be struggling with her own mental health. When I ask Jay to elaborate, he tells me that she lost her car keys and eventually found them in the trash.

"I occasionally do things like that too, Uncle Jay. Inadvertently throwing something away."

"No, hon. She told me she threw them away on purpose because they were dirty. She ran them through the dishwasher and when they didn't look clean enough, she threw them away and forgot about it."

"What about her kids? Do they know what's going on?" I ask.

"They're nowhere to be seen."

I sigh heavily, knowing at some point I'll have to deal with Penny's failing mind. But right now, she's not the priority.

I tell Jay I'll visit the following week, then hang up and allow myself a good cry. I feel like I'm in an earthquake. Whenever I manage to find stable footing, an aftershock comes and cracks the ground again.

As my personal world crumbles, clients provide some respite. I put my overactive mind on hold as I tend to their needs, finding emotional release through sex. Several guys comment on my zeal, telling me they hope I keep it up. The more thoughtful, intuitive people ask if I'm okay. I always smile, thank them for their concern and say, "I'm fine."

That is, until Thomas comes to visit.

He walks into the apartment and pulls me into a hug. I sink against his broad chest, inhaling his clean, fresh scent, then close my eyes and allow him to just hold me, simultaneously comforted and annoyed that I need consolation. After a few moments, I push him away and throw him a nasty smile.

"Follow me."

We have sex on the new couch, utilizing the buckled restraints and reclining options. Normally Thomas is a vanilla sex guy. But since seeing each other regularly, he's become more adventurous, exploring restraints and small amounts of pain.

I jokingly refer to it as the Two Shades of Thomas.

When we're done, I feel him looking at me.

"You didn't ask for the money up front."

"I didn't?"

He smiles knowingly. "No. You did not."

He's right. What's my excuse now? *Letting emotion lead the way is a rookie mistake.* I haven't done that since my very first client. Back then I didn't know any better.

I tell him it's because I trust him, and he nods slowly. Then, wearing a smug grin, he hands me three hundred dollars. He knows the truth and is smart enough not to comment, even if his face isn't. I pause before accepting the money, feeling like I got more out of the hour than he did, then chastise myself for becoming soft. I snatch the cash and hop up, telling him I have another client. Although it's true, I'm also trying to distance myself from the conflicting emotions waging war inside my head.

"Oh. Okay," he says sadly.

He gets dressed and pauses at the door. "Listen, I know I'm just another client, but I want you to know that if you need anything, I'm your guy. I just… really like you."

A tightness in my chest expands, followed by a rush of warmth, like a warm water balloon burst inside. Then I remember his wife passed away less than a year ago. He may believe he cares for me, but I'm the rebound girl. I thank him as I gently shut the door, reminding myself that the last thing I need is more drama. I've always lived by the KISS (keep it simple, stupid) principle. Now isn't the time to change.

The next client is an out-of-town finance guy I see about four times a year when he comes to Boston on business. Because his fantasy is fucking his boss, I dress conservatively in a plum skirt and white blouse, with tan heels and a scarf secured with a faux gold broach. I pull my hair into a low bun, apply minimal make-up then order an Uber, per the client's request.

A half hour later I'm at the front desk of a boutique Boston hotel asking if Mr. James Scanlon has left anything for Ms. Pereira. The young clerk holds out an envelope. When I try to take it, he doesn't let go.

"You look familiar," he says.

Some hotels have spent millions educating their employees to spot sex traffickers and prostitutes. Many sex workers on this side of town use this hotel specifically because it's privately owned and less likely to have trained its associates. But Trevor's not wrong. He's been on duty the last three times I've seen Jimmy. He clearly pays attention, making me wonder if I need to find a new venue.

I shrug, commenting that I have that kind of face. His hazel eyes narrow as his head falls to the right, trying to place me.

I raise an eyebrow and harden my voice. "Is this the way you treat your guests…" I glance at his name tag as if I've not seen it before, "Trevor?"

He stands up straight and immediately releases the envelope.

"My apologies, ma'am. Have a good day."

I nod, channeling my character, then cross to the elevator. I tap the room card against the keypad and press 4.

Within minutes I'm in Jimmy's room, dressing him down for not getting me last quarter's financial report and ordering him to assume the position for punishment. He lays on his back as I stand over him, slowly undoing the buttons of my blouse to reveal a sheer lacy bra.

"Too bad we're not at the office so I could fuck you on my desk. Do you know how many times I've fantasized about that?" he asks.

I fondle my breasts as he makes himself hard, then slowly lift my skirt to reveal no panties. He pulls me down, but before he can get going, I order him to open his mouth. Jimmy is always a good time, but he can't get off without this next part. He opens wide and I spit into his mouth.

"That's what you get for being a bad boy," I whisper against his ear.

He swallows greedily. "Again," he begs.

I do it once more while slipping a condom on, then guide him inside and move slowly while leaning over him, keeping my breasts just out of reach of his mouth. He lifts his head repeatedly to grab a nipple with his

192

Pleasure to Purpose

teeth but becomes distracted when I start moving faster. I tell him how much I enjoy working with him at the office and how I've imagined us having sex in the conference room.

"Can you see it? You fucking me on the *long, hard* conference table?" I whisper before licking his ear.

When he's about to come I slow down again, then pull him out and give him a good hand job before inserting him again, bringing him to the brink each time. This goes on for forty minutes until he grabs my hips and starts directing me. After that, it's over in a matter of seconds.

As we rest and catch our breath, he tells me he got married and they haven't had sex since the wedding night. He doesn't know what to do because he doesn't want a divorce. I face him, genuinely perplexed.

"I just saw you last… how long have you been married?"

"Eleven weeks."

He's still counting in weeks. That's a newborn marriage.

I think back to the last time I saw him. It must have been the week before his wedding. "Have you talked to your wife about the sex thing?"

"I don't know how."

I tend to avoid giving advice to my clients unless they ask me directly, but this one seems ridiculously obvious. "You could say, 'Hey, honey, I was hoping we could have sex tonight.'"

He shakes his head. "Nah. That would cause a fight."

"And?"

"I don't want to fight."

So, Jimmy has no sex life with his wife because he's conflict-avoidant? I stare into the distance, wondering why rich people seem so messed up. Perhaps they have too much time on their hands. If they spent more time making ends meet, maybe they'd have less time for avoidable bullshit. I've also found that rich people tend to focus on the next big thing, often causing them to miss the good things that are right in front of them.

I bite my lip to suppress a smirk when Jimmy says that after dating for six years and sharing a daughter, he thought marriage would rekindle the romantic flame.

Getting married to revive passion is like getting a puppy to bring you closer to your partner. Several sleepless nights and four pee spots later, you're on the fast track to Splitsville. I evaluate Jimmy in his Hermes suit and decide he isn't messed up. He's just plain stupid.

After freshening up, I get dressed and grab the cash from the nightstand saying I'll see him next time he's in town.

"Maybe by then I'll be divorced," he calls out as the door closes behind me.

The elevator door opens to reveal a well-dressed woman who offers me a warm smile. "Here on business?" she asks.

I smile at Anne. "You?"

She nods. "Good to see you."

The elevator stops on the third floor and an elderly couple joins us.

Anne clears her throat. "The date for the House committee hearing has been set for two weeks from today. You'll introduce yourself, describe your work and read your fantastic letter. They may want to ask questions, so be ready for it." She lightly elbows my side. "I think we could have a real impact."

"You're going be there?" I ask.

"Wouldn't miss it."

The elevator arrives on the first floor and the couple exits first. As Anne and I walk toward the entrance, I glance left toward the seating area where I see a woman being handcuffed by the police. Although her head is bowed, I recognize the woman's build and her platinum crew cut. It's Stella, the sex worker who's testifying against Randy's pimp. The elderly couple hurry from the lobby as hotel guests gawk in fascination, several recording the experience.

Suddenly Stella looks directly at me and grins, radiating defiance. My earlier concern about her wellbeing pops like a balloon. She's not just a survivor. She thrives on rebellion. She looks away, not because she's ashamed, but because she's doesn't want to implicate me. She's honoring an unspoken pact to protect a colleague, even though we don't really know one another. I used to feel guilty in a situation like this, believing I should help a sister out. But until sex work is decriminalized, there's absolutely nothing I can do for her without implicating myself.

I swivel my head to see Trevor filming the spectacle. We lock eyes and recognition dawns, followed by a smirk. I'm used to getting the look from hotel staff when I leave at three in the morning, but not during the

Pleasure to Purpose

day. I'll have to be more careful the next time I see him because the look he just gave me tells me he's an enterprising young man who might demand some money or a blow job to keep quiet.

In another profession, Trevor's demands would be considered blackmail and extortion.

Punishable by law.

But not for us because we don't have the same rights. Assholes like Trevor and Randy's pimp think they can hide behind the fact that we're sex workers. They assume we won't report them for fear of retribution or out of self-preservation.

As I look back to Stella, I imagine she feels as I do: tired of being a player in someone else's game.

It's high time I join the team who makes the rules.

The silent declaration empowers me. I stand straighter and lift my chin. I realize now that everything has led to this moment, even though I've been blinded to clues I conveniently ignored. Dealing with Franco's illness and building a relationship with Dad taught me that I have the strength, empathy and confidence to negotiate new challenges. Joining the Sex Worker Support Group reminded me I'm capable and not alone, and writing the letter helped me find the voice that's been suppressed for so long. Finally, allowing Thomas into my personal life injected faith and warmth, two traits I didn't know I'd lost.

My life has shifted more in the past few months than ever. I think all of us are children of the Light. Patience, empathy, kindness and strength are the factors that allow us to remain buoyant so we can help others achieve the same state.

Although I don't live with many regrets, rejecting Randy's request for help and her subsequent death haunt me.

Perhaps running into Anne in the hotel and seeing Stella's arrest is my call to action. An opportunity to make things right.

I'll start right now.

I return to Trevor and nod toward his phone, then extend my hand.

He gives me a *no fucking way* look.

I glare, daring him to make a fuss. We remain locked in silent combat for several seconds until he rolls his eyes and slaps the phone into my palm. I delete the video of Stella, then hand it back.

"No one deserves that kind of humiliation, Trevor."

I offer him a genuine smile, then wink and say, "See you in three months," before fixing my gaze straight ahead and following Anne through the revolving doors.

196

Chapter 28

I spend the next two days obsessing about Franco and Dad and my upcoming Massachusetts House speech. When reading my letter out loud in front of a mirror, I quickly realize I have so much more to say. I write three separate speeches, all of which end up in the trash. Then Thomas calls to say he'd like a sleepover because he bought a hot tub and wants to try it out. He doesn't even finish describing it before I'm on Velma, zooming toward relaxation and stress release.

We spend the night having sex in the hot tub and watching a couple of rom-coms before dozing off at about 2am. If I'm honest, it feels more like a date than a session, except for the fifteen-hundred-dollars tucked away in my wallet.

I wake up the next morning in a great mood, momentarily forgetting that Franco is no longer eating and Dad is now in a nursing facility. William finally made his way to Delaware and reports that since Dad moved to the nursing home, Penny's like a boat without a rudder. Although I try to muster some empathy, my depleting emotional well is reserved for Dad and Franco, who is emotionally distancing himself from me as his body shuts down, choosing to remain in his stall during my visit yesterday.

After cleaning the stall, I sat on the dirt floor, humming and sliding thin apple slices his way, all of which remained untouched. The final straw came when I placed my forehead against his and he turned away, the equivalent of his asking me to leave him alone. I cried all the way home, understanding that his soul had already started the final journey.

As the peace of sleep falls away, the weight of imminent loss returns, and my core feels empty as a foggy pain settles on my brow. Thomas senses the shift and kindly allows me space, fixing a dippy egg on toast before going outside to mow the small front lawn. I eat slowly, grateful for the meal and thinking about the last time a man made me breakfast.

It was the sort of spring morning that promised a warm afternoon when I awoke to the smell of bacon and eggs. I asked my fiancé why he did it. "Just because," he'd said.

I remember feeling loved. I ate quickly and rewarded him with a quick romp before I left for my job at the nursing home. When I went to the ATM to deposit my paycheck at the end of a twelve-hour shift, I was shocked to see a zero balance in our joint account. I called Aaron to say someone had stolen our savings, but he didn't answer. After texting and receiving no response, I pinged the location of his phone and discovered he was in Hawaii. Although he never confessed to stealing the money, I heard from mutual friends that he and my money had a great time in Hawaii, drinking and carousing his way across the islands.

I return to the present, watching Thomas slowly push the lawn mower across the front yard. When I go to leave, he jogs over to give me a kiss. He says, "Have a good day, hon." The scene is disturbingly domestic. Before I can think of a clever retort, however, I call out, "You too!"

I arrive at the farm to find Franco standing in his stall, oblivious to the flies buzzing around him. He doesn't blink as they crawl into his eyes or shake his head when they investigate his nose. He stands perfectly still as I approach with an outstretched hand, almost as if he doesn't see me. I touch him and he flinches. Concerned, I reach for him again, but he steps backward, swaying his head from side to side. He seems uncomfortable in my presence. My stomach cramps as I realize he doesn't recognize me.

Dr. Martin said that as sabulous cystitis progresses it can affect the central and peripheral nervous systems. She also said that if Franco ever

Pleasure to Purpose

showed neurological signs, he would most likely have a secondary infection that would hasten death.

"No, no, no, no," I mumble as sadness scrambles my thoughts and the phrase *I'm not ready* repeats in my mind.

I offer a sugar cube. He adamantly ignores me, shifting on his feet and stomping to make a point. Holding back tears, I place my chin atop the stall door and simply watch my beautiful boy. So much dignity, grace and power, even now.

I flash back to the horse book from my childhood. Just as the dream horses carry the little girl's nightmares away, I relied on its message to carry me through troubled times. As an adult, Franco's wounded soul found mine just in time for us to support one another. I will miss him. He has given me so much purpose and strength right when I needed it most.

I silently thank Franco for being my dream horse, trusting that he hears me on some level. After several minutes, I extend my hand again.

"Hi, handsome. It's nice to meet you."

He throws his head as if in surprise, then stares hard at me for several seconds before walking forward and draping his head over the door. Relief floods through me as his hot breath wets my ear. I cry happy tears that he recognizes me, even as I understand what needs to be done. When Franco steps back, I go outside and dissolve into tears, doubling over to stay quiet so my boy doesn't hear me. After several minutes I draw the phone from my back pocket. Moving as if under water, I dial the vet.

Twenty minutes later Dr. Martin arrives wearing a somber expression as she grips her black bag. Her handshake is cool and strong, a physical reinforcement of my decision. "I didn't bring a helper. I figured you might want to help instead?" She looks at me questioningly. After a short conversation that outlines Franco's ugly fate if left to die naturally, we agree it's better to let him go while he still recognizes me. It's ironic how some death decisions come unchallenged, as if the soul overrules the brain. You know it's the right thing to do, though certainly not the easiest.

As we approach Franco's stall, he whinnies softly, then backs up. I'm a stranger once more. He's calm as Dr. Martin examines him, staring into a future only he can see. She's silent as she listens with the stethoscope, her furrowed brow expressing what words cannot.

Pleasure to Purpose

"His heartbeat is erratic. I wonder if an infection is settling in there. If it is…"

I lift a hand indicating she doesn't need to complete the thought, then look away while searching for any other solution. Finding none, I swallow hard and nod. "Go ahead," I manage before slapping my hand over my mouth to stifle a sob.

Ever stoic, Franco shows no signs of pain or worry as I gently place a halter on him. Wiping tears as quickly as they come, we walk to the pasture where I let him graze in the warm sunshine. Several horses converge on him, then scatter suddenly as if sensing something's wrong. When he lifts his head to look at me, the pain in his expression lets me know it's time.

I walk toward him and extend my hand, hoping he'll recognize me. He nuzzles my palm. I wrap my arms around his neck, smothering him with tears and wet kisses. I whisper how much I love him and thank him for trusting me.

"I'll never forget you, Franco. You showed me the meaning of courage and grace. I'll see you in my dreams." My voice falters at the end, and he gingerly backs away. Somehow *he* seems in charge, guiding us in the final, gut-wrenching decision to end his life. As Dr. Martin approaches with a syringe, Franco eyes her warily, then swings his head back to me, as if asking permission.

I stroke his nose, my breath coming in short bursts as my chest feels like a boa constrictor is wrapped around it. I lift my chin, determined to be as brave as he is. I owe him at least that much. My voice trembles as I offer encouragement. "You're gonna be okay, buddy."

He bobs his head as Dr. Martin strokes his side and works her way up to his neck, where she talks to him quietly while injecting the sedative. He sways for several minutes, his head drooping before he yanks it up again trying to regain control. I watch in quiet agony as my champion fights against the medication that will ease his journey.

"Let go, Franco. It's okay," I say through broken sobs.

He lifts his head once more, gazing in my direction, then gives in. His shoulders relax while his head descends slowly. Dr. Martin approaches and carefully injects the heart-stopping medication. It takes effect almost immediately. She places her hand on his neck to guide his slow fall as his front legs buckle. His massive chest thuds to the ground, quickly followed

Pleasure to Purpose

by his hind quarters. Completely distraught, I rush in and fall to my knees, cradling his massive head on my lap. I stroke his nose and whisper in his ear. "I love you, Franco. It's okay. You can go." When his regal head relaxes, I hear his breath change, becoming more shallow and more infrequent. Then, as if a switch is thrown, he stops breathing. Suddenly gravity releases and I feel Marco's spirit leave his body. It rises and slowly floats away as I cry happy tears that he's finally truly free. I open my eyes as the sound of birdsong carries to me. I smile while looking up at the sky.

I don't know how much time passes before I feel Dr. Martin touch my shoulder.

"You okay?"

No. Not even a little okay. "Yeah. Thanks." I lean forward and bury my nose in Franco's neck. "I'm so sorry I couldn't save you. I love you so much. Sleep well, baby."

As Dr. Martin confirms death by checking Franco's corneal reflexes and heart, I watch the other horses working through their own grief and worry.

After a minute Dr. Martin faces me and nods. "He's gone."

The moment steals the breath from my lungs with its finality.

A familiar hand lands gently on my shoulder. I turn to find Pat kneeling next to me, her crestfallen face a reflection of my own. "I'm so sorry, honey." She opens her arms. I let her hold me for a minute before pulling away. Unable to speak, I mouth a silent *thank you.*

After a moment of shared sadness, she says, "I hope you don't mind, but I've arranged for Franco's cremation."

I stare blankly, realizing I was so focused on Franco's life, I'd given no thought to his death. She asks if I'd like to pick up the ashes afterwards. I nod dumbly, not trusting my voice.

"He loved you, you know. I could tell. You're a good horse mom, honey."

Feeling like an emotional dam is about to burst, I mumble my appreciation to Pat and Dr. Styles before running to Velma. I throw a leg across her while latching my helmet, then fly down the dirt road. A torrent of pent-up emotion erupts as the wind whips my face, blowing tears against my hair and into my ears. At one point I scream in frustration, the sound

Pleasure to Purpose

swallowed by the pine trees lining the road. I arrive home a snotty mess, my hair knotted and black mascara streaked in odd patterns.

Reality rears its ugly head too soon when my hoe phone rings. Although it shocks me into the present, I ignore it, then consider how expensive Franco's cremation will be. Wiping my nose on a sleeve, I answer in a voice made huskier from crying. Within seconds I know it's Bobby from Hyannis, a man in his late seventies whom I not-so-affectionately refer to as a time waster.

Like several other men, he calls every few months asking if my hourly rate has changed. When I say no, he complains, then wants to talk. Normally, I find some compassion and chat for a while. But not today.

"I don't have time today, Bobby."

"But I have money."

Going to Cape Cod on Velma would take almost two hours. Plus, he's never followed through. I waver, balancing those two points against the cost of cremation. Then I consider what might happen if I decide to go in my current emotional state and he doesn't have the money or tries to give me less than my rate. It wouldn't end well for Bobby.

"I can't. Sorry."

"But—"

"I said *no!*" I roar, surprising myself.

He disconnects and I immediately feel terrible. There are so many lonely souls seeking a connection in a digital world that has little compassion for people who don't fit inside the box. In the past I've been a haven for people like Bobby. Today I have to draw a line in the sand.

Don Rickles winds around my legs as a knock sounds. I pause, wishing the world would somehow intuit my grief and just leave me alone, then drag myself up and open the door to find Thomas holding a bottle of wine.

"Thought you might need a drink after a hard day working at the barn."

Although I appreciate the gesture, I'm not in the mood to entertain. The best I can offer is a wan smile.

"I don't drink. You know that."

He grins. "I do know that, which is why I brought this as well."

He holds up a big fat joint. I melt a little while opening the door. It's just like Thomas to be thoughtful, yet it's so much more than that. He doesn't just consider my feelings; he somehow manages to get inside my head, to know what I'm thinking even before I've recognized it.

He places the bottle and fatty on the table, then takes me in his arms and starts rocking back and forth. I settle into the embrace.

"Are we dancing?" I ask.

"Yes, ma'am." He pulls back. "Listen, I've been thinking. I know you think I can't handle your job if we're together, but I can."

A red light flashes in my brain. I appreciate his kindness, but this is the last thing I need right now. I just don't have the energy to coddle his ego. Instead, I hit the issue head on. I disengage and tilt my head to the side.

"You can handle me sleeping with other people? *Really*?"

He takes my hands and rubs them gently. "I'm an adult, Scarlett. I like you for you. You're a great person and I'm not going to tell you what to do or try to change your behavior. I just want to be with you."

My brewing anger melts under his intense gaze. His face is hopeful and sincere yet determined, like he's thought this through and isn't going to accept anything but yes. His confidence unleashes a dormant desire for our relationship to be real. *Does Franco's death have me thinking irrationally?* I dismiss the idea, realizing it's the opposite.

Losing Franco has clarified the fact that great love is worth the loss. I opened my heart to Franco and received so much more than I gave. Why shouldn't I allow that possibility with Thomas?

Before I can truly consider the question, however, the answer presents itself: people aren't like horses. They're untrustworthy.

They break you and kick you when you're down. Thomas is special in that deep down in my soul, I feel his warmth like a roaring fire on a snowy evening. I know Thomas is different. But he can't be *that* different.

I finally look at him, patiently awaiting my response. Although I'd love to have a relationship, I'm not ready to trust anyone with my heart. Not even Thomas.

"You sure you don't just want sex?" I offer.

He smiles, then pulls me close and starts dancing again.

"Well, of course I do. You're fucking amazing. But I also want to hold doors for you, get you something before you know you need it, give you a robe so you won't be cold getting out of the hot tub—"

"Bring me wine after a crappy day," I add. His whiskers tickle my ear as he smiles.

"Franco died today," I whisper. The admission is shocking to hear out loud.

He pauses, then resumes swaying, holding me more tightly. "I'm so sorry. I know how much you loved him."

I absorb his compassion, allowing it to wash over me like baptismal water as I sag into his warmth. I review the day, not believing how bizarre it's been. I've waited my whole life to be loved unconditionally. I never had it with my family, thought I had it with Aaron; yet each time I was disappointed. Until now I'd found it only with Franco. Then Thomas appeared, a widower with a huge heart and generous spirit. I want to run. To shout, laugh and cry. Instead, I remain silent with my head against his chest, enjoying the feel of being touched but not groped, of being loved but not screwed. *And that's what it is*, I marvel. *Love. Pure, no-strings-attached love.*

Can this work? Could I really have a boyfriend and still be a sex worker?

I push complications aside and focus on the sensation of his arms around me, the way we sway perfectly in synch, his scent and his compassion. I soften as I lean into him, immersed in his strength. After several moments, I mumble into his chest.

He pulls away. "I couldn't hear you. What did you say?"

I examine the honest, open visage smiling down at me. The curve of his round nose, the bushy eyebrows that need a trim and the happy eyes that crinkle in the corners.

"I said I'll think seriously about your offer."

Pleasure to Purpose

Chapter 29

With Franco gone, I turn my full attention to Dad. Death has so invaded my consciousness that when I phone him twice, I break down in the middle of both conversations. The second time it happens Dad mutters, "What the hell!" and hangs up the phone.

Feeling guilty, I consider going to Delaware but can't find the emotional energy the visit will require. The last thing Dad needs is a crying mess unable to help herself. Besides, that's Penny's role. After speaking with Uncle Jay, who insists Dad can wait until I'm feeling up to it, I decide to take some time to grieve before visiting.

The next few days are a blur, purposefully overfilled with clients, Thomas and speechwriting to take my mind off the fact that I no longer go to the barn every day. Pat appears on my doorstep with a basket full of goodies: homemade banana bread and blueberry jam, dark chocolate wafers sprinkled with sea salt and pretzels. I thank her for her unending kindness and promise to return the favor if ever she needs me.

We take a long walk, reminiscing about bad times with Serenity and good times with Franco. She updates me on Xena, who has bonded with a new horse named Huckleberry. When I inquire about Xena's health, Pat says, "She's really slowing down but still has a good appetite, so…" and lets the words trail off. I feel almost buoyant in her presence.

When Pat leaves, I find my happy Franco memories start to crowd out the sad ones. Visions of his death are replaced with him running around the paddock, searching for a hidden apple in his hay or nuzzling with Xena.

Thomas is invaluable regarding my upcoming speech, listening to many versions and offering suggestions regarding wording or timing. Through working closely with him I've learned that he has a knack for performance, teaching me how to pause for dramatic effect or make eye contact with the legislators for maximum impact. I give him free sex to thank him for his time, but after several sessions he insists on paying because he feels guilty I'm not making money seeing other clients.

By the end of the week, I have a solid presentation that I deliver in a "heartfelt, forthright manner," according to Thomas. It isn't until the sun is setting that I realize I'm scheduled to pick up Franco's ashes the next day. Thomas recognizes the anxiety creeping into my body and offers to drive me. I politely decline, thinking I can't ask one more thing of him, until he points out that the volume of ashes won't fit in Velma's basket.

The next day when he arrives to pick me up, he presents a forest green velvet box. I open it to find a sterling silver locket with a picture of Franco etched into it. When I look at him in astonishment, he shrugs. "I copied a photo from your phone. I figured you wouldn't mind." I stare at it, dumbstruck at his thoughtfulness.

"But that not the best part," he adds.

He removes the locket from the box and presses a small button on the side. It pops open.

"You can put some of Franco's ashes in here. He'll always be with you."

I shake my head, unable to put into words how I'm feeling. Sad, happy, grateful, seen and loved, all mixed together. When I finally look up, I break into a teary laugh. His expression is hopeful: eyebrows peaked, wide eyes and a tentative grin. I kiss him lightly on the lips and tell him the locket is exquisite. I know he's anxiously awaiting a response regarding the boyfriend question. But with my life in chaos right now, I don't want to rush into a decision we might both regret.

On the flip side, Thomas is an incredibly good person who deserves an answer soon. Having spent so much time together, I can't imagine my life without him in it.

Actually, I can… but I don't want to.

I'm quiet as we listen to a classical station on our way to the farm. The music lulls me into a meditative state where I find myself remembering the toss of Franco's head and his hot breath on my face. I find the memories brighten my mood, almost as if he's telling me he's okay and giving me permission to move forward.

As we travel the road leading to the farm, I feel a sense of weightlessness and butterflies in my chest. Then a countering feeling of *I can't do this* rushes up my back and settles like a knife between my shoulder blades. As my breath comes faster, I feel Thomas' hand on mine. I glance over and he's staring straight ahead while smiling and nodding. *You **can** do this*, he says without uttering a word. When we round the final bend and I see the paddock without Franco in it, the doubts scatter, leaving the simple beauty of a horse farm in their wake. Although it's not the same without my champion, the farm is still the most wonderful place in the world.

Pat greets both of us with warm hugs, then comments on the beautiful locket that dangles from my neck.

"Thomas gave it to me," I say.

An eyebrow raises slowly as she nods and stares at Thomas. "I don't know, honey. I think this one's a keeper."

Thomas points at Pat while looking at me. "See? Even Pat knows," he jokes.

Pat asks how I'm doing.

"Much better today."

After chatting for a bit, I say hi to some of Franco's horse friends who greet me like a lost relative. At first, seeing them makes me sad. But as they continue to jostle me with their large heads and reach into my bag for treats, the goofiness makes me laugh. At the end of the visit, I realize their attention bolstered me. Franco's spirit lives on in every horse that provides respite for a needy human soul. With a sense of relief and hope, I recognize healing has begun.

On the way home I take stock of my emotional state and decide I'm strong enough to call Dad. He opens by asking if I'm going to break down, which only steels my resolve to remain stoic. He's more lucid and upbeat than I've heard him in a while, not confusing me with someone else while telling me about his favorite shows.

"Anyway, people need to stop worrying so much. I'm dying but so is everyone else, dammit! Mine's just more front-and-center."

Having dealt with the elephant in the room, I find his no-nonsense attitude refreshing. It reminds me that perspective is what you choose it to be. I tell him I'm coming down tomorrow and he whoops, something I've never heard him do.

"It'll be great to see you!" he adds.

I glance at Thomas, who's heard every word and gives a thumbs-up.

"Is Uncle Jay there?" I ask.

The next thing I know Penny's on the line, complaining that the nurses don't come very often, Dad hasn't eaten in five days and he's not allowed to get out of bed.

"He needs to walk!" she announces.

I close my eyes while remembering she's supported Dad through every phase of his illness. There's no question that she's stuck by my father, so I inhale some patience before drilling into the details.

Based on her report, it sounds like Dad is eating only part of a meal each day. It's disheartening but not surprising as his body shuts down. At least he's receiving some nutrients.

"As for not getting out of bed, are the nurses turning him at least?" I ask. I'm concerned about decubitus ulcers forming where the skin is in constant contact with the mattress.

"No. They say they're short staffed."

After the COVID pandemic, this is common. But my father needs better care. I hear Dad whoop again in the background, then laugh. I've never heard him so happy.

"Is he on morphine?"

She clicks her tongue. "Too much, in my opinion."

The man is dying and doesn't have appropriate nursing. As far as I'm concerned, he can have an entire vial of morphine if it makes him happy. And from what I'm hearing, Dad's pretty happy.

I tell her I'm coming tomorrow and we should discuss letting Dad pass away at home. Penny balks at that, saying she's already stressed and can't imagine having to be a full-time nurse too. I stare straight ahead, remembering why I dislike her so much.

Suddenly she says, "I gotta go, hon. I have a nail appointment. Here's your dad."

She hands the phone back to Dad, who says, "What?"

"I didn't say anything. But listen, it's great to hear you so happy. Hey, remember the time we went fishing and you taught me how to cast?"

"'Course I remember!"

"I pulled the rod all the way back and tried to whip it forward, but the hook was stuck in your cheek?"

He remains silent, so I finish the story.

"You could've gotten really mad, but you didn't. You were super calm, telling me to put the rod down while you were taking out the hook. Remember?"

I glance at Thomas, who's following the story, his face screwed up in empathetic pain. A long silence follows.

"Dad, you there?"

"Who the hell is this?" he growls.

Before I can put a label on the feeling of vacancy that fills me, Thomas reaches across the seat and squeezes my hand.

"It's your Princess, Dad."

He sighs heavily. I can't tell if he's remembered me or given up. Either way, the earlier lightness I felt dissipates, replaced by the momentous weight of impending death.

"It's okay, Dad. I'll see you tomorrow, okay?"

"You're coming tomorrow?"

I swallow hard, desperate to stifle the sob that's crawling up my throat. "I'll be there by four in the afternoon. I love you, Dad."

"I love you too, Princess."

After returning to the house, I ask Thomas to wait on the stairs while I update William and Mom about Dad's situation. Mom listens attentively, arms across her chest, then returns to her apartment without a word. William nods solemnly, saying he'll go to Delaware when he can, but he has a "nine to five job and what else do you expect from me?"

I hold up my hands, saying I just wanted to keep him in loop, then follow Thomas up the stairs to my apartment where we have sex,

Pleasure to Purpose

tenderness turning to an urgency borne of emotional release. Afterward, two clients text asking to meet. I decline both, choosing to spend the afternoon lounging with Thomas. In the early evening we enjoy a casual dinner at a local restaurant. After driving home, we linger near his car. He removes his wallet to pay me, but I grab his hand.

"Leave it."

His eyes scan my face questioningly.

I nod.

"Does this mean you've made a decision?" he asks quietly.

I kiss him lightly, then agree to try a relationship. "But if you can't handle it, I need to know before frustration turns to resentment," I add.

He promises, then informs me that his two daughters think my work is cool.

"You told them I'm a prostitute?"

"And a dominatrix. No secrets. I told you I like you for you. You're a smart businesswoman and I'm proud to be with you. In fact, one of my daughters wants you to teach her about BDSM."

I laugh out loud. "No way! That would be weird!"

I kiss him again and he jumps in his truck, rolls down the window, and grins.

"I'm a very happy man right now!"

His excitement is infectious, and I find myself beaming like a lovestruck teenager. I kiss my palm and throw it to the air as he pulls away. He snatches it from the air and pumps his fist, leaving me laughing and breathless.

I'm definitely nervous about having a boyfriend. Even the word evokes a history I'd rather forget. But Thomas makes me feel good about myself, him, and the rest of the world. I feel attractive and smart when I'm with him. I feel valued and important. Plus, in the short time we've been seeing each other, he's helped me through two major life events.

He's seen me at my worst and keeps coming back.

I climb the stairs slowly, thinking about the House hearing next week. Nerves are making me question whether I should scrap the speech and just read my original letter. After all, Anne told me it was perfect, even if it only scratches the surface.

Pleasure to Purpose

As I pass Uncle Steve's apartment, he calls from the open window. "How's that fairytale working out for you?"

The comment is thrown sarcastically, meant to stick in my side like a burr. I stop on the stairs, ready to toss my own verbal grenade. As I open my mouth, I realize I no longer want to play this hurtful game.

Although we may never be close, I can do my part to mend the relationship by choosing kindness. Maybe not every time, but this time.

I return to the window and smile warmly. "It's working out beautifully! Thanks for asking, Uncle Steve. Have a good night."

I leave him open-mouthed as I run to my apartment where I feed Don Rickles before sitting down to review my speech. Two hours later, I read through the rewrite, pride oozing from my pores. I pick up the phone to share the good news with Thomas. Just before I can call, my father's number appears on the screen. I answer, excited to share my achievement.

"Hey, Dad!"

It takes less than one second to recognize Penny's sobbing.

Without a word, I know my father has died.

My heart slams in my chest like monkeys trapped in a cage. Then suddenly I feel hollow. I stand, knocking the chair backward and ask how it happened. She tells me he suffered several ministrokes after getting off the phone with me, and finally passed away minutes ago. It occurs to me she could've called before now to let me know about the strokes. Yet in the same instant, I understand it doesn't matter.

Death levels the playing field in that everything and nothing matter simultaneously. Things that would normally send me over the edge fade to gray as ridiculous details spring to life. The feel of Dad holding my six-year-old hand, the arch of his eyebrow, the smell of his aftershave. It's all there, rushing at me, then falls flat at my feet as I listen to Penny sob.

"What am I gonna do? What am I gonna do?"

Chapter 30

Four days later I sit at Dad's service listening as the rabbi tells a delightful story of two people who met, fell in love and lived happily ever after until one of them died from leukemia. I have to give Penny credit. She coached the rabbi beautifully, conveniently leaving out the parts about Dad's mentally distressed son, his two angry ex-wives and his other kids who rarely saw him while growing up. In fairness, I suppose no one wants to be remembered the way they really were, although it might be cathartic for those left behind. The rabbi offers the floor to Uncle Jay who gives a beautiful eulogy that focuses primarily on their lives as children and Dad's war years, two sections of his life where he was a hero. Following Jay's speech, the rabbi invites us to another building for a brief reception.

I cross through a breezeway to a smaller building where two soldiers stand at attention near the casket. Dad's body was shipped to Massachusetts and, against Jewish law and tradition, embalmed so he could have an open casket and be buried in a military cemetery. I avoid looking at the body, preferring to close my eyes, remembering him as he was. A vision of him smiling down at me makes my heart skip a happy beat and when I open my eyes, I'm steady once more. Although I understand some people find closure in seeing their deceased loved one, I find the mannequin-like body with cake makeup somewhat disturbing. My father's body might be here, but his soul is soaring high above, returning home.

Penny enters the room on shaky legs, then sinks into a chair. I evaluate her non-traditional funeral attire—an overly large black t-shirt, black sweatpants and a black knit hat—and realize she's going to need help moving forward. She's relied on my dad for so long that I'm not sure she can function on her own. I stare at her while remembering what I said to Dad. *I'm responsible for my family. It's just who I am.* I look around the room, hoping to find Penny's kids so we can have a serious conversation about her mental health. Seeing none of them, I close my eyes and take a deep breath. *I might be taking care of Penny. Cross that bridge if you come to it.*

The soldiers stomp their feet in unison to draw everyone's attention. They step forward and fold a flag ceremoniously in front of us, snapping the fabric and turning it so the triangular edges are crisp. I follow their movements carefully, impressed with the precision. Something about the exact way they hold, snap and turn brings a measure of comfort from that control. The large flag becomes compact as they work, and they tuck the final edge inside, all neat and tidy. It's the opposite of my grief, which feels like a flag flapping precariously in high winds.

They offer the folded flag to Penny who weeps openly as they raise their hands in salute. We're asked to turn toward the window where three soldiers stand at attention outside. They raise their rifles in exact unison, then point them at a forty-five-degree angle. I jump as a series of three shots echoes against the building. Although I appreciate the respectful ceremony, the bullets hammer home the finality. Dad is truly gone. His memory lives, but I can't touch or hug him.

Silence is soon replaced by polite discussion about the service and then outright chitchat about the Patriots and Red Sox. I'm amazed how quickly people want to resume their normal lives. I was expecting to reflect on a shared past.

As I stand in the corner observing Penny soaking up sympathy from her three young grandchildren, Uncle Jay kisses my cheek.

"Hiya, hon. You holding up okay?"

I'm wondering why he never became a father. Something stops me from asking, yet I'm sure his warmth and kind spirit would've made him an amazing dad.

Pleasure to Purpose

"I'm alright. What about you?"

He shrugs. "I witnessed the slow deterioration. He's in a much better place." He grabs my hand. "You know, you're a great daughter. Given all that's happened, you could've just walked away. But you didn't."

I bite my lip and nod. I can't do anything else without risking a crying jag.

He looks around. "Your mom didn't come? Can't say I blame her."

Mom and Dad were never really friends after the divorce and haven't spoken in years. In fact, when I went downstairs to tell her about Dad's death, she simply nodded and quietly closed the door, shutting empathy out and solitude in.

Uncle Jay squeezes my arm and walks away, replaced by a man who introduces himself as Raymond, Penny's son. I learn that he and his sister haven't spoken to Penny in a year because of a disagreement.

I watch Penny fawning over her grandchildren, marveling at her ability to compartmentalize. She told me she speaks with her kids every week. That's clearly a lie, like so many other things. A sadness sweeps through me with the knowledge that Penny and I might have had a chance to mean something to each other if she'd been more maternal and I weren't so angry. Not to mention the stepbrother and sister I could have enjoyed.

"Forgive me for being blunt, Raymond, but I'm a little worried about your mom." When he asks what I mean, I tell him about the Nitroglycerin pills, keys in the trash and a statement about her hands not working right.

"Also, the last time I was here, I noticed your mom didn't shower the entire week. I used to work in a nursing home so I know memory-impaired people often avoid showering because the water looks invisible. They think it could hurt their skin."

His brow furrows, he runs a hand through his hair. "Yeah. Just today I've noticed some stuff. I was actually wondering about that."

"I'm not trying to butt in, but you may want to consider patching up your differences so both you and she can enjoy the time she has left, especially with those kids. They yours?" He nods as we watch the littlest grandchild play peekaboo with Penny, both of them collapsing into giggles. Penny seems genuinely happy, which makes me smile.

Ray extends his hand. "Thanks. It was good to finally meet my stepsister."

Pleasure to Purpose

I smile warmly while shaking his hand. "You too. Take care."

My eyes travel the room and land on William who lifts a hand in greeting. He's standing next to Tyler. My brother is gazing steadily at me through a medicated haze. I wonder briefly how Tyler got here, then see Uncle Jay approach and lead him away. He must have taken custody of Tyler for the day.

I feel a sudden urge to try one more time at a relationship with Tyler. I consider following him to say hello, but my feet won't move. I try again. My gut mandates my feet remain still, perhaps protecting the little girl Tyler consistently bullied. With deep sorrow I acknowledge that the big brother I played with died years ago, leaving a broken shell behind.

My thoughts wander to Thomas. He offered to come with me. I briefly considered it, then realized it's too soon to subject him to more of my broken family. Besides, although we've been through a lot together, I'm not yet ready to let him all the way in.

I glance at Dad's casket, sad that he and Thomas never met. It would've been fun to see my two guys bond. I'm sure they would've liked one another very much. The idea makes me smile as Dad's last words, "I love you too, Princess," play on a loop in my mind. I don't focus on regrets. To me they're a waste of time. But not being with Dad when he passed… it breaks my heart.

I think about what Uncle Jay said, that given our rocky past I could've walked away from Dad and left him to fend for himself.

That's just not me. I care for the wounded when others walk away. I'm not patting myself on the back. I often pay for my kindness in heartbreak or by being used. But I can't **not** do it.

It's who I am and how I express a love I sometimes can't put into words. It's part of the reason I'm a sex worker, offering happiness to those who can't find it elsewhere.

I think of Franco (used and abused his entire life), Dad (a war veteran who gave so much for his country that perhaps he didn't have a lot left to give at home). I consider Mom and our troubled relationship, knowing despite everything, I'll be there if she needs me when the time comes.

Then I glance at Tyler walking away, wondering if my heart is forgiving enough to ever again find compassion for him.

I approach the coffin.

Placing my hand on the casket's smooth, dark wood, I whisper, "I'll miss you, Dad. I love you," before walking outside into the sunshine.

Chapter 31

After returning from the funeral, I take several days to decompress before the committee hearing. In preparation I attend a support group meeting in which I read my speech out loud. I feel confident and speak clearly, secure in the statement I so carefully crafted. Some girls express envy that I'm coming out of the shadows, that I have the guts to be "outed." Most express relief that it's me in the spotlight instead of them. Overall, the admiration in the audience's eyes boosts my confidence. As I'm leaving, Misty pats me on the back.

"You're gonna be great," she says giving me a toothy grin.

I return the smile, enjoying the camaraderie. "Thanks, Misty. It all started because of you."

She shakes her head. "I might have started it, gurl. But you're the one bringing it home. Go get 'em."

I'm bursting with pride as I zigzag home on Velma, feeling as free as I can ever remember. I call Thomas to share my joy.

"I'm so frickin' proud of you. I'll be there tomorrow. Count on it."

The following morning when I wake up the euphoria has vanished. A sense of dread overtakes me. I question wanting my perspective to be heard. I was critical of Stella for testifying in honor of Randy, insisting she was placing herself in danger. Yet here I am, putting myself out there for the world to criticize. The hearing will be recorded and televised… my hands tremble as I realize how much I'll be judged and potentially humiliated. No matter my good intentions or clear conscience, there are always people who will see me only as a woman whose sexual exploits drag every other woman into the gutter.

I call Thomas in a panic. He reminds me that I can't change someone else's mind. I can only educate them so they might alter their perspective. He also tells me to remember the disenfranchised group I'm representing, astutely pointing out I'm succumbing to the same egotistical disorder swallowing our current legislators: thinking the government is about them and their needs instead of the constituents for whom they work. "Remember, babe, this isn't about you. It's about the cause."

Duly humbled, I dress carefully in a navy-blue pantsuit Thomas called business chic when I modeled it for him last week. I draw my hair into a bun, then decide it looks too severe. I pull it free, smiling as it falls loosely around my shoulders. Glancing at the time, I realize I have to get downstairs for the Uber. Although Thomas offered to drive me, I decided I wanted my arrival to match my attire. All business.

Twenty-five minutes later when the Uber arrives at the state house, I step out of the car and let my eyes travel the extravagant structure. "I can't believe I'm here," I whisper. Blowing out a mouthful of air to steel my resolve, I start up the stairs, counting as I go to calm my nerves. I enter the building to people rushing around me, completely absorbed in their own lives. *I'm a cog in a very large, complicated wheel.* The thought centers me as I make my way to the representatives' chamber.

I open the large doors. The room is crowded and loud, making me feel wonderfully invisible as I walk to the front of the room. Anne waves to me and I rush to her.

"You made it! Sit here," she says. Her pupils are dilated. She's as nervous as I am.

Anne reviews her notes while I fidget in the hard, straight-backed chair. Suddenly Anne leans over and whispers, "You ready?"

Before I can answer a door opens behind the high, wooden dais. My mouth is slack as I watch the committee members file in, outfitted in expensive suits accessorized with Givenchy ties and Gucci scarves. They look like a tribunal ready to impose my sentence.

"I can't do this!" I hiss. As the floor starts to wiggle and the walls close in, I feel a hand on my back.

"You have to breathe, Scarlett. I swear you can do this. You're stronger than you think."

I shake my head as a TV camera swings toward me, its light blinking red like a panic button.

"I can't!"

"Look at me!" Anne orders.

I face her.

"The committee liked your letter a lot, but you need to know that *I* chose you."

Time slows, making me deaf to the chaos as people move in slow motion. I lean in for an explanation.

Anne looks exasperated. "I could've picked someone else, but I chose you because you have this thing. A… light that shines. That's what told me you're the right person for this job."

The chairwoman bangs a gavel to silence the large gallery.

"You can do this. It's just a speech."

No. It's so much more than that.

Anne's voice reaches me from far away, yanking me back to reality. "You are Scarlett fucking Pereira, and you **can** do this."

Suddenly my phone dings. I fumble nervously, almost dropping it in my haste to silence it. In a haze, I glance down to see a text from Pat.

Might have new draft mix for you. Bowed tendon in back leg & spine issues. Was in barn fire so can't be in stall.

You got this, girl… More info later

"You got this," I repeat. Does she mean the horse or… *is Pat here?* She knows my secret, and it would be just like her to show up in support. I turn quickly to scan the crowd but don't see her among the hundreds of people in the gallery. My eyes grow large as I realize in horror that every seat is occupied. Hundreds of potential haters will know my secret. I turn back around slowly, trembling as the chairwoman gathers her papers to

Pleasure to Purpose

begin. Although she gestures toward Anne and me, I've mentally left the room.

"Scarlett? Please tell me you're going to speak," Anne pleads.

I hear her but am paralyzed with fear. Then Dad's voice floats on the air, settling around me like a fine mist. *I'm proud of you, Princess.* His presence is suddenly everywhere, swirling around me. I note in my peripheral vision that Anne has grabbed my hand. I glance at my phone screen.

Might have new draft mix ... Was in barn fire...

Years ago a psychic told me I would own a horse who'd been in a barn fire. She also said I'd become involved in politics. I blink, fully returning to the moment, then face Anne. A slow smile spreads as I marvel at the universe's twisted way of putting us on the right path.

Anne leans forward. "Does that smile mean you're going to speak?"

I hold up my finger, then answer Pat.

I'm all in! You're right... I got this!

The gavel comes down hard again, opening the hearing. The chairwoman greets the committee members and the gallery, commenting on how large it is given the subject matter, which draws ripples of laughter from the crowd. She then turns her attention to Anne, who speaks eloquently about the current state of sex workers in Massachusetts, using Randy's death as an example of how unevenly laws are usually applied.

Hearing Randy's name emboldens me, reminding me why I want to be here. I'm speaking for those who can't speak for themselves due to the fear of being punished. I represent the marginalized, underserved members of society who people walk by without a thought, categorizing them even before dismissing them with a cursory glance. I watch Anne deliver her remarks, sitting bolt upright while beautifully articulating each point, accenting salient information by using a closed fist to stamp its approval. Forthright but not demanding. Educational without being preachy.

As I observe her, I begin to understand the light she referred to in me. It's the desire to do good and to inform so that equity and equality become a reality instead of a dream.

It's a hand reaching out to someone who's down and can't see a way to rise. It's kindness and empathy.

It's choosing love over hate and understanding over judgment.

Anne wraps up her remarks.

I briefly scan my prepared statement. *It's not enough.* I have one shot to make a powerful impression, and I'm going to take it.

I turn to the gallery. Thomas waves to get my attention. I smile and nod, which prompts a huge grin and two thumbs-up. He motions to the size of the gallery and then points to me. *They're here to see you,* he mouths. I glance to my left and right where two television cameras are trained only on me.

This is the moment.

I close my eyes, thinking of how much I've grown in the last few months. Opening my heart to Thomas and walking through the valley of grief have left me stronger, kinder, more self-aware and empathetic. It's no longer just about me. It's become much bigger than that, and I'm up for the challenge.

My name explodes through the speakers when the chairwoman introduces me. I inhale slowly, then push my prepared statement aside. The action draws a panicked look from Anne, but I place my hand on her arm. "It's okay. I'm Scarlett fucking Pereira, remember?" I smile.

She looks like she going to cry in relief as she nods and leans back in her seat, ready for a show.

Placing my folded hands on the table, I lean into the microphone. Today I choose to step forward into the light. I'm all in, and I don't want anyone to miss a word.

"Good afternoon, Madame Chairwoman and esteemed members of the Committee…"

I pause, letting the smells and sounds of this historical place wash over me. Once I testify, there's no going back. The entire world will know who I am and what I do. I picture Uncle Steve's smug face and Mom's shocked expression once the truth is exposed.

Then I remember I can't control others' thoughts or actions. Only my own.

Dad's energy reappears, strengthening my resolve. I straighten my back and lift my chin.

When I finally speak, the words are confident and clear.

"Polite society doesn't like to discuss the worldwide, multibillion-dollar sex industry, though many engage in it and many more secretly want to know about it. When I tell people what I do for a living, they fall silent while their imaginations take flight. The words prostitute and dominatrix conjure imaginary orgies and sex slaves. Those things are indeed real. But I'm here to tell you that's not *my* story or how *I* got into this business. My name is Scarlett Pereira. I'm a prostitute, a dominatrix and a proud horse rescuer …"

Letter to the Reader

Dear Reader,

Thanks for reading *Pleasure to Purpose*. Please leave a review on Amazon and Goodreads if you're able.

As long as humans have existed, sex has been exchanged for money or favors. Scarlett describes the sex work business as a Whorearchy that classifies workers by how and where they conduct business. Escorts who work out of apartments or hotels are more highly regarded than street workers, for example. Strippers who don't engage in sex feel morally superior to those who do. Scarlett finds these classifications ridiculous and misogynistic, based on hundreds of years of women being taught that sexuality is okay only within marriage and only in the bedroom.

In some cases, pimps & madames represent their sex workers on the up-and-up, protecting them and providing shelter and food. Others aren't so gracious, like Randy's pimp in the book. They lure workers by offering what the person's missing in their life, then give drugs and take the lion's share of any hard-earned money. People being trafficked for sex is also a major national and international problem that should not be conflated with sex workers who choose the profession, like Scarlett.

When a friend told me about a dominatrix who spends most of her money saving abused horses, my first thought was that she must be an incredibly compassionate person. We met in person over a three-hour lunch and spoke mostly of horses, only getting into her sex work toward the end. When I told her she must be very compassionate to do what she does, she thought I was referring to the horses. But I was actually referring to her sex work. For a kind person (which she is) to inflict pain willingly is not easy. It requires connection, trust, and empathy. When I expressed those thoughts, she thanked me, saying most people don't appreciate that fact.

Franco and Dad did pass away within two months of each other, and Xena is still alive (with Lyme disease but not cancer) as of the publishing date. Franco and Xena were truly close in real life, and the horses' desperate reactions to being separated was described exactly as it happened in real life. Scarlett's family stories are true. The client stories are based on her real-life experiences, changing names and small details to protect privacy.

Serenity is based on two people rolled together into one irritating character. Pat is based on a real person who's been enhanced to show how impactful she was in Scarlett's life.

When I was more than halfway done writing the first draft, Scarlett called and said, "Guess what? I have a boyfriend!" So, as often happens, the story took an unexpected turn with the introduction of Thomas, who has brought love and light to Scarlett's life. Thomas became a rescuer as well when he and Scarlett adopted the draft horse Pat texts about in the last chapter.

The letter Scarlett wrote to the legislator is real, and she (along with some other sex workers) spoke and answered questions in a legislative briefing. The state house briefing led to other meetings with state senators. The goal is to educate politicians so they understand that not all sex workers are victims and that decriminalizing sex work will enhance sex workers' lives.

Randy is not a real person, *per se*. Rather, she is a conglomeration of young sex workers across the United States. When I read about a sex worker who was strangled in July 2024 in Las Vegas, the idea of Randy's death being the catalyst that prompts Scarlett to action was born. That real-life sex worker was the mother of two young children and had gone back to school. According to HG.org, a legal website: "Prostitution is one of the most dangerous professions in the country; worse than Alaskan fisherman, or loggers, or oil rig workers. According to recent statistics, the death rate for prostitutes in the U.S. is 204 out of every 100,000. For fishermen, it is 129 out of every 100,000. Also, the average prostitute gets physically (but non-lethally) attacked approximately once a month."

When I entered Scarlett's world, I was completely unfamiliar with the sex worker's life. Having become a little more educated, I now support sex work decriminalization. The goal of this book was to tell Scarlett's story. But like Scarlett's speech to the House, it's become bigger than that. In writing *Pleasure to Purpose*, my hope is that Scarlett's story will spark people to see sex workers as people, not objects. I also hope to spur an interest in learning more about decriminalization and the challenges sex workers face on a daily basis.

For more information on the decriminalization movement, please visit www.aclu.org or www.decriminalizesex.work. To learn more about

Pleasure to Purpose

living as a sex worker, check out Kaytlin Bailey's The Oldest Profession podcast and Bella Robinson's website www.coyoteri.org.

Thanks again for reading and leaving a review. Feel free to reach out to Scarlett and me through my website at

www.elizabethsplaineauthor.com.

Sincerely,

Elizabeth B. Splaine

Acknowledgements

It takes a village to birth a book, and I'm so fortunate to be surrounded by so many wonderful villagers.

First and foremost, I'm grateful to Scarlett for opening up to a stranger about her most personal memories. Over almost two years and many hours of conversation and face-to-face meetings, we shared our lives and became friends. I'm humbled by Scarlett's trust and hope I've captured her life as she'd like it recorded.

A big shout out to my beta readers (over several versions) who took the time and effort to not only read *Pleasure to Purpose*, but to give feedback to improve the manuscript. These folks are the unsung heroes of writing.

Thanks to my publisher, Trisha Lewis of Van Velzer Press, for believing in the book before I wrote a word. And to my editor, Rose Alexandre-Leach, who always helps make my books better.

Special thanks to sex worker/podcaster/comedian Kaytlin Bailey (Old Pros Podcast and Whore's Eye View) for reading the book and giving us a blurb.

Special thanks also to Bella Robinson, Executive Director of C.O.Y.O.T.E (Call Off Your Old Tired Ethics) of Rhode Island for reading the book and taking the time to educate me on sex worker history and current laws in Rhode Island.

As always, love and thanks to my family and close friends who put up with a writer who immerses herself in the worlds she writes. This particular novel brought new perspectives and, as you might imagine, interesting stories across the dinner table.

About the Author

Elizabeth B. Splaine wrote the Dr. Julian Stryker series of "Blind" thrillers (*Blind Order and Blind Knowledge*), as well as *Devil's Grace*, the winner of the When Words Count writing competition. Her next book, *Swan Song,* an historical fiction novel, was chosen by independentbookreview.com as a "Top 35 Impressive Indie Press Book of 2021."

Prior to writing, Elizabeth earned an AB in Psychology from Duke University and an MHA from University of North Carolina, Chapel Hill. She spent eleven years working in healthcare before switching careers to become a professional opera singer and voice teacher.

When not writing, Elizabeth teaches classical voice and enjoys time with her family.

Love Books?

SUPPORT AUTHORS – buy directly from independent publishers. This puts more royalty dollars into the pockets of your favorite author – and gives them time to write their next book.

Visit us for links to our other books as well as many other vibrant publishing companies to find the book for you; join our Launch List to be the first to know about new books:

director@vanvelzerpress.com

These ARE The Books You've Been Looking For.

www.ingramcontent.com/pod-product-compliance
Lightning Source LLC
Chambersburg PA
CBHW061819190726
48289CB00007B/2260